I0573139

THE JUDAS CONSPIRACY

A JFK THRILLER

DAVID PHILIPS

Black Rose Writing | Texas

©2022 by David Philips
All rights reserved. No part of this book may be reproduced, stored in a retrieval system or transmitted in any form or by any means without the prior written permission of the publishers, except by a reviewer who may quote brief passages in a review to be printed in a newspaper, magazine or journal.

The author grants the final approval for this literary material.

First printing

This is a work of fiction inspired by true events. Names, characters, businesses, places, events, and incidents are either the products of the author's imagination or used in a fictitious manner. Any resemblance to actual persons, living or dead, is purely coincidental.

ISBN: 978-1-68513-026-8
PUBLISHED BY BLACK ROSE WRITING
www.blackrosewriting.com

Printed in the United States of America
Suggested Retail Price (SRP) $21.95

The Judas Conspiracy is printed in EB Garamond

*As a planet-friendly publisher, Black Rose Writing does its best to eliminate unnecessary waste to reduce paper usage and energy costs, while never compromising the reading experience. As a result, the final word count vs. page count may not meet common expectations.

Dedicated to the Memory of
President John F. Kennedy
5/29/1917 – 11/22/1963

For What Was and For What Might Not Have Been

ACKNOWLEDGEMENTS

This manuscript would still be gathering digital dust on my laptop if it were not for the encouragement and support of certain people. They made this work infinitely better than it otherwise would have been, and I am forever grateful for their insight and guidance.

First, I would like to thank my agent, Kirsten Schuder, of Apex Literary Management for her invaluable editing skills, literary knowledge and market experience. I would never have got this work off the ground without her professional expertise.

My thanks also go to my A.L.M. writing buddies, Mark McQuown and Al Stoffel, for their fonts of wisdom and their sound advice. I would also like to extend my appreciation to my fellow Black Rose Writing authors, Candace Lucas and Stephen Briggs, who guided me toward a better way of expressing some of my dialogue and paragraph structuring. Thanks also to Black Rose Writing for taking a leap of faith in an unknown author.

Last, I would like to extend my thanks to all my family and friends who read the raw manuscript for their kind words and helpful suggestions.

THE JUDAS CONSPIRACY

PART 1

CHAPTER 1

Spring/Summer 1967

Although it had been building for some time, it was on Friday, April 7th. that the world awoke to the indisputable fact that there would be another war in the Middle East. On this day, provoked by the constant bombardment of their settlements below the Golan Heights, the Israelis finally retaliated. The Israeli Air Force struck at the perpetrators of these actions - their neighbors to the northeast, the Syrians. The resultant attack destroyed seven Syrian MiGs.

Jews around the world held their breath, awaiting the Arab backlash that would surely follow, as Syria, influenced by the Soviet Union, invoked its defense treaty with Egypt.

As the weeks went on, it became even clearer that another confrontation between Israeli and Arab was inevitable, and it was not if, but when it would occur.

From around the globe, Jews sent aid, either financial or in-kind, and many left their own country to volunteer help. Even those who did not consider themselves to be religious could not stand by and see their spiritual homeland threatened once again by the overwhelming might of the gathering Arab armies.

One of these was an idealistic and impressionable 14-year-old Jewish teenager from Glasgow, Scotland, named Sam Nathan. Although he understood he would be too young to fight, Sam still had the overpowering urge to do something, anything, that would help Israel. At whatever cost, and by any means, he would get there.

His parents, horrified by his intentions, forbade him to do anything which would get him hurt, or God forbid worse. "Sam," his mother began patiently, "there are important issues at stake here. Things you don't understand..."

"But I do understand! I understand more than you think. Do you believe I don't know exactly what's at stake? All the Arab countries surrounding Israel want to invade it and kill all the Jews..."

"Yes, Sam, they do, and we don't want our son to be one of the fatalities, God forbid. I know you mean well, really want to do something, but there is no way in hell your father or I would allow you to... to do anything that might get you hurt, or worse. I can't begin to imagine how all the Jewish mothers in Israel must feel right now, seeing their children going off to fight. They must be worried sick, but we can't fight their battles for them. Not like this. They..."

Sam cut across his mother. "But this is just how we can help them. I've heard of guys doing this, even girls, women, going to Israel to support the troops. Even if we don't fight them ourselves, for every one of us who goes, it frees up someone who can fight. I'm not stupid. I know I won't get near the front line or anything, but I need to go, Ma. Don't you see? Israel is in terrible trouble right now. They need all the help they can get."

"Yes, and I'll tell you what they don't need," his mother shouted, anger rising in her voice. "They don't need any farkakteh help from a fourteen-year-old snot-nose kid who can't even piss in a straight line. You're too young, don't you understand? Even if we let you go, first, they would think we were crazy for allowing you. Second, what do you think they would do with you? Allow you to wander around the streets of Tel Aviv or Jerusalem by yourself? Someone, some poor soul whose sons or daughters will be fighting for their country, would have to babysit you. So instead of just having to worry about their own family, now they would also have a British brat to care for. Is that what you want? To give even more tzorres? Grow up, Sam. The world doesn't revolve around Sam Nathan."

"But Ma..." the teenager pleaded.

"No 'buts' Sam. That's it. Final! I want you to promise me, Sam. I want you to swear to me you'll put this mishigas behind you, and we'll hear no more talk about loyfing off to Israel. Promise me, Sam!"

The boy lowered his head. "Promise, mum," he mumbled, bowing his head in resignation.

His mother relented slightly. She did not like to see her son so agitated by something he truly believed in, especially when it was to do with Israel. Maybe there was a way. She brought out the Jewish Echo, Glasgow's only Jewish newspaper. "Look," she said. "There's all these fresh groups springing up to support Israel. They're looking for volunteers to help them raise funds; make everyone aware of what Israel is fighting for, things like that. That's what you can do. That's something positive that will help Israel. If you want to do something worthwhile, join some of these groups. They're crying out for people, just like you, with your enthusiasm. That's how you can contribute. What do you say?"

"Yeah, I guess so," he replied without enthusiasm. "But, Ma, don't you understand, don't you care? Israel is fighting for its very survival right now, and..."

"Enough!" screamed his mother. "How dare you? How dare you talk to me like that, you arrogant little sod? Do you think you're the only Jew in Glasgow who worries about what's going on over there? Now you listen to me. I'm getting fed up with this. You are far too young to be getting involved in things like this. Yes, we know you're worried about Israel, and so is the rest of the Jewish community, not just you. Now I'm prepared to give you some latitude and let you do what I said. There's going to be a rally outside Motherwell town hall next week. It seems the councilors there have passed a motion condemning Israel for everything, as usual, the dirty anti-Semites. Why don't you join the protest? I'm sure you'd get a lift. Just be careful. Now, what do you say?"

"OK, I suppose so."

"And that's my last word. Take it or leave it. Now, do we have a deal? I let you raise funds and go to protest meetings if you stop all this nonsense about going to Israel. Deal?"

Sam nodded his head reluctantly. Why couldn't she see what he could see? It was all very well to collect money and go on protest marches, but he needed to do more. And he would...

• • •

A few days later, Sam was in his modern studies class. Although the curriculum focused mainly on recent Scottish and British history, it also included contemporary past historical events from other countries. As the United States played such an influential part in the United Kingdom's affairs, its recent history was also part of their studies. The class was learning about the aftermath of the Kennedy assassination and what happened in the days following that tragic event. One of Sam's classmates, Kenny Watson, stood up and declared, "My dad says he's glad that Kennedy was killed. He says that Kennedy was a Catholic and was an instrument of Rome. Everyone knows it was the American Freemasons who were behind the murder. They killed him to stop him from obeying orders from the Pope." And turning his gaze to look at Sam, he continued, "My dad says that Kennedy was nothing but a Jew-lover who used their money to get elected."

The boy's teacher could only gape in astonishment at her pupil's outburst. It was well-known that Watson's father was a prominent member of the local Orange Lodge and had a bitter hatred of Catholics. It was bad enough that he should express such antagonistic feelings towards other religions, but indoctrinating his son to harbor similar sentiments was unforgivable.

"And how does your father know such things? No one else seems to have mentioned the Freemasons." she asked, shocked by his outburst. Watson shrugged his shoulders. His father had declared it; therefore, it was true. No further discussion seemed necessary. And if the truth were to have been known, his father would have tolerated no further discussion in the Watson household.

His teacher could not let her pupil's remarks go unchallenged. "Your dad says a lot of things, doesn't he? You can tell him from me he has besmirched the name of one of the best presidents America would ever have had, his religion notwithstanding. Your father is nothing but an ignorant bigot, and it's just a pity that he's bringing you up to follow in his footsteps." She shook her head in dismay. "You're better than this, Kenny. Please don't believe everything your father tells you. That's all I'm saying." She would have liked to say more, but to do so might have crossed a dangerous boundary she was not willing to do. She was there to teach, impartially and objectively. Her own personal views must have no bearing on the subject she taught.

The boy looked at her smugly as he resumed his seat. He had gotten under her skin, which was his intention. His friends gloated with him while the rest of the class stayed silent. Like everyone else, Sam was a mere a bystander at this pupil-teacher exchange.

Although it wasn't part of the curriculum, their teacher raised the current crisis in the Middle East. Despite attending a non-denominational school, Sam's religion was no secret, so it was unavoidable that his teacher sought his opinion of the situation. As every eye turned in his direction, it was here that he dropped his bombshell. Perhaps it was because of Watson's overt reference to Sam's faith. Watson was a bully who picked on Sam. Despite being smaller in stature than his tormentor, Sam did not allow himself to be intimidated by the stronger boy. He always retaliated in kind, so Sam's aggressor made sure that he always had two or three friends around when he accosted him. Maybe it was just to prove something to Watson, or maybe just to himself. He didn't know. Whatever the reason, he didn't mean it to happen. It just came out; unannounced, unpremeditated, unplanned. "I've written to the Israeli embassy in London. I've offered to go to Israel to help them." He asserted this in such a calm and matter-of-fact manner, that his teacher took a few seconds to assimilate this startling information. Even Watson's slack jaw opened in amazement.

As a buzz of excitement permeated the room, he realized he'd made a mistake; a big mistake. He should never have disclosed his secret. Not here. Not in this way. But he couldn't help it. It was out now, out in the open, and, he reasoned, why not? If Scotland was in danger, wouldn't any of them have done what he wanted to do?

Mrs. Samson was fond of the boy. He had an aptitude for her subject, and she was sure he would do well in the forthcoming exams. She tried very hard not to show the alarm she now harbored for him and sensed, more than knowing for sure, that he was aware of her concern. Patricia Samson was a matronly woman in her mid-forties. Unlike most of her colleagues, many of her pupils regarded her with affection. She had just the right knack of getting on their wavelength, and even the most disinterested of her charges found they were swept along by her enthusiasm for her subject.

"You don't understand. This is important to me. I'm a Jew, and it's Jewish people who are being threatened, whose lives are in danger, Jewish kids like me. I can't stand by and do nothing." He pointed to the sleeve of his jacket draped behind his chair. On it was sewn a round cotton patch emblazoned with a blue Star of David on a white background. In the middle of the star was the legend, 'Never Again.' "Thirty years ago, Adolf Hitler tried to wipe us out, people like me, just because we were Jews. We did nothing to hurt him, but he still wanted to kill us all. This badge reminds me of that time; it says we won't ever allow ourselves to be put in that position again." Sam stared hard at Watson. His meaning was crystal clear. "There was no Israel then, nowhere for the Jewish people to go, nowhere for them to run to. No country would take us in. That's why it's so important for Israel to be there, just in case. Now, do you see? That's why I have to go."

"But Sam, what happened in Germany at that...."

"Please, Mrs. Samson, please don't say it couldn't happen here. Only someone who isn't Jewish could think that way. The Jews in Germany didn't imagine what happened there could happen either, but it did. It did..."

"Are your parents aware you've written to the embassy? What do they think about this?"

"Oh, yes, I've told them. They're ok" His response was just a little too quick, and his immediacy of response and lack of eye contact did not escape her. She read the signs and now understood there was only one course of action open to her. If his statement were true, his parents would need to be told as soon as possible. It was unlikely that he would ever get any further east than Glasgow Airport. However, even in the improbable event he ever got to Israel, no one would let him get into danger. But she could not stand by and do nothing. Not now she knew. Mrs. Samson had now forgotten Watson's earlier rant. This new situation was far more important. She had a duty of care to all her pupils, even those who seemed hell-bent on putting their own young, impressionable lives in peril, no matter how noble, not to say problematic, the cause.

And so it was that, on Wednesday, May 24th, Sam's mother opened an envelope to find a letter from his headteacher inviting her and Hyman, Sam's father, to a meeting a few days later. It read, 'Dear Mr. and Mrs. Nathan, one of Samuel's teachers has brought a matter to my attention of which you may not be aware. I should stress that he is not in any trouble, nor has he done anything which warrants any disciplinary action. It is, however, something which may cause you some concern. For this reason, I would be grateful if you would come to my office on Monday, twenty-ninth May at nine-thirty a.m. It would be better if you did not discuss this letter with Samuel in the meantime. I look forward to seeing you on Monday. And the letter was appended with the headmaster's signature.

Sam's mother clutched the envelope to her chest, brooding, nursing her wrath until her husband returned home from work later in the evening. He had barely come through the front door when she thrust the letter at him. "Read this," she shouted.

"What is it?"

"Just read it. You'll see."

Hyman scanned the document, then looked up at her in some confusion. "This says nothing."

"Exactly. It's what it doesn't say that's worrying me. What's that little bleeder been up to now, eh?"

"Well, I'm sure we'll find out on Monday. Look, you're making a big thing out of this. It's probably nothing...."

"If it was nothing, why did his headteacher write to us? You don't write letters like this for no reason. He's done something; you can bet on it."

"But the letter says he's not done anything wrong, so it can't be that bad, surely."

"Where is that little tow-rag? Never mind waiting until Monday. I'll find out what this is all about now!"

"No, Millie!" Hyman shouted. "The letter says we should wait until Monday, and that's what we'll do. He must have said that for a reason, and we might make things worse if we do anything now. Leave it and carry on as normal. Monday will come soon enough."

"Very well," she answered, "but if he's done anything wrong, God help him."

"If he's done anything wrong, we will punish him appropriately." Hyman agreed. "Listen, I might not be able to come with you."

"Why not?"

"If I go with you, it'll mean taking a morning off work. I probably won't get paid for my absence, and we can't afford to lose any money right now."

"Do you mean that mamzer you work for wouldn't pay you to see about your own son?"

"Probably not." Hyman scratched the back of his head nervously, anticipating his wife's response.

"It's about time you stood up to that swine. For all the hours you put in and the work you do...."

"Let's just leave it, eh? We, I need this job too much just now to rock the boat...."

"Rock the boat? What do you mean, 'rock the boat?' If it weren't for you, that company would go to the wall."

"Look," he replied, exasperated, "I won't make it on Monday without losing some wages. We can't afford that right now."

Millie shook her head sadly. "No, I suppose you're right," she finally agreed. She was happy to be going on her own. If her son had done anything untoward, she would be the one to administer whatever punishment she felt was necessary, not her husband, who was more lenient towards their wayward son. Monday could not come soon enough.

• • •

Derek Arthur, the headmaster, had been in a predicament. This could all be for nothing. Maybe the boy's outburst was just early teenage swagger.

He was duty-bound to act on the intelligence furnished by Mrs. Samson, but what if her suspicion was wrong? What if his parents knew of his actions? What if he'd done it with their blessing? He did not see how this could be possible, but the idea still gnawed at him. If this were the case, what else could he do? He had never come upon a situation like this. Yes, he'd seen parents who had neglected their kids, children who arrived at school unwashed, malnourished, poorly clothed, and barely awake. He had even seen a few who were the worse for alcohol. Such circumstances he could handle. He had precedents. There were the authorities. They could sanction the parents; teach them to raise their kids better. The children could even go into care.

But this was something different, which was why he had found it necessary to craft his letter so delicately. Might these parents be so oblivious to the dangers their son could face? Was it possible they had condoned, even encouraged, his actions? Might he be curtly told to mind his own business?

His secretary interrupted his thoughts. "Mrs. Nathan is here."

"Only one parent?"

"Yes, the husband is at work. Mr. Nathan cannot come."

Well, at least he would only have to face the wrath of one of them if his fears were justified, although he still didn't know the best way to handle this situation. He had never met either parent and didn't understand their make-up, their character. He didn't even know the boy that well, which wasn't a bad thing. The only pupils he ever came across were those who merited special attention; a few because of some outstanding achievement, and others who required discipline, such as exclusion or expulsion. But this young lad had come into neither category; just an ordinary, average, everyday schoolboy. Or at least he had been until last week. Now this anonymous child had done something extraordinary. He had offered to put himself into the front line of a war. What makes anyone, let alone a boy of fourteen, want to do anything like this? He wondered. He breathed in through his nose and then nodded.

Arthur was an educator with many years of experience. This was his third posting as head teacher, and Glencroft Senior Secondary was the largest school to date, of which he had been in charge. Approaching fifty, Arthur was tall and imposing, with silver-grey hair shorn into a crewcut.

He wore glasses that were perched precariously at the tip of his aquiline nose. Arthur knew this was an affectation, but it was one he cultivated, wishing to appear as being a rather stuffy character, which, by nature, he indeed was. He could, however, and when the circumstances demanded, be as tough as a Marine. Many pupils had fallen victim to his unassuming demeanor, wrongly believing him to be a soft touch. His staff respected him rather more than they liked him.

Although many of his peers had discarded the black gown, it was part of his 'uniform,' signifying his authority. He would no more allow himself to be seen without the garment, than he would go without wearing trousers.

"OK, give me a couple of minutes, then show her in."

He stood up as she entered and extended his hand, smiling. He did not want her to feel threatened or intimidated or think that her son was in trouble. Instead, he wanted her at her ease.

"Mrs. Nathan. Thank you for coming. Please sit down. Would you like a cup of tea?"

Well, she judged, at least it doesn't seem as if they were going to expel him. Do you offer cups of tea to parents whose children you're going to kick out?

He pressed the button on his intercom. "Julie, two cups of tea, please." and turning to Mrs. Nathan, enquired, "Milk and sugar?" Sam's mother, Millie, nodded. Arthur instructed his secretary accordingly. "I'm sorry to bring you up at such short notice, but, ah, something has come to my notice, which you ought to know...."

If she knew about Samuel's letter, now would be the time for her to mention it. He was sure she would read the signs and react accordingly.

She only stared blankly back at him, concern growing on her round but otherwise not unpleasant features. "What's wrong? What's wrong with Sam? What's he done?" Her concern seemed genuine, which made it that much easier for him to continue. If she did not know about her son's communication, it was more likely that, as his mother, she would be even more appalled and worried than he was. "Sam has told one of my staff something... about his, um, immediate intentions."

She still regarded him with bewilderment, willing him to continue. "He, ah, told one of his teachers he had, um, written a letter...."

"Please, Mr. Arthur, what are you talking about? What has Sam done? Written a letter...? Written to whom? What concern is it of his teacher? And why are you involved? Why have you brought me here?" She was now becoming truculent. This was good. She certainly didn't know what was on her son's mind, and, he considered, I wouldn't like to be him when he gets home tonight.

His secretary entered his office with the refreshments, allowing Arthur a few extra seconds of thinking time.

"Mrs. Nathan..." he began and then stopped. If she didn't already know, how would she take this momentous news? He had to handle this sensitively. "Mrs. Nathan, Sam has written to the Israeli embassy...."

"Yes, he wants to get involved. He's been raising funds, going to meetings. I know we should be...."

"No, Mrs. Nathan," he interrupted. "I don't think you understand. Sam told one of my staff he intends to, ah, to... go... to Israel. He seems to -" He got no further. Sam's mother shook as she visibly paled. She trembled as she placed the cup down, some of its contents spilling onto her coat. Arthur pressed the intercom. "Get Mrs. Nathan a drink of water, now!" His secretary had rarely heard him bark an instruction like that, so stridently. She was back and in his office moments later. "Here, drink this," he said. Now that he understood they were on the same side, he was sure the boy would never get within a thousand miles of The Promised Land. "I take it you were unaware of Sam's ambitions?" he asked when he saw a little color returning.

"You're bloody right I wasn't. Just wait 'til I get him home. In fact, why wait until this afternoon? Let me see the little perisher now! Israel? I'll fuck, oops, sorry. I'll give 'im Israel! We sp'ifically told him not to do anything stupid. We warned 'im. 'E promised! Just wait 'til I get my 'ands on 'im. 'E'll not be in a fit state to fight anyfing!"

Arthur had not known the boy's parents, let alone that she was a Londoner, a Cockney, by the sound of her accent, and he smiled inwardly. These people had been through the Blitz! If she couldn't control her own son, he would be surprised. Still, he felt he had to come to Sam's aid. After all, the boy had done no great harm, and was motivated by what he deemed to be right. Now he knew there was not the slightest danger of the child leaving Glasgow, Arthur could afford to be magnanimous on his pupil's behalf. "Mrs. Nathan, please do nothing you may regret. I'm sure Sam did what a lot of Jewish boys his age would like to do. He just took it too far, that's all. Besides, I'm certain the Israeli authorities would never let a youngster anywhere near their shores at a time like this, even with the consent of his parents. How you discipline him is up to you, but please think before you act. That he was willing...."

"Mr. Arthur, do you have any children?"

"Yes, as a matter of fact... oh, I see...." Arthur smiled. He considered his reaction, should his son, who was a good deal older than Sam, have behaved similarly.

Millie Nathan had now fully recovered from her initial shock and thanked the head teacher for bringing these unpleasant facts to her attention. As he saw her to the exit, he wished her good luck.

"It's not me who'll be needin' luck." She was still not smiling.

• • •

Sam's parents had now barred him from attending the meetings and raising funds. Not only that, but he could also only go to school, run chores for his mother, and attend Sabbath morning synagogue. He was also scrupulously timed and had to be home from school no later than four-fifteen p.m. Grocery errands would take only forty-five minutes there and back, and it meant big trouble if Sam was home after two o'clock on Saturdays. This was not punishment. It was preventive medicine. He could call it 'being grounded,' whatever that meant, but he had shown them they couldn't trust him. He had betrayed his parents, the two people who should have been the most precious to him. Yes, Israel was important. It was the ancient, sacred, and spiritual home of the Jews, but they would just have to learn to survive without his farkakteh help.

This was bad enough, but it was worse at school. Even kids he didn't know were mocking him. Once word got out about his non-adventure, it was open season on him. He couldn't understand how people could be so cruel, especially those he considered as friends. Surprisingly enough, the one person who did not ridicule him was Watson. Lesson learned, perhaps, or did he suddenly find a new respect for his victim? Time would tell. For over a week, his classmates teased him mercilessly. Then, as suddenly as it started, it died. Everyone found a new scapegoat, a girl who'd dyed her hair green for a dare, but then couldn't wash it out. He wanted to pity her, he really did, but his selfish streak came to the fore. As sorry as he was for her, well, it took the heat off him, so without wishing the girl ill, he hoped the colorant would last for a few days longer.

It would not have been true to say his ridiculing had ceased entirely. Yes, it practically had, but not quite. Not quite. One of his best and closest friends was Andy Marshall. Where all his other friends and acquaintances had moved on, Andy could not get Sam's story out of his head. Phrases like 'Crazy mixed-up Yid' and 'Jew-wish you could get to Israel?' were only two of the lines with which Andy would not stop baiting him. Sam's escapade aggravated an itch that Andy just had to scratch. Sam tried threats, but Andy was bigger than him and would have only retaliated harder. Besides, you didn't thump your mates just because of a little innocent name-calling. He tried not speaking to Andy, but this just made him taunt his friend all the more. He tried reasoning, pleading with him to please stop. Enough, already. These entreaties only provoked even more laughter and jokes at his expense. Sam needed to do something. Andy's teasing was just going on and on, and it had to end before Andy drove him mad. He would have to find a solution and find it fast.

CHAPTER 2

At 7.14 a.m. on Monday June 5th., after increasingly belligerent threats emanating from its immediate neighbors, Israel launched practically its entire air force in a pre-emptive strike on Egyptian air bases. While their pilots were still asleep or having breakfast, almost the whole of the Egyptian Air Force fell to I.A.F. firepower, who destroyed around three hundred warplanes still sitting idly on the tarmac. By the end of the same day, Jordanian and Syrian planes had suffered the same fate, and Israel had de facto control of the skies. The pilots of the Dassault Mirage III Interceptors had done their jobs well. Many Israelis would have found it fitting, had they known, that their country had survived because of Israeli pilots flying aircraft designed and built by a company founded by a French Jew.

At 6.30 p.m. on Saturday June 10th, a plan emerged that would stop Andy Marshall dead in his tracks. Sam had been telling two of his Jewish friends, unknown to Andy, about his problems with his classmate and friend. They knew of Sam's abortive plans, and, rather than ridicule him, had admired his aspirations. One friend was called Paul Goldberg. The other was Bernard Lowenstein.

Paul was a few months younger than Sam, a studious boy whom everybody expected would go to university. He always got good grades, and a bright future seemed assured. Paul was about the same height and build as Sam, and Sam's mother often made unfair comparisons between the two boys, usually in Paul's favor. Paul was a gadget freak, and there wasn't a television, radio, telephone, vacuum cleaner, or any other household appliance that he had not taken apart to study its internal workings. Not only could he disassemble them professionally, but he had also put the parts back in the correct working order. He had also rigged up his own intercom system with parts scrounged, 'borrowed' or downright stolen from Post Office Telephone engineers. Paul also had in his possession a couple of highly illegal items, and it would be these devices that would help end his friend's torment and persecution.

Bernard was unlike his two friends. For a start, he was almost two years older than them, and a good four inches taller. The boy was also very slim, so much so that all his clothes just seemed to hang on him, like a better-than-average dressed scarecrow. Sporting glasses with wire frames and thick lenses, he was almost blind without them. He was also the most imaginative and articulate of the three.

Bernard's father, Ben, worked for a publishing company and was more indulgent towards his son than perhaps was good for either of them. However, when Bernard asked his father to get him certain items, even the good-natured and placid Ben cocked an eyebrow at his son's strange request. What Bernard had requested from his father was blank foolscap sheets with Hebrew writing on the top.

"So, what did you say when your dad asked why you wanted them?"

"I just told him I needed them for a school project. That did the trick; easy."

"And did you do what we agreed?" asked Sam, excitement evident in his voice. "Is it ready?"

"I just need to change one or two words, but, yes, it's almost finished." They regarded Bernard's handiwork with nothing less than awe. "Wow, this is fantastic... God, if I didn't know better, I'd swear this had come straight from Jerusalem, or somewhere." enthused Sam. "You've done a bloody good job. Remind me to double your money."

"What money?"

"Well, if I were goin' to give you any, I'd have doubled it."

Later, Sam could never quite remember who had come up with the plan. The chances were that it had just developed from vague ideas suggested by all three boys, most of which they realized were unworkable. However, the idea eventually coalesced, solidified, and became whole, became one. Sam would be on his own and would have to carry out the scheme by himself. He would have to practice so that when he did it for real, that's how it would appear - real, genuine. Could Sam do it? He would give it a bloody good try; anything to get Andy off his back. The schoolboy began by rehearsing on his friends, and to start with, it did not go well. It was so outrageous, he could not stop laughing, but eventually, they all settled down, and by the time he had left Bernard to return home, he got into the part he would play.

By the following Monday, the conflict was almost over. Israel had miraculously beaten her enemies once again, but for Sam, the actual battle was just about to begin.

"Hey, Sam, heard a joke. There's a little Israeli soldier sitting under a tree smokin' a fag. His captain comes up to him, and says, 'Private Levy, what are you doing smoking under that tree. Don't you know we're outnumbered sixty to one?' 'It's ok, Captain, I've killed my sixty...' good, eh?"

Sam smiled. He'd heard the same story a week earlier, but his humor was not just because of hearing the repeated tale. He was laughing because of what he was about to do to Andy. It was at the morning break, which when they had been at elementary school they had called 'playtime,' but were now older, and too grown-up to call it by such a juvenile name. "I've got something to tell you, something to show you, but not here. I'm going to walk behind the boys' toilets, and I want you to wait five minutes, and then follow me."

Andy looked at him with suspicion and bewilderment. "You're not turning funny or anything, are you? Why...?"

"Just do this and don't ask questions. No, I've not turned queer. Just do as I ask, and it'll all become clear. Oh, and come by yourself. No uninvited guests."

Without giving Andy time to respond, Sam spun around and headed off toward the rest rooms. He wasn't sure if Andy would take the bait, but would have been surprised had he not done so. Sam was not disappointed and, suspecting Andy would not wait the full five minutes began counting down from one hundred. As he mouthed seventeen, Andy appeared. "Now, what the fuck's...?"

"Keep your voice down. We need to be quiet. This is important."

"What the hell are...?" he lowered his voice. "What the fuck is this all about? If they catch us here, we'll never live it down. It'll be all around the fucking' school. Andy and Sam, bum buddies, shirt lifting specialists..."

"Well, the sooner you be quiet, the quicker we can get through this."

"Get through what?"

"Just shut up and listen. Do you remember when I wrote to the Israeli embassy?"

"Yeah! Don't think I'll ever forget that one. Why?"

The fun and games were about to begin.

"I've... had a reply," Sam started, as if almost reluctant to say any more.

"Yeah, so?"

"They want me to work for them."

"Who's 'they'?"

"The Israelis; they want me to work for them."

"Yeah, right, and I'm The Man from Uncle!"

"No, straight up." He pulled Paul's set of walkie-talkies from his pockets. They resembled cheap transistor radios, except for the fascia, which was all black, and there was only one dial, a combined on/off switch and volume adjuster. There was no frequency changer or channel guide. A push-button 'transmit' device at the side of the unit was the only other control. Also, the aerial extended to about three times the length of a conventional 'tranny'.

"What the fuck? So you've got two radios; big deal."

"Look again, you fuckwit. Take one and go stand over there." He pointed toward the girls' lavatories. "Say nothing. Just put the radio near your ear and listen. Do it." Andy, too dumfounded to argue, did as Sam directed.

"Are you getting this...? Over... If you can hear me, press the button and speak, over."

For a few seconds, Andy heard nothing except static and silence. He had replied but forgot in his excitement to take his finger off the transmit button, so had not heard Sam's response. Sam raced over to where his friend was standing, mindful of Paul's injunction not to keep the devices on for too long at any one time. This equipment was illegal to use in the U.K. as it interfered with the emergency services signals, and anyone found with them faced a hefty fine and even imprisonment. Sam repeated his instruction to Andy to listen for his, Sam's voice. Then to press the transmit button when he wanted to reply, but remember to release it after he had finished. He ran back over to his place of concealment and repeated his call. This time, Andy did as instructed, and Sam heard his voice clearly in reply, "Christ, these things work; I mean, they really are two-way radios! Where'd you get them? Uh... over."

"I told you. The Israelis have recruited me to work for them. Over and out." He turned off his unit before racing over to Andy's hiding spot. Andy returned the other device, which Sam immediately de-activated. "They want me to attend anti-Israeli meetings, demos, that kind of thing. Let them know who goes. Try to get friendly with some of them. Find out if they belong to any pro-Arab groups." Sam was relishing his role so much that he felt he actually was working for Israeli intelligence. This was fun. But it wasn't over yet. Not by a long way.

"You're fuckin' me about. How would they want you to work for them? We're only fourteen years old, for fuck's sake!"

"That's the beauty of it. Who would suspect someone as young as me? To anyone else, I'm just a kid. And I don't look very Jewish, do I?" Andy had to admit that his friend didn't appear to be too Semitic looking, but still... "Do your mom and dad know about this?"

"No, and you'd better not tell them. I've taken an oath to secrecy. No one must know, especially them. If you tell them, they'll be in danger; so will I. I could be killed."

"If nobody's supposed to know, why're you telling me? This isn't funny anymore."

He was doing it! It was actually working! Andy was falling for the bullshit. "They said I need a backup, someone to cover for me. Say I've been somewhere when I've been somewhere else. You know…"

"Someone to lie for you, you mean."

"Something like that, but it has to be somebody I can trust, someone who won't let me down. You're my oldest friend. Who else should I have picked?"

"I don't know… I mean… won't I be… in… danger…?"

Sam threw him a withering stare. "No, you coward! No one will know about you, except me. All you need to do is back me up. I'll tell you in advance when I'll need you to help me; a piece of piss. I'll be the one in trouble, maybe worse…"

"And you're… willing… to go along with this… this… undercover stuff? What if you get hurt or killed? What the fuck am I supposed to do then when it comes out? It'll bloody all come out. You'll be dead, and it'll be me who… no, fuck it, I'm not doing this! It's crazy… find someone else to play fuckin' James Bond with." He looked at Sam skeptically. "How do I know any of this is real? You could have got these things anywhere!" he asserted, but with little conviction. Two-way radios had been commercially available for many years. However, to a young boy from one of the post-war Glasgow social housing estates, it seemed incredulous that his friend could have access to this equipment. Andy had only seen such things on the TV, or at the movies, and it never occurred to him, he would see them in real life, never mind use them. Sam, also, until his friend had shown the apparatus to him, supposed you could only get these things in the United States.

"Oh, yeah, like I'm going to fly over to America on a jet, go into a shop in New York, or somewhere, get them, and then fly back in time for supper." Sam was now savoring his role. A couple of minutes back, he was finding it difficult to keep his calm façade without 'corpsing,' but that time was past. He may not have been on a trans-Atlantic airliner, but he was flying! "Look, I need someone I can rely on. It has to be you!"

"Wait a minute. What about one of your Jewish mates? Surely you Heebs should stick together. Why not ask one of them? You could, you know. You fuckin' should!"

"Yeah, I know that, but none of them live close enough. I need someone I can depend on at short notice, like late at night or something. I'm not sure."

"The war's over. Your lot won. Why do... why d'you still need to do this...?"

"Andy," Sam began and knew what he was about to utter was the only kernel of truth in this entire charade. "This war will never be over. Do you think for one minute that a hundred million Arabs are just going to go away? I wish it would, but it won't. It will happen again sometime. We have to be ready, to prepare for it. I want, I need, to help them."

"Why, for fuck's sake? You live in Scotland, not Israel. This is your home, not Jerusalem."

"I don't know why, I just do!" And he did. That much was also true.

"If this is on the level, I want to see proof; a pair of fuckin' two-way radios isn't good enough. How did they contact you?"

"They wrote to me, replied to my letter. I told you. They said I was too young to go to Israel, but I could work for them here in Glasgow. Said if I was interested, I should phone a number, and they would tell me more. So I did..."

"This sounds weird. What if your mom had opened that letter?"

"My folks don't open my mail. And besides, it just came in an ordinary envelope. And when I read it at first, I thought they just meant, you know, doing something like I was already doing, raising funds, that kind of thing. I didn't realize they meant... and if I didn't get what they had in mind, I don't think my mom or dad would, either."

"I won't promise anything, but I want to see this letter. Show me that, then I'll think about it."

This was working out better than any of them had hoped. Andy was falling for this nonsense hook, line, and sinker. He couldn't credit how easy their plan was slotting into place. "Wait until I tell Paul and Bernard about this," he thought. "Of course you deserve proof, but I've got to get your commitment first. If you agree, I can show you the letter, but only if you say yes. Otherwise, I walk away, and we never discuss this again, ever!"

Andy hesitated. That was when Sam was sure. He had reeled him in.

"OK, show me the letter, then I'll do it.

"It's not as simple as that…"

"Why…how?"

"Well, first, I had to get your agreement. Now I've got that they'll check you out. Make sure you're kosher." Sam laughed at his little piece of irony, a kosher Christian.

"What do you mean, make sure I'm kosher? You've known me since… Christ, I can't remember ever not knowing you!"

"Yeah, I know you, but they don't. So, they'll do a background check on you. Make sure you're not working for the Arabs or anything…"

Andy eyed him with suspicion. "And how long will this take?"

"Shouldn't take any more than a few days; took them two days to do me. But they'd probably done some checking before they wrote to me. Oh, they'll also investigate your mom and dad, your immediate family, too. No skeletons in the closet, is there?"

"I wouldn't fuckin' tell you if there was."

"You won't have to. My Israeli mates will do that." Sam smiled. "In the meantime, keep shtum. I mean, keep quiet. Not a word to anyone, and I mean anyone, not even your priest."

"That's Catholics, you ignorant fucker!"

"Cathies, Proddies, you're all the same to us." Sam smiled at Andy's stiffened response. "You're all fuckin' heathens. Come on; the bell's about to ring."

CHAPTER 3

Hyman had earlier lifted the embargoes on his son, despite Millie's continuing deep anger and hurt at what Sam had done to them. Sam suspected that there had been a lot of arguing about him, and he was correct. There had been, but Hyman believed Sam had learned his lesson and would do nothing so foolish and foolhardy again. Now that his parents allowed him to come home later from synagogue, Sam called at Bernard's home after the service. The teenager hoped to acquire the letter he needed to seal Andy Marshall's fate and turn the tables on his friend. How would Andy like it when he showed everyone what an idiot his friend had been? Imagine believing for one minute such a ridiculous story. How could he have been so stupid?

The boys had decided that if Andy fell for their fables, they, or rather Sam, would spin it out for a few weeks to make the denouement even more explosive. Imagine stringing him along for a month, telling him increasingly outrageous stories about his exploits, what he had done, the 'dangers' he had faced. The excitement was practically unbearable. The joke had now almost taken on a life of its own, which none of the boys seemed able, or predisposed, to stop.

Sam had received a reply to his letter from the Israeli embassy. This was the letter they used as the template for the document, which was now ready to be used in the second phase of their plan.

Bernard had taken one folio with the Hebrew writing and inserted it into his Adler typewriter, which he had received as a bar mitzvah present. Below the existing Hebrew, he had added the letter which he had concocted the week earlier, using the original message to Sam, and adding a few more lines of his own invention. It certainly looked impressive. As the oldest and most articulate of the three, Sam had left the wording up to him. Bernard knew what he needed to do, and he did not disappoint. Sam read it aloud for Paul's benefit and to refresh their memories. "Dear Sam, Thank you for your kind message of support and your offer of help in this uncertain and volatile time. While we appreciate your concern, we feel it would be better to continue with your studies and come to Eretz Yisrael on a more favorable occasion. There are, however, other ways in which you might help us here in the U.K. If you would like to consider this, please contact us at the number at the top of this letter, and ask for Yossi. We hope to hear from you soon. Thank you once again for your support. Shalom. Yours..." and Bernard had appended a scrawl, just above the author's name, the writer of the original letter, Avram Ben-Yaacov Metzler.

"Well, do you think it will do?" Bernard asked, fully confident of the answer.

"I told you, it's bloody brilliant. Yeah, it'll do. It'll more than do. I can't wait to show this to him. And this is so good I've just had another idea. We could do a second letter...."

"What do you mean, 'a second letter'?"

Sam relayed the proposal he had just thought of. Paul was enthusiastic, but Bernard was more cautious. "Don't you think we're taking this too far, Sam? Just show Andy the letter as we agreed, and leave it at that, eh?"

"It has to be realistic, doesn't it?"

"Ye...es," Bernard conceded.

"Well, then think about it. Don't you see? A second letter would have to be written if this were real. It would need to be."

Paul came to Sam's help. "He's right, Bernie. It would be necessary." Bernard only reluctantly, and with some reservations, accepted the logic and acknowledged that to make the practical joke more authentic, a second note would have to be composed. The boys then spent two more hours discussing the wording the new document would contain. Finally, they agreed on its construction, and Bernard was, once again, tasked with the job of producing the finished manuscript.

• • •

On the following Monday, Sam confirmed Andy had passed the 'investigation' process. He revealed the letter, which Andy accepted as genuine, more than he had believed Sam's first 'evidence,' the two-way radios.

"So it's true, you really are a… what the hell are you, a spy?"

"No," Sam laughed, "I told you. All they want me to do is go to a few meetings, see what's going on, what's being said, and by whom, that sort of thing…."

"In other words, to spy!"

None of the boys had considered this interpretation. Still, Andy's assessment had been correct, or would have been, had the situation been for real. Sam was pretending to be a spy! "Yeah," Sam smiled as the realization dawned upon him, "I suppose I am." The word 'spy' had never occurred to him or his friends, so his initial reluctance to accept this soubriquet had been sincere. It was Andy who had uttered the 's' word, not him.

"Are they going to give you a gun?" Without hesitation, Andy now believed his friend. Sam smiled. As much as he would have loved to say 'yes,' he knew this was impractical for two reasons. First, Sam did not know how to get a firearm, which Andy, no doubt, would want to see. Second, it was unlikely that they would entrust someone as young as him with such a weapon.

Sam had no intention of slipping up now, not when he had achieved his goal. "No, and I doubt they'd give me one, either. That's why I've got the radios. There will always be someone close by I can contact if I get into trouble; at least, that's the plan."

"How will you know if they're there?"

"I won't. They'll know me, but I won't know who they are. That way, if I get caught, I can't tell anyone what I don't know."

"Oh, Christ, this is getting heavy. Do you know what you're getting yourself into? Have you thought about what would happen if you get hurt or killed? What about your mom and dad...?"

"I've written them a note... they'll find it if... anything... " Sam was now so focused he believed this pretense himself. For just the briefest of moments, he seemed to remember penning a 'confession'! Also, he found he was crying, for God's sake!Andy rested his hand solemnly on Sam's shoulder. "Don't worry. I'll be here. You can call me whenever you need to, night or day, just not on a Thursday between seven-thirty and eight o'clock in the evening."

"Why not then?"

"Top of the Pops." This was a U.K. television program that showcased new popular music songs, occasionally with bands and solo artists performing live in the studio.

Despite Andy's attempt to lighten the tension, Sam did not fail to notice the trembling and unsteadiness in his friend's voice. Andy really cared about him. Perhaps he should end the deception. Right here, right now. He'd accomplished his aim. He had made, or he would make, Andy look so foolish when this all came out. It had been far more straightforward than he had expected. Actually, there was no need to carry it on. For about ten seconds, Sam considered this option, during which he was staring straight at Andy. Misunderstanding his friend's behavior, Andy thought Sam was regarding him with affection, the friendship between two boys who had known each other all their lives.

No, Sam resolved; let's see where we can take this. Let's see how far we can really go.

CHAPTER 4

There was a slight problem on the following Saturday. Paul's parents had given him a new Fidelity record player for his birthday. It boasted all the latest features, including a four-speed auto change facility, and the inquisitive boy could not resist the temptation to investigate its mechanics. Although he had stripped it down effortlessly, he just could not re-assemble it correctly. It didn't play, and no matter how often he dismantled it and readjusted its internal mechanism, the record player would not work. When his parents noticed he was not using the appliance, the boy had to admit his culpability.

"'Fourteen guineas,' that's all he keeps saying," moaned Paul to his friends. "'Aroisgevorfene gelt. Money down the drain.'" he mimicked in a voice not unlike that of his father. "Christ, you'd think I'd broken it on purpose. Anyway, that's why I can't come out. They've grounded me."

"How long for?"

"Listening to my dad, about seventy years."

"Why didn't you just say you didn't know why it wasn't working? That's what I would've done," said Sam.

"Because you pferde, they knew that if I'd found it like that, I'd have told them right away. Think about it. They only discovered it because they realized I'd not used it. My folks are not daft," he conceded. "They know what I'm like."

"So, are your mom and dad going to get it fixed?" this from Bernard.

"Well, my mom wants to, but my dad doesn't. He says they ought to teach me a lesson."

"Do what I would," volunteered Bernard. "Say you'll pay for it out of your own pocket money. They won't have the heart to keep your dosh from you, and it would look at least as if you were sincere. That ought to do the trick."

"So you can't come over to Bernie's house, then?"

"Are you kidding? I'm lucky they're still feeding me!"

Sam turned to his friend, smiling. "You don't work for Israeli intelligence without learning a few tricks," he said.

"What do you mean? You don't work for Israeli intelligence. You and intelligence shouldn't even appear in the same sentence."

"Do you want to come to Bernie's or not?"

"Of course, but...."

"Then shut up and leave the rest to me."

As Paul was seeing his friends off at the door, Sam slipped and hit the floor hard, going down heavily. Mrs. Goldberg came out to see what the noise was, appearing in time to notice Sam raising himself from the carpet.

"Are you all right, Sam? What happened?"

"Don't know, Mrs. Goldberg. It must have been my shoelaces or something," and turning to Paul, he continued, "Sorry you won't be able to come for dinner. Mum's made your favorite...."

"What's this about dinner, Paul? You didn't tell me Sam's mom had invited you over...." The boy almost didn't take the hint until he saw Sam silently prompting him.

"Sorry, mom, I must have forgotten." Her son replied, embarrassed.

"Well, I don't suppose we can let Sam's mom down, can we?" she sighed. "Not after she's gone to so much trouble. Ok, you can go, but you'd better be back here by nine o'clock, or there'll be hell to pay. I mean it!" she added, wagging her finger to emphasize her demand.

"What about dad?"

"Don't worry about your father. It'll be fine." She smiled. Even though it would cost money to repair the record player, yes, they would get it fixed. She still doted on her son. Julia Goldberg, née Rosenbloom, had married late in life and did not believe she would ever bear children. This was the son she had never expected to see, a nes, a miracle.

Sam had somehow understood that if he'd gone to his friend's mother and just asked her if her son could go for supper, she could not lose face in front of Paul. Discipline would need to be maintained. But pretending to have fallen in her house, under her roof, letting her see him in some 'distress.' Then suddenly springing on her his own mother's invitation to supper, well, she could hardly refuse, could she? He would catch her off-guard, off-balance. Discipline had to be maintained, yes, but she couldn't look like a complete bitch, could she? At least, that's what he hoped. And it had worked. "Well, am I good, or am I good?" crowed Sam, as the trio left Paul's house.

"Yeah, but what about me? Your mom didn't invite me over, and now my mom won't feed me either. I'm going to be hungry." wailed Paul.

"No, you're not. Don't worry; I'll get my mom to fix you up something. I think we've got some cat food somewhere. You ungrateful bastard, I got you out of a grounding, and all you can think about is your stomach."

"Well," Paul pouted, "I've got a large appetite."

"You've got a large arse as well, but never mind, eh?"

"That was a nice piece of work you did in Paul's house." Bernard allowed.

"I told you…"

"Yeah, yeah… Israeli intelligence, more like dumb fucking luck if you ask me."

"Well, nobody's asking you. Did you do the second letter, by the way?"

"Yeah, and you'll like it. I've tinkered with it, but it looks better. Wait and see."

When they arrived at Bernard's house, they went to his room, where their friend displayed his handiwork. As before, Bernard had printed the letter on the vellum and included the same Hebrew characters. Sam admitted it had been better than he expected and couldn't wait until Monday to assault Andy with the next phase of his plan. He now considered the entire project to be his. After all, wasn't he the one who had instigated the entire thing and was carrying it out by himself, unaided? Yes, Paul and Bernard had helped, but only peripherally. He was the powerhouse who was driving it along and would see it through to its conclusion. Didn't Sam just free Paul from being kept indoors on a bright summer's evening, not that he'd even received much appreciation for his efforts? And that staged fall hurt more than he would admit. And hadn't Bernard only reluctantly agreed to this second letter at Sam's insistence? He forgot, or chose not to remember, that Paul was as eager as he, that they should write a further letter.

• • • •

Andy was two or three inches taller than his friend and heavier built, and there wasn't a sport at which he did not excel. Their sports teacher always chose him to pick his side's numbers, a natural-born leader, someone who his team would listen to and obey. He played football for a local team and had won many prizes for swimming. He had also taken up golf. Unlike Sam, Andy had come to his headmaster's notice before, but for positive reasons.

During the morning break, a few days later, Sam gently nudged Andy away from their friends. When they were alone, he furtively drew out from his pocket a crumpled envelope. "I've had another letter. It's really for you, but they sent it to me, in case your mom or dad opened it. By now, Andy knew what Sam was talking about, although, of course, he did not know the contents of the document.

He took the letter from Sam and read. "'Dear Andy Marshall, we understand from our Glasgow agent, Sam Nathan, that you are to be his support officer, and we understand he has instructed you on your duties accordingly. While we do not perceive any danger befalling you, you must discuss this operation with no one, especially your family. We can only act efficiently as long as everybody plays their part effectively, no matter how great or small their role. If we believe your actions have compromised any of our agents, we will investigate the source of the problem and respond appropriately. We hope you will both work successfully together for a long time. Welcome to the family of The House of Israel. Shalom. The Office of the Sanhedrin.'"

Sam made sure he got the letter back, explaining that he had to keep hold of it for 'security reasons.'

It took Andy some time to understand what he had just read. What the fuck was a 'support officer'? Just what had he gotten himself into? This couldn't really be happening, could it? Was he, a young Christian boy, really being recruited to work for Israel? The very idea seemed impossible, and yet he had seen and used the radios, and he had read the letters. And what did they mean, 'respond appropriately'?

Sam assured him that this was just a standard letter of introduction, and all they were doing was covering themselves. Besides, he would never get into that position. Not unless he told anyone, and he wouldn't do that now, would he?

And who, or what, was the Sanhedrin? This was a point which the boys discussed when they were planning the letter. Sam would have liked to invoke Mossad, the real Israeli intelligence organization, but they feared if word of their escapade ever got to the ears of anyone connected to this group, unlikely as this was, all of their arses would be in a sling, and what they were only doing as a joke could end up backfiring on them big time. Mossad did not take prisoners, and even being Jews might not save them from the service's wrath. The real Sanhedrin was a biblical entity, the Jewish High Court of pre-Christian times, which the boys had learned about in Hebrew classes. It no longer had any currency or relevance to modern life, and the boys were sure that using this term would not endanger them. And besides, it had a nice dramatic ring to it. Sanhedrin. Sanhedrin. Yes, that would do nicely, indeed.

Sam lied that the Sanhedrin was the cover name for the intelligence unit running them, which was controlled by the embassy who reported back to Jerusalem.

"So, when do I start? When's your first gig?"

"This Saturday, but don't worry. I won't need you this time."

"Where are you going?"

"That's the one question you never ask! I can tell you after, but not before. It's for your own safety—and mine!"

"Yeah, I understand, I guess.

The bell rang to end the morning break, and they walked back into the school building together, just two friends side by side. Everything was working out just fine. Soon, Andy would understand what it was like to be at the receiving end. It was all coming together according to plan.

CHAPTER 5

The following Saturday, the three Jewish friends got together again to devise a scenario that Sam could relate on Monday. Sam had envisaged bringing in an imaginary agent, a young Israeli girl, just to spice things up. He imagined her to be in trouble, and he, Sam, would rescue her just in time from the clutches of some evil band of cut-throat Arab sympathizers. She would have to show her appreciation, and there was only one satisfactory way she could do this.

"Your name is Nathan, Sam Nathan, not James bloody Bond. And besides, if she had any sense, I bet she would rather be murdered by those mamzers than shag you!"

"No," agreed Bernard, "Paul's right. Let's keep it simple. The more lies you tell, the more you'd have to remember. You're bound to slip up."

"Why wouldn't he believe it?" reasoned Sam. "He's believed everything else. What's the point of pretending to be a spy if you can't get laid?" He wasn't giving up without a fight. "Christ, James Bond, even Napoleon Solo, gets a bird in every show, at least one. If it's OK for them, why can't I? Let's face it; they're only pretending to be spies, too. Mind you, I wouldn't half mind that Stephanie Powers. She's a bit of all right."

"These guys are old, well, at least twenty-five, and they're, well, smart, like...suave, you know... look, it's only a bloody T.V. show, they're not real bloody secret agents!" They eventually abandoned the idea, much to Sam's chagrin. Bernard had an idea where to place Sam on his first 'mission,' and it did not take the boys long to work out a likely scenario that Sam could relate to Andy.

"OK, if we're done with this, who's for a game of Monopoly?" asked Bernard eagerly.

. . .

Andy was looking forward to Monday morning with a strange mixture of emotions. Excitement at what Sam would tell him about his adventure, but also trepidation, almost bordering on fear. What if he didn't show up at all? Suppose 'they' had caught him doing... God knew what? What if they'd beaten him up, hurt him, or worse?

He would have liked to see Sam yesterday, Sunday, but this would have been out of their routine. Andy didn't want to do anything which could compromise his friend's safety. Sam arrived at school, knowing Andy would be waiting for him. He sauntered up to his friend, grinning widely.

"Well, how did it go?" he whispered. "What happened? Are you ok?" And so Sam retold the story the three boys had concocted two days earlier. "They sent me to listen to a speech by some pro-Palestinian group. They demanded that Israel give back the territories it had captured in the recent conflict and release all war prisoners. There was also a call for a United Nations resolution condemning Israel for starting the war in the first place. A few followers wanted to call for a jihad, and...."

"A what?"

"A jihad; it's Muslim for a holy war against any other religion, but usually Jews."

"Shit. Sounds like us Proddies and Cathies."

"Yeah, something like that–well, actually, nothing like that. Anyway, I talked to some people, especially the loudmouth who insisted on starting a Holy War against the Jews. I asked him to explain more and got his phone number and address. I told him I would get in touch so we could talk some more. Needless to say, I've got no intention of doing this, but I will give his details to Sanhedrin. I'm sure they'll be interested." He shrugged this off as if it had been only going for a walk, but Sam could not fail to notice the awe and admiration in Andy's expression.

This idea came to Bernard from an item he had seen in The Jewish Echo a couple of weeks earlier. His parents still had the paper, and Bernard had brought it out for them to read. The anti-Israel meeting had been held at Strathclyde University in George Street, chaired by Tony Cliff, a well-known Marxist and anti-Zionist. There was very little copy about the conference itself, but the paper's editorial lambasted Cliff for his stance and asked how a Jew, born Yigael Gluckstein, in pre-Israeli Palestine, could take such a posture on the country of his birth and his religious heritage.

"I might need you to cover for me this weekend. Well, Saturday anyway. Is that ok?"

Andy now had no doubts or hesitation in agreeing to Sam's request and couldn't wait to do his bit. His friend understood he could disclose nothing he did for Sam now, but later, when they were both older and no longer involved, boy, would he have a story to tell.

"Yeah, sure, just say where and when."

And so, for the next few weeks, the boys invented various events at which Sam had been, some of which required Andy to 'cover' for him. The situations that Sam pretended to find himself in, the adventures he related, became more outrageous each week. Sam picked the pocket of one of 'them,' only to find a piece of paper detailing a proposed assault on a local synagogue. Invited to one of their secret meetings, he heard some people discussing the next war against Israel. He listened in on how they were going over to volunteer, as he, himself, had intended, only to fight for the Arab side.

However, in due course, the boys began to run out of ideas, and even Bernard found it difficult to invent new plots. Sam, too, was becoming tired of the pretense, so they decided to bring the whole thing to a close. But Sam had one more scheme, which would bring the entire deception to a spectacular finale. When he outlined his proposal, he fully expected Paul and Bernard to go along with him. The prankster was unprepared for their reactions, which were nothing less than mutinous. He was in control of this operation. How could they go against him? How dare they? This would be the best wheeze of all, a real ball-breaker.

"Listen to what you're saying," shouted Paul, the discussion becoming more heated by the minute. "What we did before... the letters... the scams, that was ok, but this is going too far. No, you shouldn't do this. It's too much; it's way over the top."

"Paul's right, Sammy, think about it. You don't know where this might end up. It's fuckin' serious, and I want no part of it. If you really want to do this, you're on your own. Neither of us will help you. Please, just let's end it now, as we planned. You, we... you... did it. You screwed your mate. Just think of the look on his face when you tell him the truth. Think of how he'll feel. He..."

But Sam could not stop now. The whole thing had taken him over and was now in control. It was his addiction, his obsession, and it compelled him to finish it in the way he had planned. Nothing and no one could stand in his way, not now, and if he had to complete his aim on his own, well, so be it. He didn't need these two... pussies. No, he was determined to see this through, in his way, and he would allow no one to talk him out of it, not for any reason. Couldn't they see it? This would be a real 'Candid Camera' stunt, an absolute showstopper!

Bernard felt he had to give it one more try, to get his friend back from the planet he now inhabited, a very lonely, dark, and scary place.

"You're not considering the effect your little 'joke' will have on Andy. What do you think this will do to him? Have you thought about that?"

Sam shrugged his shoulders, indifferent to Bernard's objections. "Who cares? He'll get over it. It's only a fucking gag; it's not real."

"You know that, and so do we, but he doesn't. Don't forget; he thinks all this is real. What if it was the other way round? How do you think you'd react to...?" He now understood it was no use. Sam was too far gone. There was a look in his eyes that worried him. Paul saw it as well. Sam had become someone else, someone neither of them liked very much. They didn't know who this new person was, only that he was dangerous and could never be a friend to them.

• • • •

As he watched his friend approaching, Andy knew something was wrong. There was no jaunty step, no conspiratorial glance, no smile of recognition even, only a grim determination set on Sam's face. He pulled Andy by the shoulder, insisting they had to talk, now, in private!

For the first time since Sam's initial revelation, Andy was worried. He'd never seen his friend like this before or since his 'recruitment.' Something was up. Sam was in a state. He looked as if he hadn't slept, which was true, but for different reasons than his friend believed. Sam couldn't sleep for excitement, his nerves almost on fire waiting for this very moment.

He pushed-propelled his friend to the back of the toilets, where this episode had all begun. Sam quivered with anticipation, about to pull the stunt of the century.

"I've had word from someone in Sanhedrin," he began, feigning anxiety. Andy regarded him with expectation. "So, what do they want you for this time? To save the world, again?" he laughed.

"This wasn't for me. It was about you."

"About me?" he almost screamed. "What about me? What have I done?"

"It's not what you've done; it's who you are, or rather, who you're not." As if reluctant to continue, Sam closed his eyes, afraid to reveal the rest of his knowledge. However, he had rehearsed this drama over and over during the last forty-eight hours.

Andy felt as if his stomach had suddenly emptied, had turned into a hollow shell, devoid, even, of vital organs. Just a vacant space where they should have been. He knew this would not be good, wanted to run away and forget all about the past few weeks. Andy had the urge to put his hands over his ears, anything to blot out the information Sam was about to impart. "There's no easy way to say this. I wish there were. I... I don't know how to tell you. Oh, God..."

"Tell me what?" Andy screamed, no longer mindful of any discretion. "What the fuck's going on? What have I done?" he calmed down before continuing in a lower voice, "I've told no one about our... secret. I swear, no one. If anyone knows who you are, they didn't hear it from me. That's the truth."

"I know..."

"Then what the fuck's going on? What have I, am I, supposed to have done?"

"Nothing, you've done nothing wrong," Sam assured him.

"Then, what, for fuck's sake?"

"There's been a screw-up. It's not your fault. It's mine, theirs...."

"What do you mean, 'screw-up'? If it's not got anything to do with me, why am I involved? It's your balls in the vise, not mine."

"It's not what you've done; it's about you."

"What about me?"

"You're not Jewish."

"So...?"

"They didn't tell me...."

"Tell you what?"

"I was only supposed to recruit someone Jewish to be my backup. I won't be able to use you anymore."

"Is that all? I thought it was something serious." Andy said, relief palpable in his voice.

Sam took a deep breath. "No, I'm afraid that's not all. There's... more. I'm sorry; I'm so very sorry...."

"What? What more? What are you not telling me?"

"They... they now think you... you're a liability...."

"What are you talking about? What 'liability?'"

"I've told you things I shouldn't have, things that can endanger our mission...."

"I would never say anything that could get you hurt. You know that!"

"Yes, I know that, but they don't. As far as they're concerned, you need to... oh, my God. I don't know how to tell you this...."

"Need to what?" Andy demanded.

"You know what," Sam replied quietly.

"No, I fucking don't... oh, Christ, you mean... No! No! No!" Andy screamed, rocking his head from side to side. He stared at Sam, gazing all around him but seeing nothing, unwilling to believe what his friend was telling him. "You can't... I helped you, remember? I was your fucking alibi. I'm on your side. No, this isn't happening. You've got to do something. Surely there's something you can do! They can't kill me; they can't! I won't say anything to anybody, honest. You can't let them do this!"

"There's nothing I can do. I tried, I really tried, I did! I begged them not to... it was no use. They've done what they call a damage limitation plan. Once that's put into effect, no one can stop it. They're playing for high stakes; the highest of stakes, the security of Israel itself is in danger...."

"Not from me!" Andy cried, "Not from me!"

"I'm sorry, really sorry... I told them you're no threat, but they refused to listen. They're determined to... It's only a matter of time..."

"When...?"

"I don't know. It could be at any time. They didn't tell me, only that it would be soon - before you became a greater liability."

"Fuck, this has gone too far. I'm going to be killed because of a mistake you made. Fuck them! Fuck you too. I'm going to the police. I would never have revealed our secret to anyone; you know that, never, especially when your life could have been in danger. But it's my life that's on the line now, for something that's no fault of mine. I didn't fucking ask to be your backup. You came to me, remember? Fuck, they even investigated me. They know I'm no threat. Why did this all not come out when they did their checks? It must have been fucking obvious that we weren't Jews, with a name like 'Marshall.' I thought you Jews were supposed to be smart— some fuckin' smart. I'm going straight to the cops. They can sort it out. I said I'd help you; I didn't agree to die for you!"

"You can't do that," Sam said with determination.

"Can't do what?" Andy replied, anger and fear rising in his voice.

"You can't go to the police."

"Oh, can't I? You just fuckin' watch me, pal!"

"No, you can't! We, that is, the Sanhedrin, have people everywhere, even in the police. If you go to them, Sanhedrin will find out, and that will make things even worse."

"Even worse? How can things get any worse than they already are?"

"If they find out you've tried to go public with this, they'll have no choice. They'll kill your family, too. Your mom, your dad, your little sister...."

"Sarah? They would kill Sarah? A seven-year-old child? What likely threat could she be to you, to Israel? No, no way. That's not going to happen. It's bad enough threatening to kill my parents, but to murder an innocent little girl...? What sort of people are you...?"

Sam shrugged his shoulders. "It's out of my hands. There's no more I can do. I'm sorry."

"But how do they possibly think they can kill my entire family and me with no one getting suspicious? This is just crazy!"

"They've done it before, they said. The last time, they made it to look like a car accident...."

"The last time? How often do these people go about killing innocent families?" Andy was dumbfounded.

"I don't know. I only know that you can't go to the authorities. It would be too dangerous."

Andy now broke down completely. He sobbed, staring wildly around him. Maybe they were here now, waiting, in hiding, disguised perhaps, ready to strike. One thing was for sure. He couldn't go into classes, not in the state he was in, yet maybe that would be the safest place. They couldn't hit him in a room full of pupils, could they? Could they? Would they? Andy did not yet know the meaning of the word 'paranoia,' but he would learn all about it over the next few days.

CHAPTER 6

It had been four days since Sam had perpetrated his cruel hoax, during which he had not seen or heard from Andy. Now, he had achieved his ultimate aim, the total, complete, and utter humiliation of Andy Marshall.

Since the time he heard the fateful news, Andy had been too afraid to go outside his own front door. His parents noticed the change that had come over him, and he ached to tell them, was desperate to unburden himself of everything, but believed that to do so would lead to their deaths. He pretended he was unwell but could not overplay his hand in case they might call the doctor. Andy knew that any examination would show the only thing he was suffering from was fear.

He pretended to go to school but hid in a nearby tenement building, disguising himself as best he could until he was sure his house would be empty. When he was confident that he would be alone, Andy returned as discretely as possible, to draw as little attention to himself as he could. He froze at every sound, trembled at every passing car, scanned the street, secreted behind the curtains for any unfamiliar face, any activity out of the ordinary. The postman delivering the mail. Was it the regular one? Somehow, he looked different. He hid behind the settee in the front room, listening as the letterbox cover opened, the soft rustle in the otherwise quiet house, of envelopes falling gently, landing on the carpeted floor. Was it only mail that the postman was putting through the aperture? What if it were more, what if it were a letter-bomb? Could you get such an explosive between the narrow space? Was it possible? He strained his ears. There was no hissing, no sound of a fuse burning. Could you hear a fuse burning down? He listened intently, but heard nothing suspicious. Did the postman leave? He couldn't remember hearing departing footsteps fading into the distance. What if he was still there, waiting just behind the front door for Andy to collect the mail? Then, phut... phut... two quick shots through the letterbox from a silenced gun, and it would all be over. But would they make it appear so obvious? Surely his demise would have to seem like an accident. If it were a murder, all of his friends would come under scrutiny, Sam included, and they wouldn't want him implicated, would they? No, he decided, thinking almost rationally, and regarding his fate objectively, like an academic exercise. It would have to seem accidental, unforeseen. For the next four days, Andy went through the same purgatory, each day becoming worse, knowing it was another day nearer his death. Accepting his end could come at any minute, any second, he could face it no longer. Fuck them, fuck them all!

At 4.30 p.m. on the fourth day of his self-imposed confinement, the doorbell rang. This was it, he thought. They've come. They're finally here. Well, I'm not going to make it easy for them. If they want me, they'll have to break in and come and get me. Nothing will make me go near that fucking door. The bell rang a second time, louder and more persistent. Andy still did not budge from his hiding place. He then heard the letterbox rattle, and a familiar voice assailed him. "Andy, it's me, it's Sam. It's ok; you can come out. Everything's ok."

Andy's brain went into overdrive. Would they send Sam, a fourteen-year-old boy, his friend, to kill him? No, impossible, but what if he was only there to lure him out into the open? What if they were forcing Sam to do this, being coerced by a similar threat? Co-operate with us, or we'll kill your family. What if the killer was standing beside him, waiting with a hypodermic needle or something? No, his best bet, his safest bet, his only choice was to stay put. Wait it out. His folks would be home soon. Oh, God, what if his mother arrived? She could get it, too, with his little sister. Afraid as he was for his own safety, he could not have his little sister, whom he adored, suffering, dying because of his selfishness, his cowardice. Andy screamed out in fear, anger, hatred, frustration, impotence, despair. He was only fourteen years old. He didn't want to die. He didn't deserve to die. Neither did he want his mother to die or his little sister. How could Sam have allowed them to get into this mess? There had to be a way out; there just had to be!

"Andy," Sam repeated, shouting through. It was the first real clue he had had of his friend's total terror. "It's ok. It's all been a joke, a gag. There's no killer; there has never been. You're not in any danger. You never were!"

"Yeah, right, maybe not from you, but what about the bastard standing behind you with the fucking needle?"

"Needle, what needle? There's no one here except me. I promise and swear to you; this has all been a lark."

"I... don't... fucking... believe... you..."

Sam shouted once again, "Do you have an encyclopedia in the house?"

"A what?"

"An encyclopedia; do you have an encyclopedia?"

"Why the fuck do you want to know if I've got an encyclopedia? It's a fuckin' strange time to want to know something!"

"Get it. Go to the word 'Sanhedrin.' It's got nothing to do with Israeli or any other secret organization. I promise. Please. Just look it up."

Andy could not see where this ruse could be going, but realized that nothing he did would save him. Why not humor his pal? There wasn't much time left, anyway. It was all he ever wanted to know. He would die all the happier for learning the meaning of this strange word. He leafed through the pages, alighting at the name, 'Sanhedrin, the highest judicial and ecclesiastical council of the ancient Jewish nation, comprising seventy-one members. It was dissolved after the destruction of the second temple by the Romans in AD70.'

"Can you see it? Have you read it?"

"Yeah. This doesn't prove shit. It's still a Jewish word. I don't care if it goes back to Roman times. Go away. Just fuckin' go away! All you're trying to do is confuse me, make me come to the front door. Look, I'll do a deal with you. Tell your guy he can take me, but don't hurt my mom or my sister. Ok?"

"Andy, please, no one will hurt you; you or your family. It was only a practical joke. I made the whole thing up. Honest."

"Don't fucking insult my intelligence. I saw the letters, and I used the walkie-talkies, remember?"

"I had… help, two of my Jewish friends. Andy, I swear. Look, I'm leaving, but I'll be back in ten minutes. I'll prove I'm telling the truth. Please wait. I'll be back…"

Andy heard Sam's footsteps hurrying off, but this proved nothing. Someone could still be out there, listening, just waiting for the chance to finish the job. Please, God, just let it be me, not my family, too. They wouldn't fool him that easily, not Andy Marshall! He would wait until he'd heard Sam's voice again before saying or doing anything else.

In less than the time he'd said, Sam returned, panting, out of breath. "Andy, I'm going to put something through your letterbox. It's a Jewish prayer book called a siddur, and it's very holy. It belongs to my mom and dad. Pick it up, please. Just look at it."

Andy had resigned himself to his destiny. It might as well be now as never. He crept to the door, scooped up the prayer book, and rushed back to his place of concealment. Sam had heard him and knew he had retrieved it.

"Open it, Andy, please, so that you can see I'm telling you the truth. I've sworn on that siddur, and I'll do it again now. On the lives of my mom and dad, you are in no danger. No one is trying to kill you. No one ever was. It was a practical joke, all of it. That's all it ever was, the radios, the letters, everything. Please, I swear to you. Please open the door and let me in. I'm here on my own."

Could it be true? What was real, and what was make-believe? Andy didn't know anymore. Was he being reprieved? Were his family out of danger? Were they ever in danger? Was he? He just didn't know. What had Sam done to him? If they were going to kill him, better they did it now. He just couldn't face it any longer, the uncertainty, the tension. They'd won, as they were bound to win. Only please don't hurt my folks, my little sister… Cautiously, he opened the door. Sam put his face to the gap. Andy could see that he, too, looked anxious. That much, at least, was for real. But why? Was it because he knew his friend was about to be murdered? He slammed the door closed and fled back into the relative safety of his living room. Andy sat behind the sofa with his knees bent up to his stomach in the fetal position. His eyes stared wildly into vacant space, his breath coming in small sharp gasps.

Sam shouted through the letterbox again. "Please, Andy, come to the door. There's no one here except me. I promise. There was no secret organization, I swear to you. Please come to the door. You don't even have to open it if you don't want to. Please, just let me explain."

Andy so desperately wanted Sam to be telling the truth, but how could he be sure? How could he be sure of anything? The distraught teenager rationalized that nothing he did would make any difference now. If he didn't come to the door, they would gain entry anyway. He may as well listen to what his friend had to say. It would be the last time he would see Sam. He opened the door a mere fraction, still half-expecting to be hurled back inside by the killer, but it was only Sam who remained at the partition.

"Please, Andy, let me in so I can explain. I really am on my own." Nervously, Andy allowed Sam to push the door, still tensing himself against a sudden incoming onslaught. None came.

Sam slid inside rapidly, in case his friend suddenly changed his mind. Andy slammed the door behind Sam. He still wasn't sure and wasn't taking any chances. Once inside, Sam picked up the prayer book he'd given Andy. It had landed on the floor, and without thinking, Sam performed the time-honored ritual of kissing it, as a gesture of atonement, as he picked it up. Sam took his parents' siddur in his right hand. "What I'm about to tell you now is the truth. You know I wouldn't lie on this book, don't you?"

Andy assented. And so Sam confessed to everything. He explained how he came to have the radios in his possession, how the boys had prepared and written the letters. He even admitted that his two friends did not want him to carry through his last part of the scheme. This he had done without their blessing, never mind their help.

The burning question came to Andy, the one he had to ask. Why? So Sam explained the reason for the whole thing, right from the start. Andy barely believed what he was hearing. He had gone through hell for four days so that Sam could get even? For a few bits of name-calling? It was hardly credible that he would go to such lengths for something so... so trivial. "Fuck's sake, Andy, it was only a bit of fun. I was only trying to..."

"You bastard; you fucking bastard. Have you any idea what I've been through? Not just me; my parents. They knew something was wrong, but I couldn't tell them, could I? Do you know what you've done, you fucking shit?" Fear and anxiety had now given way to anger and rage. "You're a fuckin' maniac, do you know that? A fuckin' dyed-in-the-wool psycho. You're a dangerous head case. D'you know something? I wish you had gone to Israel. Do you know why? Because you might have got your fucking head blown off! You fuckin' deserve to have. You've no idea what I... Do you know what I think? I think Hitler didn't do a good enough job. He should have finished off the lot of you! You're all a bunch of fuckin' lunatics." With that, Andy let fly a well-aimed punch at Sam. Sam saw it coming and could have avoided it. He chose not to. Andy followed up with a string of blows that Sam only half-heartedly parried, allowing many of them to land. He did not even try to hit back. Andy extended his arm once again, and Sam braced himself for another pummeling. But the boy merely stretched out his hand, pointing at him. "I don't want to see you, or talk to you, ever again. Don't think about saying sorry, because even if you apologize until the day you die, it wouldn't be enough. Not for what..." and he lost control again. "How could you do this to me, to me? Your best friend! Get out. Just go. And never come near me again. Go. Fuck off. How often have I got to say it before it goes into your thick fuckin' Jew head?"

"Andy, please..." but he realized it was no use. Andy had never, ever cast up his religion before in such a derogatory way. Yes, he was bound to be upset, but this was too much, and what he'd said about Hitler... no, this friendship was over, dead and buried, say Kaddish, and move on.

It would be almost four years before the two boys would speak again. And because of this conversation, Sam would be plunged into a nightmare so dreadful that it would make what he did to Andy pale into insignificance...

PART 2

CHAPTER 7

January 1971

In the immediate days and weeks following his disastrous self-indulgent actions, Sam tried everything he could to apologize, to make amends for what he had done. But the wound was too deep and would not heal so quickly. Although Andy's ordeal lasted only four days, it took a lot longer for the psychological trauma to leave him. For weeks afterward, he awoke periodically in the small hours, drenched in sweat. Half-remembered forms swimming tantalizingly just out of reach, mocking him remorselessly. Vague shapes in human outline, images, dark, mysterious, threatening shadows were coming at him through the mist, black diaphanous ciphers about to strike the fatal blow. He could never take his parents into his confidence. The shame and embarrassment known only by only a fourteen-year-old forbade him to reveal how frightened he had been. Even after Sam had revealed the danger to be nothing more than a malevolent invention, his legacy was still there. It was in the background, brooding, out of reach but not out of mind.

However, the nightmares eventually faded, slowly at first, but gradually losing their potency. Finally, they became nothing more than a minor irritation, reluctantly receding into the crevasses of his memory.

Although the boys shared many of the same classes, Andy refused even to acknowledge Sam's existence. Everyone realized something had happened, but an unspoken, tacit agreement between them meant that neither would discuss the reason for their enmity. It had been enough for both to say that they were no longer friendly; there had been a disagreement. The subject was now closed. Move on.

Sam's relationship with his two Jewish friends remained not so strained. This was because Sam could never admit to them the depths to which he had sunk and the anguish to which he had subjected Andy. Having realized the enormity of what he had done, he had lied to his friends and abridged the last five days into one. Sam said that once he had told Andy the Israelis were going to execute him, he almost at once revealed the whole thing as a hoax. He had even taken the siddur to school so that Andy would accept his apology without question. He further compounded the fiction by declaring that, although angry at first, Andy eventually saw the funny side. After this, the trio never again mentioned the events of the past few weeks. Despite this, the boys' relationship cooled, and although still friends, limited their meetings to the times they met at synagogue.

It was with some surprise, therefore, not to mention delight, that on a dark, wet and windy evening in January 1971, Sam received a phone call from Andy. Could the division, the separation, of the last three-and-a-half years be about to end? Sam hoped so. There had not been a day that had gone by without his thinking about that time. His very psyche wished he could somehow recapture it, make it different, make it never happen at all. Sam realized their friendship could never go back to what it was. After all, they were nearly four years older now. Still, at least they could have a relationship of a sort, even if only to go for the occasional pint. At first, Andy hesitated, as if regretting his decision to make contact, but he slowly and nervously regained his assertiveness. It had been a long time since they had last spoken during that highly charged afternoon in Andy's house.

Although the boys had had no direct contact since that time, both knew how the other had progressed, mutual friends keeping them informed. Sam had left school and found a job working in an office. The work did not challenge him, but his wages were not too bad, and there was always scope for advancement. He hadn't yet really decided what he wanted to do with his life, and considered this position as only a stopgap until something better came along.

Andy had gone to university to study architecture, although, like his former friend, he, too, did not yet have any long-term ambitions.

"Hi... Sam? It's Andy. Andy Marshall. Ah, long time no speak. How are..., how are... you?"

Sam couldn't credit it. Could this be Andy? Had he found the generosity of spirit to forgive, at least, if not forget, Sam's atrocious behavior? Well, here he was, on the other end of the phone. Sam couldn't deny that much, at least.

"I'm fine, Andy. I'm well. How are you? I heard you'd gone to uni. You must be brainier than I thought. You're doing, what is it - architecture...?"

"Yeah," he replied. "Well, it beats working for a living. How about you? I was told you'd landed an office job. Any good?"

"Well, it pays for my keep, I guess...." There was so much he wanted to say, to tell Andy, again, how sorry he felt, how stupid he'd been, but somehow, this didn't seem the right time. He was sure Andy hadn't phoned expecting an apology. Besides, perhaps this might not be the time to open old wounds. Let sleeping dogs lie, and just be grateful for Andy's welcome gesture.

"Look... ah... Sam, would you... I mean... do you fancy going out for a pint some time? We could... ah... catch up, perhaps."

This was what Sam had dreamed about for so long: a final rehabilitation in Andy's eyes. "Yeah, sure... when... where... do you think...?"

Andy appeared to think for a few seconds before he replied. "Do you know Denholm's Bar?"

"No. Where is it?"

"OK. It's at the bottom of Hope Street, just around the corner from Argyle Street. It faces the back of Central Station. You can't miss it. Maybe we could have a drink this coming Saturday."

"I'll find it," Sam responded, still overwhelmed by Andy's phone call.

Saturday was three days away, and for the next seventy-two hours, Sam could hardly concentrate his mind on anything else but for the expected reunion. There was so much he wanted to say, so much to think about. How, for example, would they greet each other after all this time? Would they shake hands, embrace, or merely nod in a friendly but distant response? Who would be the first to break the silence? What did etiquette demand? Should it be Andy? After all, it was he who had instigated the meeting, or him as the no doubt guilty party? Should he offer to buy the first round, or should Andy, as the 'host' (well, this meeting place was his suggestion), who does the honors?

Listen to him, he thought; anyone would imagine this was the first date with a girl, rather than a meeting between two old... acquaintances. He could not bring himself to use the word he wanted to–friend. One thing was for sure. He did not want to be late. That, he felt, would be the ultimate insult.

•　•　•　•

He arrived at the pub a few minutes early, not wanting to keep Andy waiting, but neither did he want to seem too keen. Andy, however, was already there. Who was the more eager of the two? He wondered.

At that time of the evening, the bar was still quiet. It would be another hour or two before it got busy. It would then fill with customers coming in after their weekly trip to the cinema or theater or just to pass the evening away drinking. There were still a few stragglers who had arrived earlier after leaving one of the local soccer matches. It took a couple of seconds for Sam to realize that Andy wasn't alone. There seemed to be someone else seated beside him, although it could have been a stranger, sitting just a little too close. But the pub had plenty of empty spaces...

Sam strolled over cautiously. This wasn't how he had meant it to be. Andy had mentioned no one else, and Sam had assumed it would be only the two of them, trying to put right the wrongs, Sam's wrongs, of so long ago.

Andy rose at Sam's arrival and extended his hand in greeting. "Hi, Sam, nice to see you again." Sam felt something in Andy's welcome, but what was it? He was smiling, and his approach seemed sincere, yet something was missing; warmth. That was it. There was no warmth in his voice or his manner. It must be his imagination, he thought. Andy had been the one who invited him. If he didn't want this to happen, why phone in the first place? He let these uncomfortable thoughts drift to the back of his mind. It was a time to heal, not a time for suspicion.

"Hi, Andy, it's good to see you, it absolutely is." and Sam was sincere; he really felt the pleasure he hoped he was exuding and hoped his enthusiasm was not lost on Andy. "How's uni.?" Sam continued. He did not know or understand much about university life and struggled to ask any other appropriate questions about this topic. "What's the talent like?" As soon as the words had left his lips, he wished he hadn't said them. How corny could you get; how pathetic? Here he was, hoping he could finally lay the ghosts of the past, and all he could think about had been laying female students in the present!

Andy only smiled at Sam's inquiry and did not bother to reply. The question did not even merit a response. Not at a time like this. Instead, he introduced his companion. A thought flashed through Sam's head. Was Andy... could this be his boyfriend?... Oh, no... surely not. Not Andy. Was that the reason he hadn't contacted him before? When... how... then the horrible realization... could it have been because of what he did...? Did the shock of those events turn him? Was that possible? Even if this had been the case, why ask Sam to meet him? To rub his nose in it? Look what you've made me. See, because of you, I've become queer. And it was only with this last thought that Sam took stock of the other man sitting at the table because that's what he was; a man. Sam studied him, trying to discern in his features some personality. Even sitting down, Sam could see that the man was above average height. He had short mousey-gray hair and was clean-shaven. The newcomer wore eyeglasses, but which seemed to stress his masculinity rather than detract from it. If he weren't a guy's guy, Sam thought, he wouldn't have too much trouble with women. Sam judged he had to be at least in his late thirties. He couldn't be studying with Andy, could he? There were mature students, of course, but...was he... one of those, or one of those...? These impressions raced between his mind faster than light, but he still did not hear Andy's introduction, so full as he was of his own thoughts.

"Sam, did you hear me? Are you ok? You looked as if you were miles away."

"Further than you'll ever know," Sam thought. "I'm sorry, Andy, it's just the thought of you being, I mean... being here with you... like this... I... I'm sorry...."

"Andy, this is a... friend of mine. Colin," he repeated, with some asperity. "Colin, this is Sam. I'll get the drinks, give you two a chance to become acquainted," he offered, casting Sam a meaningful glance. The look might have been more meaningful to Sam if he knew what it was trying to convey. Had Andy merely been hurt at his shameful display of inattention, or was he trying to say more...?

Sam smiled uneasily, unsure of how to start the conversation. Luckily for him, Colin was more adept and opened the discourse. "Andy tells me you two have been friends, had been friends," he corrected himself, "for many years. I understand there was some unpleasantness...."

What the hell is going on here? Sam wondered. Both boys had reached a silent understanding years ago to skirt around this issue, to leave it unspoken. Yet, here he was, a stranger, well, a stranger to him, not only cognizant of it but bringing it out into the open. How much did he know? Did Andy tell him everything? If so, why? Even if they were together, what business was it of his? Why mention it now, here?

Unwilling to reveal more than Andy might have told him, Sam said, "We had a sort of... misunderstanding a few years ago, and things... cooled between us after that." Sam shrugged, as if to feign detached indifference. "If you don't mind, I'd rather leave that time where it belongs–in the past." Something which he expected Colin to understand, a subject he did not wish to discuss any further. Not here, not now, and definitely not with him!

Andy returned with the drinks, and the talk veered to less contentious matters. For almost an hour, the three discussed various subjects, but never the obvious one, and Sam noticed Colin seemed to want to concentrate on one particular topic. He asked Sam if he had any political affiliations. The teenager responded his father had been a lifelong socialist, so guessed that it would be Labour if he were to support a political party. However, he had no actual interest in the subject. He admitted he believed that whoever you voted for, nothing much changed.

The bar filled, and Andy announced he would have to leave. Sam expected Colin to go with him, but he seemed content to stay. Andy's parting shot to them was only a vague "See you around..." Sam promised he would keep in touch and phone him during the week. Andy only responded with an indifferent shrug as he walked away. As his former friend left the bar, Sam thought, "Something strange is going on here, but what the hell is it?"

Again, there seemed to be an embarrassing silence between them. Colin realized his earlier foray into unwelcome territory, and Sam's apparent rebuke, had been a mistake. However, it was one he had to endure. Without Andy acting as a conduit between them, there seemed little further scope for discussion. It was with plain relief that Colin, too, excused himself, explaining he had another engagement. Shortly after Colin's hurried departure, Sam also decided his night was over. Well and truly over if it had ever started.

His evening might have been curtailed, but it would not be the last time he would hear from Colin. Tonight was only the start of Sam's relationship with this man, and their next confrontation would change Sam's life forever...

CHAPTER 8

The events of that Saturday evening troubled Sam. Why had Andy not told him he'd be with someone else? And who the hell was Colin? Was he, as Sam first suspected, a boyfriend? If that was so, why did they not leave together? For appearances? Had they left separately but rendezvoused later? Why organize the meeting at all, especially if he knew Colin would be there too? If Colin's presence had been an unforeseen complication, surely Andy would have somehow made Sam understand this. And why arrange the whole thing in the first place, then appear so cold, so distant? If the entire purpose of Andy's initial approach had been to exorcise the demons of the past, why hadn't he at least hinted at it? Why had he not been more optimistic about a further opportunity for them to meet? Sam desperately wanted to call him and ask him these questions, but would give him a couple of days to explain himself. Suppose he couldn't do what he'd planned, not in front of Colin, whoever he was. If Andy didn't phone him, Sam would make the call. He didn't intend to allow the link to be broken, now that it was made, however strange the circumstances.

The following Monday evening, he took a phone call that threw all of his plans into disarray. It was from Colin.

"Hi, Sam. This is Colin, Andy's friend. Remember, we met on Saturday?"

"Yes," Sam replied, recalling the unusual events of a few nights ago.

"I... uh... I just wanted to apologize for what I said. I hope I didn't upset you...."

"What you said...?"

"Yes, about you and Andy. I'm sorry if I offended you. I didn't mean any - I had no right to trespass on anything that happened between you."

"No, that's ok. I was just surprised that Andy had told you...."

"Yeah, I realize that now. Listen, I enjoyed our chat, believe it or not. Andy mentioned you were a 'folkie.' As it happens, so am I. Do you manage to go to any concerts?"

"I usually go to see The Corries when they perform at the City Halls in Candleriggs. How about you?"

"Yeah, when I can. I like the Irish folk group The Clancy Brothers. I managed to go and see them in Dublin the last time I was there. Unfortunately, I don't get as much chance to go to their gigs as I would like. My job tends not to give me much time."

"What do you do?"

As if he hadn't heard him, Colin continued, "Listen, Sam, what do you say we start over? Maybe we could meet up sometime, get together, and discuss the folk scene. Folkies like you and I are thin on the ground. We should stick together, eh?"

Sam had been a fan of the genre since he could remember. From the days of The White Heather Club and Highland Air on STV with John Bannerman and Alasdair Gillies, the 'The Singing Dentist,' although most songs on that program were sung in Gaelic. While all his friends were into Manfred Mann (Ha, Ha Said the Clown - what the hell was that all about?), Jimi Hendrix and all, give him The Corries and The MacCalmans any day. This music would last forever, certainly longer than the fleeting illusion of the current pop music scene. Well, if this bloke made any inappropriate moves, Sam would soon mark his card, and damn quick. He had nothing against gays and considered himself more tolerant than some of his friends, who were blatantly homophobic. Live and let live; that was his motto. But it didn't mean he had to fraternize with them. Or go for drinks. Sam considered Colin's offer for a few more seconds. He didn't want to seem too keen, which he wasn't, anyway.

"Why don't we meet midweek, say Wednesday? It'll be quieter and give us a chance to chat. We could go to the same place; it's pretty central. There's one other thing...."

"What's that?" asked Sam.

"Have you been back in touch with Andy?"

"No, not yet."

"It might be better to leave it for a few days, just...."

"Just...?"

"It must have been quite a shock for him to see you again after so long. Why not give it another few days to see where you both want to go? Tell you what; why don't we get together on Wednesday, then give him a ring after that."

"Well, I thought I might..."

"Trust me, I think Andy will appreciate your leaving it in the meantime, honestly."

"OK, but I don't want to lose him again. Fine, I'll see you at about seven o'clock." And, Sam thought, it might just answer a few of his own questions, such as the relationship between his ex-friend and this stranger.

Sam did not tell his parents (he was still living at home) about this phone call. Somehow, he didn't think they would understand, and besides, knowing them, they would jump to the same conclusion he had, that Colin was a faygeleh.

• • •

Despite the day and the hour, Denholm's was busier than expected. A stag party had come in, who had started their drinking binge elsewhere. They were already fighting drunk when they arrived and became even more belligerent when the manager refused to serve them. Chairs and tables hurtled through the air like guided missiles, and one or two just missed Sam. Colin suggested a quieter spot elsewhere before either was hurt in the melee and chose the bar of the Central Hotel. Here, at least, they could be sure of some peace and quiet. It was much more sedate than its neighbor across the road, being the cocktail bar of one of the most prestigious hotels in the city.

The hotel had played host to such celebrities as Frank Sinatra, Laurel and Hardy, and Sir Winston Churchill, among others. Future President John F. Kennedy took a suite in the hotel during his trip to Glasgow in September 1939. The visit was at the behest of his father, Joseph, who was the American Ambassador to Britain at the time. His trip was prompted by a U-boat attack on the passenger liner, the Athenia, en route from Glasgow to Montreal just hours after the declaration of war. The ship was torpedoed, despite Hague Convention protocols protecting civilian vessels from such attacks. Over one hundred people drowned, including some twenty-eight American citizens, and threatened to plunge the United States into the European conflict. It was only the firmly held isolationist policies adopted by America during this period, which stopped the U.S. from also declaring war on Germany over this tragic event.

Colin began by apologizing once again for his earlier gaff, but then said something which took Sam by surprise. "Listen, Sam, do you, ah, think, we could, um, discuss that episode; you know, the one with you and Andy...?"

Sam glared at his questioner. Colin held up his hands in supplication, trying to lessen the distance between them. "Why? Why, after all this time...?"

"Look, I understand if you would prefer not to, but there is a reason I'm asking you. It's just..."

"What?"

"Could you? I mean, could you talk about what happened back then?"

"I suppose so. It might even be good to get it off my chest, I guess. A chance to cleanse my soul; if I've got one, that is. Where do you want me to start?"

"Well," Colin smiled, "the best place is usually from the beginning."

"How much do you know?" Sam asked.

"Almost everything, I think. That's where you come in; to fill in the blanks. Andy could only tell me his side of the story. I need to know from you the parts Andy didn't know, couldn't know; your angle, so to speak. So I can get a clearer picture of the whole thing."

"Why? Why do you want to know now, so long after the event? What interest can it be to you?"

"I will tell you why, I promise, but first I need to get a fuller idea of the whole story."

"Well, why don't you tell me what Andy told you, and I'll come in when I see you've missed anything out?"

"Ok," Colin agreed and began from the time Sam told the class about his letter to the Israeli embassy. Sam interjected at the appropriate gaps, until finally the entire episode had been retold, in turn, by both of them.

"That is one of the most incredible chain of events I've ever heard. You made him think..." Colin shook his head in amazed disbelief, although he knew it all to be true.

"Yeah, and it's not something I'm proud of. How come Andy told you? What does any of this have to do with you? And why are you so interested? I've kept my part of the bargain. It's time for you to keep yours."

"I will. I promised, but there's something you need to know first. Before I tell you, I should warn you; it will come as a shock. Are you ready?"

"I'm eighteen, not eight."

"I know how old you are, Mr. Nathan."

Sam did not miss the formality of his response. Mr. Nathan! Mr. Nathan? What was this 'Mr. Nathan' shit? Who was this guy?

"OK, go on."

"There's one thing you don't know about that time, one part of the story that you've never been aware of."

Sam snorted in youthful arrogance. "I think if anyone knows all about that time, it's me, wouldn't you say?" The unspoken sequel was that there was nothing he didn't know, and couldn't remember about that episode, that it was burned into his memory like a brand. Colin ignored his contemptuous remark and continued, "First, I must ask you. Do you remember what time it was when you arrived at Andy's house?"

Sam considered the question for a few seconds. "Yeah, it was after school; must have been around the back of four o'clock."

"Nearer half-past, to be more precise."

"So...?"

"Had you arrived five minutes later, Andy Marshall, your friend, would have been dead!"

"Dead? What the hell are you talking about, dead? It was only a joke, a practical joke. He never was in any danger."

Colin explained. Andy had endured four days and nights of sheer terror, expecting to be assassinated somehow at any minute. Sam had made sure, by his threat, that Andy could tell no one. He was only fourteen years old. Consider it. Consider what must have been going through his head. Without realizing it, Sam had conditioned him to believe his own demise, possibly violent, was imminent, about to be perpetrated by an unseen hand. To happen any second and there was nothing he could do about it, no one he could tell; no one to save him. He could stand it no more. His young mind had snapped. Rather than wait for it to occur, Andy had run a bath, intended to lie in it, and... Sam knew the rest. He didn't have to be told. He felt himself go cold and began to shake uncontrollably. "God, what have I, did I... I never meant, I swear... I never thought he'd..." Colin's revelation had come as a dreadful blow, and the adolescent experienced a mélange of emotions, abject shame, self-loathing, self-disgust, self-hatred.

It took Sam a few minutes to compose himself. So much was now falling into place. Andy's offhand and indifferent manner, his attitude, now it all made sense; sense Sam didn't want to contemplate.

"OK, that's all very well, and I'm truly sorry for what I did. If I had known... but wait a minute. This doesn't explain where you come into all this. How come Andy bared his soul to you? What are you? A shrink or something? Listen, if you think you're going to get me as a patient as well, you can fucking think again. The last thing I need is a fucking psychiatrist!"

"No, it's not that."

"So where do you fit into all this, Mr....?" If Colin had ever intended this to be a friendly meeting, he had sure miscalculated, but big-time.

"Colin will do just fine, Mr. Nathan."

"If you think I'm going to lie on a fucking couch for you to tell me what a cunt I was, don't bother. I think I've worked that one out all by myself."

Colin modulated his voice before continuing. "I'm not a psychiatrist, Sam."

So it was 'Sam' again, was it? Did Colin think talking softly was going to make him roll over and get tickled? He could fucking think again. This meeting was over. But he couldn't go yet. Colin said he wasn't a brain-curdler. If not that, then what?

"I'm not so sure I want to continue this discussion, Sam. Perhaps I made a mistake. Finish your drink and go home. This was wrong, all wrong. I'm sorry."

"You explode a fucking nuclear bomb under my arse, then all you can say is 'sorry'? Sorry doesn't quite cut it, don't you think? You tell me I almost killed, no, murdered my best friend, and the rest of what he suffered. Then you expect me to walk away without knowing why you're involved in all this? Just who the fuck do you think I am? I think you owe me more than 'sorry,' don't you?"

Colin did not respond for a few seconds, as if considering Sam's outburst. He then stared straight at the adolescent, pursing his lips before continuing.

"As I told you a minute ago, I'm not a psychiatrist. I'm a police officer of sorts." He showed Sam his I.D., and Sam saw he was a detective, but not an ordinary run-of-the-mill cop. Colin worked for Special Branch.

For the second time that evening, Sam felt himself going cold. Had Andy gone to the police about what he had done four years ago? What was the charge? Attempted murder? But Sam hadn't meant to harm Andy, not really. Scare the shit out of him, yes, he'd 'fess up to that, but that was it. And Colin appeared to believe him, so what...?

Colin expounded on his explanation. "I am... I was a detective inspector in the murder squad until about two years ago. Then I was transferred, well, actually I applied for this job. We're a bit more specialized in what we do. Similar to the American F.B.I but not so glamorous." he smiled.

Sam said nothing. He was reserving judgment until he saw where Colin was taking him.

"While you were screwing up Andy's mind," he continued, "more important things were happening elsewhere out in the big, wide world. Not nice things. It started in the United States, possibly New York. However, some think it began on Berkeley campus in California."

"What began?" asked Sam.

"Student rioting. Yes, students have been causing trouble for some years now, especially during the 'sixties, when they came out in their thousands to protest against the Vietnam War. But it was towards the latter years of that decade that many of the protests and mainly peaceful demonstrations turned violent. These street insurrections had increased in number and spread to many countries in Europe, culminating in the barricades of Paris in May sixty-eight. The protests had spread here quickly, and it even embroiled workers and professionals in the upheavals. It almost brought down the De Gaulle government. It was so bad that the General had to make his appeal for calm and tolerance on the radio. This was because many TV crews and journalists had joined the strike themselves, and television was off the air."

Sam was becoming impatient with what he perceived as a lecture. "What has all this got to do with Andy or me? I don't even go to uni. and I've only ever been on one demonstration in my life, and that was to support Israel."

Colin begged Sam's indulgence, promising that it would all become clear. All he asked was to finish his discourse. Sam was weary, physically and emotionally. Colin's revelation had affected him badly, and the last thing he needed right now was a history lesson. Especially on a subject of which he knew little and cared even less. All Sam wanted to do was to go home, try to make some sense out of what he had learned, and if this wasn't possible, just go to sleep. Perhaps when he awoke, he would find that the past two hours had only been a nasty dream. But his wish to leave was more than matched by his innate curiosity to understand where Andy and he fit into this conversation. He nodded, signaling for Colin to continue.

"The protests finally fizzled out," continued the detective, "because, paradoxically, the students didn't get the support they had assumed they would receive from the trade unions and the French Communist Party. In fact, when elections were held in June of that year, the French re-elected the Gaullists with a greater majority. No one quite knew why or how the protests just seemed to die away. Possibly back door deals had been done with the unions. In the following months, the industrial national minimum wage increased by over one third, and most workers benefited by wage rises of at least ten percent.

"That was three or four years ago. Since then, however, there has still been a great deal of student unrest, but it has never reached the levels of that Parisian Spring; until now. There are a few agitators of that time who still struggle for the class revolution that would wipe away forever the corrupt capitalist societies of the West as they see them, and replace them with, well, take your pick. Get two communists in a room, and you'll get at least a dozen ways of ruling society. Our English colleagues have spotted some of these underground figures at universities in Oxford and Cambridge, and Durham in the North of England. Trouble always seems to flare up where these 'class warriors' are, and now we've got them right on our own doorstep here in Glasgow. Well, to be more exact, we've got one of them. Our intelligence tells us that this person has been talking to a well-known local student activist, who is familiar to us. That's how we know the agitator is in the city. We've had our team monitor them with occasional surveillance on the Glasgow student. Funds aren't sufficient to mount a full-time watch on him, so it was just by luck that on one occasion when my team was following him, they spotted them both together. We're also liaising with our French counterparts. It didn't take us long to realize that we might have more trouble on our hands than a few ragged protests and some indiscriminate bottle throwing. This Continental is in favor of more 'robust' forms of action, and violence always seems to be a fellow traveler wherever he shows up. There were rumors that fires in public buildings and right-wing newspaper offices have been attributed to him. No evidence, however, has ever linked him to the causes, and witnesses who claim to have seen something suddenly find they had a severe loss of memory for the times in question. We've had to assume, therefore, that if he is in Glasgow, there's going to be some major trouble. Not only for us, well, the regular police, but probably the fire brigade, and most likely ambulance crews and hospitals are also going to be kept pretty busy, not to mention my squad."

By this time, Sam had had enough and desperately wanted to get home. It had all been too much, the revelation about Andy, and now this fucking history lesson. Why didn't Colin just get to the point? Why all this long-winded explanation?

Colin saw Sam's all-too-obvious ennui, his tiredness plainly showing. He pleaded with the teenager to give him just a few more minutes. Then he would understand where he and Andy fitted into the puzzle. "The thing is, Sam, we need to get someone into this group-to find out just what they're planning to do. The who, the where, the when, the how." They knew that the Glasgow student, Max Jordan, was part of, possibly the leader of, a student protest group. The same crowd accompanied him at any demonstration and it always seemed that it was he who was in charge. Colin's team had to get someone inside that gang to discover what they were planning. They desperately had to know what the foreign agent provocateur and his Glasgow cohorts would do. Property and possibly lives could be lost if they didn't find out in time what and where the objective of the protest would be.

Tired as he was, Sam felt the faint stirrings of apprehension, and the hairs were rising on the back of his neck. He thought he knew where this conversation was going and didn't like it, not one bit.

CHAPTER 9

Sam's head ached from the tension and weariness, and his eyes felt like hollow rings and for a few seconds, it was as if the entire floor had just dissolved beneath him. Was this Andy's way of getting back at him for what he did back in 1967? It had to be, although not very subtle, either. Had he almost caused Andy to commit suicide, or was this just another part of the game to get his conscience going into overdrive before coming out with this ridiculous story?

It surely couldn't be real, could it? Colin, if that was his name, part of some covert police force? Give me a break, for God's sake! And they wanted Sam's help to prevent some unknown catastrophe. If this was the best that Andy's imagination could come up with, and him training to be an architect, Christ, we'd all be back to living in caves.

"Look, you can tell Andy that it was a nice try, but if that's the best he and you, whoever you are, can do, then go away, far away, and don't bother me again. I think it all stinks. I thought Andy wanted to put the past behind us, to get together again, but if he's still been brooding about this after all these years, then he's not ready to move on. But I am. So, fuck off, and leave me alone."

The shocks were not yet over for Sam. More were to come. "I'm afraid I've not been totally honest with you about Andy, either." Colin sighed over his beer glass. In the background, Sam heard the sounds of the bar's other patrons, quietly chatting over their drinks, some smoking, having normal conversations. Glasses were chinking together in toasts, the bar's customers unwinding after a long day. "Andy only agreed to meet with you at my, ah, insistence. Frankly, he wanted nothing to do with you..."

"Then why the fuck did –?"

"I'm sorry, Sam, but as far as Andy's concerned, he wouldn't bat an eyelid if you got run over by a bus. I'm sorry to be so blunt, but that's how it is. He's never got over what you did to him. Honestly, I don't think he ever will. His nightmares may have stopped, but his loathing of you will last..." Colin shrugged his shoulders.

The Special Branch man suddenly changed gear, and addressed Sam abruptly, "Look, I don't have time to piss around. Come with me, and I'll prove everything I've said about myself is true. You can make your own mind up later on what I've told you about Andy."

With that, he walked out of the hotel bar quickly, not waiting to see if Sam would follow. Although still feeling drained, physically and emotionally, Sam raced to catch up with the detective. They turned the corner into Gordon Street, where Colin had parked his car. He opened the passenger door, then slipped round to the other side where he got into the driver's seat and gunned the motor into life.

"Where are we going?"

"I've got no time to fuck about, so just sit still and be quiet until I tell you otherwise. And stop feeling so fucking sorry for yourself. It's over, in the past, so deal with it and move on. Now shut up."

"I thought I had dealt with it until Andy phoned me last week," thought Sam. He felt it better to let the words remain unsaid, but would remember them for ammunition, should the matter come up again. "Andy phoned me, and now I find out that he only contacted me because they had asked him to, but how, and more importantly, why? Is Colin really who he said he is, and if so, just what am I letting myself in for?" These thoughts troubled Sam as the car turned right, down Union Street, then left into Argyle Street. From here, Colin drove the rest of the short distance to their destination, which was Turnbull Street, just a couple of hundred yards from Glasgow Cross. As they arrived, Colin drove through a covered archway into a courtyard. The detective parked the car, then switched off the engine, nodding to Sam as if to say 'end of the line.'

As they exited the car, Sam glanced about him to study his surroundings, and noticed that all the windows of the two top floors had bars on them. The teenager followed Colin up a few stairs to an unlocked outside door. Once inside, they made their way past the C.I.D. bar, where Colin nodded to the officer on duty. Although they had entered by the detective's entrance, the officer on duty, as usual, was from the uniform branch, usually a sergeant, or a seasoned and experienced constable, but in mufti for this responsibility.

The detective led Sam up two flights of stairs to a corridor with several doors behind which the plain-clothes men had their offices. At one of these doors, Colin stopped and keyed in a brief sequence of numbers into the door's combination lock. Most of the other entries only needed a usual Yale key, but Colin's office required a higher level of security, because of the very sensitive nature of his particular work. The Special Branch officer depressed the wall switch, and the room flickered into light, illuminated by two long overhead strip lights. While Colin made himself comfortable, Sam surveyed the room. A few wall shelves with bulging folders, a long desk with two phones, three filing cabinets, and a small table with a chair at each side. Those pieces of furniture, together with a coat stand, comprised the room's furnishings. A large ordinance survey map of Glasgow and its surrounding area to the north and west was pinned on the wall behind Colin's chair. Colin sat behind his desk, motioning Sam to take the seat on the opposite side.

"OK, I suppose it's time to answer your questions, so here goes. Yes, I really am who I said I was. Everything I've told you tonight is true, even about Andy. As I said before, we need someone, desperately, to get inside Jordan's little playgroup before they can cause mayhem, or at least to find out where the action will happen. Obviously, we had to be very careful about how we conducted our recruitment process. We couldn't just pull any likely teenager off the streets and ask them if they'd like to take part in a Special Branch operation. We took a leaf out of the other security services, you know, the real cloak-and-dagger guys, MI5, and contacted universities."

Sam looked puzzled by this remark, so Colin explained that British Intelligence occasionally recruited likely students, with the offer to work for them once they had attained their degrees. Colin and his team approached Glasgow University, who gave them a shortlist of candidates who seemed sound and stable enough to be considered. His friend was on that list. Colin continued, "We approached Andy, and, well, you, of all people, will appreciate the irony. He turned pale in front of me and shook with anger. He actually tried to punch me! Then he wanted to kick me! Hands and feet going like I've never seen. In fact, at one point, I'd swear he had both feet off the ground at the same time! I couldn't understand what I'd done or said to instigate such a reaction. We'd investigated him, and he came up clean. We spoke to his tutors for a background report. That was ok. There was certainly no mention of mental illness. Naturally, I didn't know at that point the history between you and what you had subjected him to. He really is a remarkable guy. To have kept what you'd done to him a secret, to have kept his sanity, even. Eventually, he calmed down and apologized for his conduct. That outburst had been waiting to erupt for almost four years, and I got it, both barrels, so thanks for that, by the way. Anyway, he declined our, ah, advances, but then he mentioned you, and what you did. At first, even despite Andy's rage and violence towards me, I couldn't believe what I was hearing, what you had made him go through. I just had to meet you. I had to be sure that what Andy had said was even half right, let alone wholly accurate. If it were, then you would be the very person, likely the only candidate for this job. Let me boil it down for you so there can be no misunderstanding. We, I, want you to get inside Jordan's group and nip his plans, whatever they are, in the bud. Will you help us?"

Sam didn't know how to reply. He had accepted that everything Colin had just told him was true. It had to be. Here he was, inside a police station, and he couldn't see any police officer agreeing to be part of a practical joke by allowing their station to be used in the ploy. So, if that much was true, then everything else had to be, too. The tiredness he had almost succumbed to before had now left him, to be replaced by a numbing shock. But there were so many other questions; it was hard to know where to begin. For a start, why didn't they try to infiltrate the group with one of their own officers?

"Because we can't. Our guys just don't fit in. They don't have the right profile. For a start, they're too old, most of them. We'd like to get younger guys in, but at the moment, we just don't have them. And often, the gang even spot our surveillance teams, the more inexperienced ones, and do you know what happens? The bastards point at them and whistle the 'Dixon of Dock Green' theme tune. I mean, how demoralizing is that? We're not even sure where they operate from. We believe it could be somewhere in the East End, but we're not certain. Hell, it might not even be in Glasgow. We just don't know. Even discovering their base would be a help." Colin did not reveal that they had tried, once, to infiltrate the gang with one of their officers. It wasn't a success, especially for him. They beat him savagely when they discovered who he really was, and he had to retire from the force. He was lucky they didn't kill him.

Sam then reminded the police officer he wasn't a student; how could he pretend to be? He'd be bound to slip up, and then what?

Colin's reply surprised him. "I don't want you to pretend you're a student. You don't have to, working in an office for a pittance of a wage. You're discontented to see your bosses swanning off to play golf, getting good salaries, while you do all the hard work. God help you if you take a day off for a cold while they get weeks off to go on overseas vacations, which, even if you could get the time, you certainly couldn't afford. It was time for the workers to take more control, and if the unions weren't prepared to get in and mix it, then it was up to the proletariat, the workers, to get stuck in. I can give you some reading material, if you like, just to give you more background, but that would be the gist of it. And I'll bet you'll not be the only non-student on any demo."

"Whoa!" Sam cautioned, "I haven't agreed to anything yet. I'm flattered that you think I'm capable, and everything, but I don't know. Won't this be dangerous?"

Colin thanked himself that he had not revealed the fate of his colleague. "I'm not saying it won't be without risk, but we'll keep it to a minimum.

We'd brief you with a false name and background, so they'd never know who you were, and we'd try to give you as much protection as possible. As long as you keep your head, there's no reason it won't work. It has to work. Realistically, you're the only chance we've got, and you've already proved you've got the qualities we need. You totally submerged yourself in the role you portrayed for Andy, and you really believed you were working for the Israelis, and you made Andy accept it. You had the resourcefulness to adapt to a situation, and it did not faze you when Andy threw questions at you that you weren't prepared for. And you can think on your feet. If anyone can carry this off, it's you. What you did to Andy wasn't just cruel; it was fucking sadistic. Oh, I know you didn't mean it to be, but it shows you have a certain natural ruthlessness. If I had any doubts at all about you being able to do this, I'd say so. But I think, I know, you can. Christ, I still can't believe you did all this when you were fourteen. I should bring you in to give lessons to my team. Possibly I will."

That was the first time Sam had seen Colin smile that evening. "I also know that you're no stranger to bravery," Colin continued. Sam looked at him blankly.

"Sorry...?"

"About four years ago. Must have been not long after the incident with Andy. You chased after a robber from a supermarket."

Sam smiled wistfully at the memory of that adventure, such as it was. It had been a Saturday afternoon. He had been buying groceries for his mother and had just been about to go through the checkout. A tallish man wearing a long beige raincoat came in through the exit door, casually walked up to the checkout he was at, plunged his hand into the till drawer and grabbed a handful of notes before scarpering out the way he'd come in. Sam stared in disbelief at the empty tray, not believing what he'd just witnessed right before his eyes. The checkout girl screamed at him, "Don't just stand there. Get after him!" Without thinking, Sam bolted out of the door in pursuit, catching sight of the miscreant just as he disappeared around a corner. Sam gave chase, running as fast as he could. The robber turned around briefly and, seeing Sam dogging him, increased his pace even more. Sam found he was losing ground and knew it would be only a few seconds before he was out of reach. The man turned around again, to see if Sam was still following him, and as he refaced front, bumped into a passer-by. This mishap allowed Sam the few seconds he needed to regain lost yards, but the felon quickly recovered and ran on, with Sam slowly catching him up. Abruptly, however, the robber darted across the road and ran into a tenement building. As Sam approached the close mouth, he realized that the opportunist might be hiding in wait for him. He hesitated before slowly entering, tensing himself for an assault. As he approached the back of the building and realizing that this attack was now less likely, ran through stealthily, just in time to see the long beige raincoat disappearing into the distance. Understanding that further exertion would be useless, Sam gave up and returned to the store, by which time the police had arrived. When he collected his groceries, they asked him to give a statement and description of the robber.

Several weeks later, Sam was summoned to an identity parade, despite remonstrating that he only got a brief look at the perpetrator. As Sam predicted, he could not pick out the person the police suspected of carrying out the robbery and heard no more about the incident. "How'd you find out about that? I mean, it was four years ago!" As realization dawned, it quickly occurred to him that the only way Colin could have known was through Andy. Although the boys were no longer on speaking terms by the time of this event, Andy would undoubtedly have known of the circumstances. Hell, the entire school knew, because the police had gone there to take him to the line-up. Several pupils and staff had seen him being led away by two uniformed officers before being hustled into the back of a police Land Rover.

Sam had been reluctant to make much of the robbery incident and had told no one what he'd done. However, he had to come clean when he returned to school, as everyone had drawn the obvious but wrong conclusion. Sam certainly didn't want to be considered a hero and believed that he only did what anyone in his position would have done. There was an exciting and enjoyable consequence of his adventure. Once it became known, a couple of girls that he liked but who wouldn't even acknowledge his existence suddenly wanted to be seen with him. A situation he exploited to the full. Yes, overall, it had been a good time.

"So," continued Colin smiling, "you've got form in the valor stakes. You're very lucky, however. Just what did you expect to do if you'd actually caught up with him? Just ask him politely if he would mind handing back the cash which had somehow fallen into his pocket, there's a good chap. This man could have done you some serious harm. Did that not occur to you?"

Sam shrugged his shoulders. "It was a long time ago. Honestly, I don't know what I thought. I can't remember. I just knew I had to catch him. He had committed a crime. That's all."

"Well, despite his feelings towards you, Andy must have admired you enough to tell me about your efforts."

"Yeah, that'll be bloody right," said Sam. "The bastard probably just wanted to drive the final nail into my fuckin' coffin. 'Yeah, Sam's your man. Chased after a villain four years ago when he was only fourteen. Can't think of anyone more suited to go undercover and join a gang of violent terrorists. You want brave, he's the man to see, and with luck, he'll get his fuckin' balls blown off, or end up doing twenty years in Barlinnie.'"

"Well, let's get back to the present. What do you think? Could you do what I'm asking of you?"

"Just a minute," Sam responded. "How do you know I'm not like them? I mean, how do you know I wouldn't do...?"

Colin answered him patiently, "When you told Andy that the Israelis had recruited you, you said that they investigated you. 'Vetted' is what we would say. Well, what you said to Andy was, of course, untrue, but we're playing for real now, Sam, so, of course, we checked you out; you and your parents and family.

"You were born in Rottenrow Maternity Hospital on the fourth of January nineteen fifty-three, the first and only child of Hyman and Mildred Nathan. Your first school was Castleburn Primary, which you started when you were five years old, graduating to Glencroft Secondary when you were twelve. Your best subjects were English, History, and Economics, but you were lousy at science and technical subjects, the latter just because you couldn't do them and science because you just weren't smart enough to understand the intricacies of the subject, despite having above-average intelligence. I wondered why you didn't go on to further education, but you chose not to go to university so you could bring in a wage to help support your parents. You are working as a clerk in a shipping company where your attention to detail is 'exemplary.' You've never been in any trouble with the police, despite growing up in an area where, sadly, this is an all too common occurrence. Your mother Mildred, or 'Millie' as she is more commonly known, was born in the east end of London in July nineteen twenty-five, the fourth of five children of Clara and David Edelstein, both now deceased. Your middle name, David, is called after him. Millie was a seamstress by trade but hasn't worked since you were born, giving up her job to devote all her time to looking after you. Your mother met your father when she came up to Scotland on vacation in the summer of nineteen-fifty. Being a religious woman, she still wanted to attend a Sabbath service and visited South Portland Street Synagogue, where she met Hyman, a chair-maker, and woodworker. Hyman Abraham Nathan, born in Glasgow in nineteen twenty-two, the oldest of six siblings, to Rivka and Shalom Netayanski. Your father had a brief love affair with communism around the time you were born, but soon saw the error of his ways. He's still a socialist, but is no longer a member of, or supports, the communist party. He anglicized his name to Nathan in nineteen forty-six. You're called after your paternal grandfather, who passed away just after the war. Apart from his fling with communism, your father does not seem to have been in any trouble with the authorities either; a well-adjusted, law-abiding family."

Sam felt icy fingers running up and down his spine, as he realized that all the information Colin had just revealed was accurate as far as he knew; however, there was one point he questioned. "You said my father has a middle name, Abraham. Are you sure? I mean, he's never even mentioned this to me. I never knew." He shook his head in amused bewilderment and tried to recall the times when the Chazan gave his father an Aliyah in Shul. Was he called up as Chaim ben Shalom or Chaim Avram ben Shalom? He struggled to remember, but it would just not come into focus.

"Oh, absolutely sure, Sam. We do our job most thoroughly. Attention to detail, just like you." Colin smiled. "There are even more facts I could give you, but I don't think they are pertinent or necessary."

"I don't think I want to know, anyway. You've said enough. Did Andy tell you about my run-in with that supermarket robber, or was that you?"

"Oh no, Sam, that was Andy. We did, of course, verify his statement, and it came up almost exactly as he remembered it."Colin returned to his earlier question. "So, Sam, will you do it? Will you help us stop this carnage from happening?"

Sam did not disguise his reluctance and his apprehension. Despite what Colin had told him, and the assurances the detective had given him, this could still be very dicey. It would only take one slip, and he'd be finished. This wasn't a fourteen-year-old's juvenile game anymore where no one got hurt if you discounted psychological trauma. It was grown-up stuff, and people could get damaged for real, worse than damaged even, and Sam tried to push this thought to as far back in his mind as he was able. This foreign guy, he sounded like a real psycho. Setting fire to buildings was terrible enough, but there was also the intimidation. This guy hurt people, and if he was prepared to use violence on witnesses, fuck knew what he would do to Sam if they discovered who he was. His whole being cried out for him to run screaming out of the office, out of the police station, and pretend this evening had never happened. Yet, something in him, he could never analyze what, stayed him in his place. He heard himself saying the words, but it was as if they were being spoken by someone else.

"Let me think about it."

"We don't have the luxury of time, Sam. We don't know what they're planning, or when. It may be too late even now, but we've got to assume we can still put a stop to whatever they're going to do. I need an answer now. Yes or no?"

"If I say yes now, can I...?"

"This isn't some fucking school five-a-side soccer team decision we're talking about. Once you give me an answer, that's it. No backing out either way. Whatever decision you make now, tonight, it'll be final. So I'll ask you again, yes or no?"

CHAPTER 10

Sam found out later that Colin had taken him to the headquarters of the City of Glasgow police force, but at that moment, his current location was the last thing on his mind. He was trying to absorb all that Colin had told him in the past few hours, the truth, the actual truth, about those last hours with Andy back in 1967. Now there was the possibility that a group of lunatic fringe students was planning some kind of havoc in Glasgow. A bunch of maniacs with a French guy in charge, and only he, Sam, could stop whatever chaos they had planned. He knew this was all too real, but somehow, it felt surreal, as if he was watching himself on some bizarre movie or TV show. He had to give Colin some kind of answer now, and whatever decision he made, that would be it. There would be no time for second thoughts later, but he had the right to know some things before he gave his response.

"If I don't agree to help you, what will you do?"

"Honestly?"

"Yes."

"I don't know. That's the truth. There is no 'plan B.' We'll just have to react to whatever this gang does, by which time it'll be too late. The damage, and I mean damage, will have been done. I'd hoped that, just for once, we could do what the French failed to do and anticipate them and stop whatever destruction they had planned."

"But you must have expected, or at least considered, the possibility that I might say no. You said you'd already approached Andy, who led you to me. You must have gone to other likely people as well as him."

"Believe it or not, Andy was the first. We had other people in mind, of course, but when I heard about you -" Colin shrugged. The rest of the sentence didn't need completion. Sam had a few more pertinent questions, which he put to the detective. Could he wear a 'wire' as he'd seen in the movies?

Colin smiled patiently as he explained to Sam. First, they were not always reliable, and the listeners sometimes did not pick up what the subject was saying. Colin also did not want to risk that the group might detect the device, and Sam himself could even cause this eventuality. He was still very young to be involved in this kind of situation and would be self-conscious about wearing the microphone. This thought alone might make him appear more nervous than he should be, which itself might arouse suspicion. No, on balance, it would be better for him, for them all, if they did not connect him remotely.

Sam was also concerned about his parents. What would he say to them? He understood that they, too, would have to be kept in ignorance about his 'activities,' probably for the best if this were the case. But what would happen if things went wrong? He wondered. Colin answered as truthfully as he could, without mentioning his ex-colleague. He knew this was wrong. Sam had a right to know, but his department needed Sam too badly to allow him to back out because of a justified fear for his safety. He was ethical enough to mention the apparent dangers that Sam would know about, anyway. If Sam found out about the undercover police officer later, well, that was just too bad. Colin could give Sam a few lessons; Christ, he'd written the book and wore the T-shirt when it came to ruthlessness. As for Sam's parents, well, they'd cross that bridge if it needed crossing.

The two men regarded each other across the desk. It was now or never. Sam had not considered himself to be civic-minded. But if the worst happened and property was destroyed, worse, that people were hurt or even killed, how could he refuse to help, even at the risk of his own safety? Especially if he could have prevented it.

He answered quickly, afraid that he would change his mind as the words escaped from his breath.

A smile played around the corners of Colin's mouth. He'd done it. Despite what Andy had told him and confirmed earlier in the evening by Sam himself, the security man knew that deep down, and not even that deep, Sam was basically a good guy and realized it wouldn't take much effort to play him.

He opened the top drawer of his desk, from which he extracted a gray foolscap size wallet. Out of this, he took a document, which he slid across to Sam. It was headed, 'The Official Secrets Act 1939, 1939 Chapter 121 2 and 3 Geo 6'. Without being asked, Colin explained what signing this document meant. He could not disclose to anyone, now or in the future, anything he did for Colin or his department under penalty of imprisonment. Once Sam signed, he would be bound by the Act, and if he should betray anything or anyone connected to this operation, Colin could not stand by him, no matter how much he would want to. Sam took the proffered pen in his hand and found that he was trembling as he appended his signature to the spot Colin had indicated.

As much as the detective would have liked to continue, he was all too aware of Sam's physical and mental state and decided that it would be best if, for that night at least, Sam went home. With the condition that he returned to Turnbull Street the following day, both men left the office, and Colin drove Sam home. Tomorrow was going to be a full day.

• • • •

Sam phoned in sick to his office early the next morning and arrived at Turnbull Street at nine-thirty as arranged, entering by the same door he went through the previous evening. A different officer was on duty, but appeared to be expecting him. He waved Sam through with a cheery nod and the teenager made his way upstairs to the room he'd shared with Colin. It didn't escape Sam's notice that he could go unescorted through the station. It said much about Colin's trust in him. As he climbed the stairs, Sam hoped he could repay Colin's faith in his abilities.

"There's a lot to get through today, so let's get straight down to it." said the detective on Sam's arrival.

"Good morning to you, too," Sam responded without humor.

Lying on the desk in front of him were eight ten-inch by eight-inch photographs, six of which showed men and the remaining two women. They were all around the same age or slightly older than Sam. All the shots had been taken without their knowledge or consent. Despite this, the candid images were good and clearly illustrated faces of the unwitting subjects. Sam regarded the photographs carefully before responding to the obvious, unasked question. No, he did not know or recognize any of the people in the photographs.

"No, perhaps you don't recognize them, but could they recognize you?" The question was not as obtuse as it sounded. Could he have been anywhere, a pub, a hotel, a disco, any place they could have come into contact with each other? No matter how fleetingly, but just enough to remember a face, a mannerism which they could recall?

Sam repeated he knew no one from the images in front of him, nor could he think of anywhere he might have been where they could have met, however briefly. And even if he had been in any club, or boozer, where this bunch hung out, so what? It wouldn't have been any more than any ordinary coincidence.

The point was, Colin insisted, that he wanted none of this lot trying to remember where they had seen a face before, no matter what the circumstances, coincidence or not. He did not want even the faintest trace of suspicion for any reason to fall on Sam. It was all about survival - his survival. With the assurance that none of the faces could have known Sam, Colin continued. The images the Special Branch officer had shown him were those of the group he was to infiltrate. He was not being told any names except that of Max Jordan.

Neither did Colin disclose the French activist's identity, the radical already behind so much anarchy on the Continent. There was a reason for this. They could not afford any slip-ups, not this time. Colin did not want to take the risk that Sam might inadvertently acknowledge or mention any name he would not already have known. Again, Colin deemed this necessary for Sam's safety. They had learned from the mistakes of their earlier attempt at infiltration. Sam wasn't a security officer. He was a civilian, and his protection had to be paramount.

As the Special Branch officer had already stated, Sam would use a false identity. Colin would have a couple of innocuous documents such as a travel pass and library card issued in this name should the need arise.

It was unlikely that the gang would entrust Sam with the cell's innermost secrets on his initiation. It may even take several meetings before he had gained their confidence, enough to give him at least a clue about their motives. Time was crucial, however, and Colin instructed him to do anything, within reason, which would hasten his elevation to a fully paid-up member of the gang. Colin gave him a number to call as soon as he left the group. It was important for Sam to relate as much as possible about what had occurred within the meeting. Certainly, to relay any intelligence regarding their intended target.

Now, for the most vital part of the operation, the method by which Sam would infiltrate himself into Jordan's radical fellowship. The detective and inductee spent some time going over Colin's plan. It was imperative that Sam was as prepared and rehearsed as he could be. If this scheme was going to work, it was going to depend on many elements.

Unfortunately for Sam, some contingencies just could not be factored into any equation.

CHAPTER 11

Anti-Vietnam War demonstrators had planned a rally in George Square, in the heart of Glasgow's city center, for the following Saturday. Inevitably, the gang would be there. Sam had memorized the members' faces and would inveigle himself as near to them as possible before embarking on his task. Perhaps because it was such a wet day, or possibly because people in the West of Scotland did not view the Vietnam cause as an emotive issue. For whatever reason, the demonstrators numbered barely a few hundred rather than the several thousand expected, and the police almost outnumbered them. This was the first problem. Both Colin and his team assumed the turnout would be greater for such a current flash point issue; in fact, they were counting on it. However, the operation would need to go ahead nonetheless.

Even in the pouring rain, Sam quickly spotted his quarries, and it was with relative ease, the crowd being so light, that he could get up close. Approaching the group, he began shouting slogans against the police, the Americans, the American military, and anyone else he could think of. Blustery winds carried his voice away from the throng, and his calls became more strident as he approached his targets. As he came up close to one of the group, Sam undid the buckles of his old khaki school haversack. He withdrew a rock, which he threw at the mounted police officer nearest the group. The missile flew wild as he aimed it to do, and Sam screamed in feigned anger and frustration.

He took out another stone and repeated his actions, calling in hatred as he hurled the rock into the air. Again, the trajectory went over everyone's head and landed harmlessly fifty yards away. By now, he was standing beside a body he recognized. Extracting another small boulder from his rucksack, he brushed his target's arm as the missile left his hand. The agitator paid him scant regard as Sam's arm once more reached into the sack to lob another rock. This time, his target noticed him just as Sam let fly. As before, the stone was supposed to go astray, but the horse bolted forward, startled by a sudden noise behind it just as the missile was hurtling downward. It hit the mounted policeman full in the face, blood spurting from the officer's cheek as he fell from his mount. For the merest fraction of a second, the crowd stopped dead, then like a pack of starving lions, they pounced upon the downed officer. This wasn't meant to happen. Before Sam could fully appreciate the enormity of his actions, he felt someone hastily pulling him away from the crowd and propelling him down a side street, away from the main demo. It was all happening so quickly; he didn't have time to gather his thoughts, and his panic was now real, not affected as he meant it to be. The regular force was not made aware of any covert action, so they would hunt Sam down unless Colin pulled a few strings if he could. He had hurt one of their own, and they would pursue him without mercy. Sam was staring wildly around him, not daring even to blink, lest a momentary lapse saw the felled officer's colleagues come thundering down the narrow lane towards him. They would have only one thought–to arrest as brutally as the law allowed, the perpetrator of the heinous and cowardly assault.

While all these ideas were tumbling inside his head, he was only vaguely aware of being bundled roughly into the back of a waiting car and being driven off at high speed. As they put distance between themselves and their erstwhile pursuers, a voice, a French voice beside him, instructed the driver to slow down to avoid drawing attention. Even as Sam's stress level was just subsiding, a thrill of exhilaration was stirring inside him. He recognized three passengers as members of the group, although Max Jordan was not in the vehicle. But here he was, sitting beside his targets, the real reason for his 'mission'. It was time to get into his role. "That was some shot, eh?" he crowed. "The fucker never even saw it coming! They'll have to identify the bastard by his dental records or his badge number or somethin'. Fuckin' brilliant, just fuckin' brilliant!"

Sam's eyes were bursting bright, his adrenalin still coursing high through his bloodstream. Now pretending some confusion, as if awakening from a thrilling dream, he looked around the car. "Who are you guys? Why did you get me away from the action? Thanks, anyway. I owe you one. Just class, man, just class..." he rambled on. "Hey, where are we goin' anyhow?"

"Shut up and listen, you stupid prick. The only reason we lifted you away is that you were close to us when you hit that cop. I don't give a shit about you, but if they had grabbed you, they could have arrested us as well. So, don't think we bailed you out for your sake. As soon as we can find a suitable spot, we'll throw you out, so keep quiet, and we might even stop the car first."

Sam had to think fast. He was supposed to penetrate this gang, and it looked as if his and Colin's plans would go up in smoke before it could even get started. Colin had tasked him to prevent injuries, and all he'd done so far was to knock a police officer from his horse. Surely it had not all been for nothing. Sam had assumed that all four other occupants were male. However, as the person sitting in the front passenger seat turned around for the first time, it was evident that this fellow traveler was not a man, despite the short-cropped hair. Sam did not recognize her as one of the gang, so right away, here was a result if he lived to tell Colin about it. There were even more surprises in store for Sam when she spoke in French to his co-passenger.

Now that he had a better chance of regarding her more carefully, he observed she had striking hazel brown eyes. She appeared to be tiny; he guessed no more than five feet. The girl was wearing an anorak at least two sizes too large, which only seemed to accentuate her diminutive stature. Although she looked only about eighteen, Sam strongly suspected that she was a good deal older. From the confident way she responded to her French companion, he thought that maybe the Frenchman wasn't the boss after all. Perhaps Colin and his Parisian counterparts had been wide of the mark.

The two Continentals exchanged a few words, most of which Sam could not understand.

"What is your name, my friend?" asked the girl.

"Paul... Paul McGregor. Et comment vous appelez vous?"

A look of surprise darted between the two French occupants. "Et bien, vous parlez Français?"

Sam suddenly realized the stupidity of his attempt at integration. He must do nothing to put them on their guard if he wanted them to accept him as one of them.

"Nah. That's about all I can remember from my 'O' levels in fourth year. Are you guys really French?"

"Oui, Henri and I are from Paris." She pronounced it as 'Paree,' with a slight glottal inflection. "But never mind about us. What were you doing there? Did you come on your own, my friend?"

"Yeah, I prefer to go to these things alone. Don't like to be marked as part of a crowd."

"And would you like to be part of our crowd?" she asked, smiling.

"And who is our crowd, exactly?"

"Just a few people who like to go to demos and do more than just throw stones at poor defenseless members of the constabulary."

"Ça suffit! Tais toi! Tais toi! Ferme ta gueule, maintenant!"

"Non, Henri, I think our little ami will fit in well. Let us see. Tell me, Paul, would you like to do more than throw a few rocks at Glasgow pigs?" She smiled as she asked, but Sam knew that behind this mild interrogation, there was a deadly earnestness.

"Fuckin' right." He snapped his fingers rapidly, as though high on some narcotic. But he quickly realized that they could consider him too much of a loose cannon if he carried the deception too far. "What did you guys have in mind?"

She smiled briefly at him. "Perhaps later we could discuss it. Je m'appelle Marie-Claire." His newfound companion offered her hand to him palm down. Sam briefly took her fingers in his hands before releasing them. Her French companion remonstrated with her in their native tongue, and Sam could only make out a few odd words. He was obviously itching to expel Sam as soon as possible, but Marie-Claire was not as keen to let him go. She replied in a gentle but authoritative manner, showing that perhaps they should not eject him yet, smiling and all the while regarding Sam warmly. She leaned over and brushed him on the knee, much to Henri's reticence and not without some distress to Sam. The adolescent found himself aroused by the caress of her smooth hand just inside his lower thigh. The French pair exchanged a few more words, but it appeared that she had won the argument as he sat back, slumped in the seat with a Gallic shrug.

"Where the fuck are we goin'?"

"You will come back with us for a little while so that we can have a... talk, then we shall see..." she replied, but Sam could not mistake the edge in her voice. If this were to go pear-shaped now, he did not even want to imagine what his fate would be. This French guy, this Henri, didn't like him one petit peut, and it wouldn't take much to rattle his cage. Sam felt a little apprehensive for the first time, but the last thing he wanted to do was show fear. The only way he could think of to hide his growing anxiety was to bluff it out, but again, he had to do so carefully. There was only one leader here, and this French lunatic would not take kindly to someone none of them knew trying to dominate the proceedings. He remembered the instructions from Colin. Don't ask too many questions. Don't give them any reasons to become suspicious. Let them come to you. The more you gain their trust, the more they'll open up to you, maybe not everything, but enough for us to understand what their plans are.

They were driving eastwards down Duke Street, a long major thoroughfare just a few hundred yards north of Glasgow Cross and near to the Turnbull Street police station. After about a mile, they turned off into Armadale Street, where the driver suddenly pulled in and parked. Sam only knew this area a little, having been to a party nearby a few months earlier. However, as he'd been less than sober for most of that evening, his memories of the event were hazy. At this moment, it seemed like a lifetime ago.

"OK, this is it, people, Dennistoun Mansions. Everybody out."

Henri pushed Sam from the stationary vehicle and manhandled him into the tenement building before he could take the time to view his surroundings. All five occupants quickly mounted the stairs to the top of the building, entering the flat to the right.

"Ah don't know what you're getting so uptight about, man." offered a protester. "This guy's done well. He fucked that pig right good and proper."

"And you remember, we are here to do more than knock a few policemen from off their horses. This stupid shit could have put all that in jeopardy," replied Henri with some anger.

"Well, I think we need some more bodies, and this wee guy might be just the fresh blood we're lookin' for. Listen, nobody knows him. He's anonymous. We can use him."

"Anonymous?! Anonymous?! After what he did? His picture will be all over the TV and newspapers. By tomorrow, this little fucker will be more famous than Bob Dylan!" Henri was not giving up without a fight. Well, he was supposed to be the leader.

Despite himself, Sam realized his adversary was right. If anyone had filmed or photographed him throwing rocks, especially the one which hit the policeman, his usefulness to the gang and Colin would be over before it had even begun. Once again, for the second time in fifteen minutes, his future as an infiltrator was in grave doubt. If Henri had his way, his future as a living, breathing member of humanity was also a matter for conjecture.

"He was standing beside Billy when he threw that rock, n'est-ce pas?" asked Marie-Claire. "Well then, Billy and the rest of us were near the back of the crowd. I do not think there is any danger that our friend will find himself on the front page of the Daily Record."

"The Daily Record disnae come oot on a Sunday. It wid be The Sunday Mail or The Sunday Post," suggested Rab, one of the other members and the driver.

"No, I think I am right. Our new friend here will continue to be anonymous, and if he wants to stay that way, he will do what we tell him, won't you, mon Cherie?"

The threat was unmistakable. Collaborate with us, or we will make a telephone call. Even Marie-Claire might eventually decide he'd become a liability. And what then? This was becoming even heavier than Colin, or the team, not to mention Sam himself, had envisaged. Christ, he'd only been in their company for less than an hour, and already they were prepared to sell him out, or worse. It seemed as if the only thing they couldn't accuse him of was starting World War III. This thought was to return and haunt him over and over in the months ahead.

CHAPTER 12

While the crew was discussing Sam's immediate future, it gave him time to study his surroundings. A typical Glasgow tenement flat of the area, but devoid of much furniture, except a few moth-eaten armchairs. There was also a dining table that had the detritus of a hastily eaten meal on it, with two matching chairs, and another two stacked against a wall, obviously not able to be used. A few posters adorned the walls, the usual black and red Che Guevara print, and a couple of large prints from the Soviet Union showing happy workers toiling in farms and factories for the good of the Motherland. The wallcovering itself looked as if it had not been changed for some time, and patches of it were peeling away from the damp-looking plaster. The sound of a toilet flushing from within the apartment at least showed that there was indoor plumbing. How many more rooms there were, he did not know.

There also seemed to be a faint, peculiar, but somehow familiar odor, which Sam felt he should know, but could not quite place. The only other fact that he knew at this stage was that the flat felt freezing, and he was shivering, and not just from fear or excitement.

"Perhaps our new friend might like to prove his loyalty to us, would you not, mon ami?" The Parisienne asked Sam, raising her eyebrows.

"Do what...?" asked Sam, as he glanced around the room.

"Perhaps you would like to go on a little errand for us, n'est-ce pas?"

"I'm not a fuckin' message-boy. If you want anyone to get your groceries, find someone else." Sam knew he was playing a dangerous game, even more so, as he had already fallen foul of Henri. But he had to make this look as authentic as possible. He understood from Marie-Claire's request that she was asking him to do more than go to the local shop for a few tins of beans, but to comply too quickly might look too obvious. Besides, he did not want to seem too curious about what they were planning, but now he realized that if he played his cards right, not only would he gain that information, but just might be able to stop whatever they intended to do.

"Oh no, Paul, we don't want you to buy food for us. Do we look like cooks to you, eh?" The other gang members sniggered obligingly. "We want you to buy a clock and some steel wool. You'll be able to get them both in the hardware store along the road on Duke Street. Do you think you can do that small thing for us?"

Sam knew there must be a reason for their strange shopping list, but had to act as if he thought Marie-Claire had gone mad. "Buy what? A clock and some steel wool? You're fuckin' crazy." He looked helplessly around the group, but none of them seemed moved by the girl's strange request. "You want me to buy a clock and some steel wool?" he repeated, as if trying to convince himself that he had heard her correctly. "What the fuck do you want those for?" It was not an unusual question for him to have asked; in fact, it would have looked odd if he did not want to know.

Marie-Claire smiled at him, replying airily, "Oh, it's just for something, nothing for you to be concerned about." She delved into her handbag and produced a purse from which she extracted some money. She held out her hand and allowed him to take the notes. "Don't buy a large clock. A small one will suffice. Rab will go with you and point out the one we want, won't you, Rab?"

Although the woman put this command as a mild question, Sam could see that there was no way Rab could or would refuse her request. "I think Rab should go with you just in case you get… lost, ok?"

"I think I can find my way to the shops. The one thing I don't need is a fuckin' escort."

"Oh, but I insist. Besides, Rab needs to point out which clock we want. There are so many kinds out there, and we wouldn't want you to choose the wrong one, would we?"

Sam saw it was no use arguing any further, so shrugging his shoulders, he opened the door allowing his new 'friend' to pass through. Turn any opportunity to your advantage, Colin had said. Well, here was such an opportunity.

He waited until they were in the street before attempting a conversation with Rab. "Is the shop far?" he asked. "So what's with the clock an' steel wool? Do youse guys no' have watches? Maybe it's tae see if you can drive faster than the cops, an' no get caught like a shit driver wid, eh?"

"Fuckin' shut up, all right. Ah don't know whit the cloak's fur, or the steel wool. Ah just do as Ah'm told, an' you'll do the same if ye know whit's good fur ye. An' Ah'm no' a shit driver, ok?"

So that was it. No further help there. Sam tried again to make conversation with the gang member, but Rab did not seem too disposed to engage with him. Maybe he was smarting at Sam's remark about his driving skills, but for whatever reason, they conducted the rest of the shopping expedition in silence.

The hardware store was only a couple of hundred yards from the tenement block. As soon as Sam opened the door, the smell of paraffin from the store's heater assailed his nostrils. It mingled with the odors of wax, varnish, and mustiness, as if no one had brushed the shop for some time.

"You go in. Ah'll wait here," said Rab.

"But Marie-Claire said..."

"Ah don't give a fuck whit she said. Just go in yourself. Ah canna stand the smell of that heater, ok? Ah'm allergic tae paraffin, if ye must know."

"Fine. But what about the clock?"

"It's not fuckin' rocket science," he retorted. "Just get a wee clock like she asked for. Christ, how hard can that be? You a retard or somethin'?" Sam ignored the barb and approached the counter. He immediately saw a clock behind the glass display case which looked ideal. Pointing at the instrument, he asked the proprietor if he could purchase it. The old, grey-haired man in the khaki overall removed the clock, placing it on the ancient wooden counter.

"Anything else, son?"

"Um, yes. Could I have some steel wool, please?"

The store owner pursed his lips. For a brief second, Sam thought he knew the purpose of the items, what they were to be used for. He felt himself shiver and go hot and cold, imagining that he was going to call the police. However, the old man merely asked him what the steel wool was going to be used for.

"I don't know," replied Sam. "Why?"

"Well, there's a few types of grades of steel wool for different applications," the man replied patiently.

"It's... um... it's for my dad. He didn't say why he wanted it; he just asked me to get it for him."

"Well, more than likely he'll want it to strip old paint or varnish off some wooden furniture," he said, regarding Sam over the rim of his tortoise-shell glasses. He reached up to the shelf behind him, taking a packet from it. "This is a mid-grade strength which should do the trick without scratching the surface. If it's not right, tell your dad he can return it as long as he doesn't open it, ok?"

Sam proffered the man the money and took the change, thanking him for his help. As he left the store, something bothered him about their little expedition. It wasn't just about the goods Marie-Claire had sent them for. No, it was something about Rab himself, but what was it? Sam didn't know. Had he seen or met him before? No, he didn't think it was that. It was something else that was bothering him. It was Rab's... attitude. No, it wouldn't come now, but maybe later...

It was as well that Rab had gone with him, as they had been away for some time, and had he been alone, it might have fostered some suspicion why he had taken so long.

Marie-Claire clapped her hands together in merriment, and even the usually scowling Henri showed signs of approbation. "You have done well, my friend. I am sure you will be a valuable asset to our team, but we have things to do that don't concern you now. Come here again next Saturday morning, say around ten o'clock, and we will let you know what we want you to do. I needn't remind you not to say a word to anyone because if I find out you have betrayed us..."

Again, it was essential to play the role Colin had tasked him to do. "Are you giving me the bum's rush here? If Ah'm in the team, then Ah'm in the team. Nae half-measures. Whatever youse do, Ah do tae. Whit are youse gauny do that ye canny do with me here? Oh, an' see if anyone ever accuses me again of grassin' youse up, Ah'll rip oot their lungs frae the inside, man. Now, am Ah in, or am Ah no' in?"

"Your enthusiasm does you credit, my friend, but honestly, there is no more for you to do here today. I can see you want to change things as much as the rest of us, but for the time being, go home and rest, or do whatever you want. Just say nothing about what went on here. Ok?"

"Are you daft? Me say anything? After knockin' that polis off his horse? Ah just want tae keep a low profile, so Ah'll no' be doin' very much the night, Ah can assure ye. Ah'll see youse next Saturday."

Sam knew he should turn right into Duke Street, as both his journey home and Turnbull Street were in that direction, but he wanted to make sure no one was following him. He needed to see Colin as quickly as possible while the events of the past few hours were still fresh in his mind. Not only that, but he just had the feeling that whatever the group had planned had not yet taken place but was not far off from happening, hence the need for the clock and steel wool.

After a hundred yards walking in the opposite direction, he stopped to look in a shop window, turning his eyes slowly rightward. He recognized no one, nor did anyone else seem to halt suddenly. He walked on for another hundred yards, then stopped to tie his shoelace. Again, no one seemed to pay him any attention. Almost now convinced he was not being followed, Sam crossed the road and walked back in the direction he had come, watching to see if anyone in the crowd came over behind him. Nobody did. He hurried back down Duke Street to its junction with High Street, then down past Glasgow Cross, through Saltmarket, then into Turnbull Street.

Making himself known to the officer on duty, Sam asked to see Colin. Sam was unknown to this desk sergeant, who did not seem to know anyone named Colin. The youth told the sergeant which floor Colin worked from and even the number of the room he inhabited. After the customary to-ing and fro-ing, in which Sam's limited patience was being sorely tried, the officer finally called the number of Colin's office. Judging by the deference shown to Sam after the brief call, Colin must have marked the sergeant's card well. The officer instructed him to go straight up as quickly as possible, and sorry for the misunderstanding, etc.

Once in the Special Branch man's office, Sam promptly related the events of the past afternoon, first by asking how the downed officer was. Colin responded he was unaware of any hurt police officer, and why would Sam want to know? Sam realized not only had Colin not known how their plans had almost gone awry, but he also did not know that he, Sam, caused the mounted officer's injury. That was now by-the-by. Once he had finished his narrative, with interruptions and questions from Colin, Sam saw a change come over his handler. In the short while he had known him, Sam had not seen Colin look so grave. His face seemed to blanch more with each sentence, and his very body seemed to stiffen as Sam's story reached its conclusion. "Sam, this odor. Can you describe it? Was it familiar? When had you smelled it before?"

Sam struggled with his memory. "I know it's kind of familiar, but... is this important?"

"It might be if my suspicions are correct. OK, I'm going to suggest something to you to try to jog your memory, but don't tell me what you think I want to hear. Just tell me if I'm right or wrong. Could the vapor have been chemical, you know, like when you were in the science classrooms at school?"

Sam looked up, a glimmer of light coming into his eyes. "Yes, that's it!" he exclaimed, remembering the odors from his days in Glencroft.

"My God. The bastards... the fucking bastards... Sam, listen, this is extremely important. Are you sure they gave you no sign of how they were going to use the clock and steel wool? Anything they said, any hint, anything that can give us a lead on what they plan to do."

Sam thought for a few seconds before replying. He didn't know yet what theory Colin had formulated, but reckoned it had to be serious for him to behave so ardently.

"No, I told you. I don't think they quite trust me enough yet to take me into their complete confidence. You know, don't you? You know what they wanted those things for? I can tell by the anxiety in your voice. What exactly have I got mixed up with?"

"Well, there's good news, there's bad news, and then there's worse news. The good news is that thanks to you, we now know at least where the bastards operate from. That's a great start, but the bad news is that the chemical stench in the flat is probably some kind of acid, either sulfuric or nitric. The reason that the flat was cold wasn't just because they couldn't afford a heater. They need the flat to be cold because if I'm right, based on what you've just told me, they're making bombs, probably from nitroglycerine. This chemical is highly unstable in a warm environment, and they sent you to buy a clock and steel wool to use as a timer. Yes, it might...no, probably would work..." He was speaking to himself now, rather than to Sam. "Yes, the steel wool would be de-stranded and attached to the hands of the clock to use as a crude, but effective timer. Where the fuck they got hold of the acid and glycerin from, God only knows. But, no doubt, they have contacts either within the university network or in a commercial business that could get these products for them either for a price or under threat."

He also now recalled some information that had come his way the previous week, which he ignored at the time, as it seemed unimportant. Now it made perfect sense. Police in Maryhill had been alerted to four or five explosions on waste ground in the area. The police station sent a constable to investigate, but he found no signs of damage other than some cratered and charred earth. Assuming it had been some kids playing with fireworks, he made his report and sent it in. The station never pursued the matter, as there had been no other destruction or reported injury. But it made sense now, all right. It made perfect sense. The fuckers were experimenting and trialing their handiwork before going for the main event, whatever that was. "I've also been giving some thought to what you said when they sent you out to buy the clock and steel wool, and it's not good."

"Not good? How could it get any worse? These fuckers are going to set off a bomb. Or bombs," he added.

"It... no... I mean, the worse news is really for you personally. Although Rab accompanied you to buy those items, you went into the shop alone; by yourself. From what you said, he cried off going in with you, saying he was allergic to the paraffin fumes from the hardware shop. Do you realize what this means?" Sam could only look in bewilderment at the older man, not understanding the point he was driving at. "They are going to make a bomb. Once this bomb goes off, there will be the inevitable investigation. Our forensic boys will know at once what they made the device from, and what kind of timer, that is, your clock, the terrorists used. The police will make inquiries from every likely shop, and it will only be a matter of time before the store you bought the stuff from makes the connection. They've set you up. Either by accident or design, your new friend Rab made sure he was well out of sight of the shopkeepers, so it'll be you and you alone who'll take the rap for this. You can bet your life that by the time the bomb goes off, your French friends will be well away, probably on their way back to Paris, and the rest of the group will have vanished into thin air. So the police will only be looking for one suspect, someone matching your description. Your face, or an artist's impression of it, will be all over the newspapers and on television. Not just here, in Glasgow, or even Scotland, but throughout the United Kingdom. In fact, if they kill enough people, it's just possible that your face will be seen on every TV set throughout the entire world!"

It was now Sam's turn to go white. It was bad enough when he thought all they would search him for was knocking a policeman from off his mount, but now... they could want him for mass murder. And that's what it would be. Deliberate; cold; premeditated. That's what he couldn't figure out about Rab. Colin had been right. That cunt had deliberately not gone into the shops with him. Allergic to paraffin my arse, he thought. He knew! The bastard knew what that stuff was to be used for. There were now some very tough decisions for both Colin and Sam to take. Sam had to decide whether he wanted to carry on with this mission. He knew he could pull out now if he wanted to. He'd done much of what Colin had asked of him, and no one would blame him if he withdrew. After all, he was a civilian and a young one at that. This was even more dangerous than Colin or his team had envisaged, and it seemed unfair to pressure him into continuing with what could be fatal consequences.

The other decision Colin had to make was whether to round up the gang now before they could carry their plan to fruition. On the surface, that was the best option, but in doing so, it would give away Sam's role in the affair, and he would never again be safe. Even if they gave him a new identity, and it was uncertain that Colin could guarantee this, his cover might eventually be blown. It would then only be a matter of time before they exacted revenge.

Something else for Colin to consider was a matter of intelligence. He knew from previous experience that although the type of bomb which the group was planning to use could be very effective, there was one grave disadvantage. It was very unstable, and unless constructed accurately and handled with great care, could detonate at any time. It was Colin's guess that they would use Sam to deliver the device to wherever they were planning to explode it. Once again, if the premature detonation of the device did not kill him, any witnesses would undoubtedly pick Sam as the bearer of the bomb. Together with his description from the shop where he purchased the ingredients, his goose was well and truly cooked. Colin's dilemma was whether to give Sam this information. It would already be infinitely harder for him to play his role now he knew what they were going to use the clock and steel wool for, and Rab's complicity. Colin doubted even Sam could continue effectively if he knew he was to be the carrier of a lethal device. One that could explode at any minute, blowing him and anyone close to him into a million tiny pieces.

Colin also had another problem with Sam. Although he had been acting under Colin's express instructions, Sam had still committed a grave felony in purchasing items to making an explosive device, and although harmless in themselves, would the authorities allow Sam to walk away unscathed if the worst happened and people were killed? Justice would require and demand arrests and convictions, and Colin just did not know whether he had the authority to override the Scottish legal system.

His real problem was that before he approached Sam, Colin did not get approval from his superiors to allow him to recruit a civilian. Not someone from within a university, but a complete outsider. There had just been no time for the bureaucracy. He, Colin, had acted on his own initiative, and now it looked as if it could all go to pot. "Shit," he thought in exasperation and anger. "Shit, shit, shit. I've put this boy's life in danger and my career in jeopardy. If the gang doesn't do for him, it's just possible he could go to prison for life. Oh, fuck, what have I done?"

CHAPTER 13

Sam knew as well as Colin that if this did not turn out well, he would be in serious trouble, serious trouble indeed, and understood that he just could not walk away now. He had to see this thing through because, he calculated, it was probably the only way the courts would acquit him. If they raided the apartment now, all they could charge the group with was having explosives. This conviction alone might carry a custodial sentence, but, as first offenders, a more lenient and misguided judge might decide to hand down a suspended sentence or even just to put them on probation. He or she might conclude that although collectively, the components could be constructed in such a way as to make an explosive device, each constituent in itself was a relatively harmless product, apart from the sulfuric acid and the glycerin. And a smart brief might even suggest a reasonable explanation for their presence.

Colin was certain that minor setbacks like these would not deter or discourage the gang from trying a similar stunt again. The only way to be sure to get them off the streets was to catch them in the act of planting the bomb. This decision would mean taking the extreme risk of actually allowing them to use Sam to take the device to its intended target, if that was their intention. So, there was now no alternative. It was up to him, and him alone, to thwart whatever plans Jordan's group and the mad Frenchman were planning. Both men spoke for a few minutes longer, and then Sam left the building. One thing was for sure. If Sam could not prevent the carnage, he, Colin, had to ensure that, as much as his position would allow, Colin would mitigate Sam's role in the affair. The Special Branch man had to take steps now to the best of his ability to protect Sam if the worst happened. It was the very least he could do.

•   •   •

The next few days passed slowly for Sam. He tried to preserve an air of normality, but his parents knew something was wrong. After all, he was their son, and Millie especially noticed the subtle differences that had come over him. She realized that to challenge him openly would only make him withdraw even more, so a bit of tact was called for. He knew she was trying to help, but could not possibly tell her the truth or anything near it. He had to lie to her and his father, but, he reasoned, it was as much for their sake as his. If they knew of the real reason for his strange behavior, they would go out of their minds with worry and try to stop him from getting even more deeply involved than he already was. What was worse, they might also give his secret away, however unintentionally, which would be even worse for all of them.

It was a girl; he said. A girl he liked a lot, one he desperately wanted to go out with, but who was already seeing someone else. This explanation his parents could understand and even believe. After all, hadn't they both also been young once?

When he was playing the joke on Andy, Sam compounded the fiction by saying he had written a note to his folks in case he was injured or killed. That had been for fun then, but he realized that he now really had to leave such a message should, well, anything could happen, and for the first time in years, he felt so much love for them. He had, like most teenagers, taken his parents for granted. They had always been there for him, always sheltered and protected him, always loved him. They had a right to know the truth. He was their son. The tears he felt welling up inside him were now for real, and his whole body, his very essence, cried out for him to be honest with them, but he knew that was the one thing he could not be. Not now. It would all have to be in the letter - everything. He wasn't sure whether Colin would approve of this, but right now, he didn't care. They were his parents. Fuck Colin.

His work, too, was suffering, and he used the same excuse on his boss as he had done with his parents. His manager, however, was not as sympathetic and told him to buck up or else. He did not bring his personal life into the office, so get on with the job in hand or find somewhere else to be miserable. There were millions out of work who could do his job and could probably do it better. For just the briefest of moments, Sam felt empathy with Max Jordan and his dreams of a socialist revolution.

•　•　•

Saturday morning eventually came, and Sam somehow found himself outside the tenement in Armadale Street, although he could not remember how he had arrived there. He had no memory of boarding the bus, of paying his fare, of the journey itself, of alighting at the stop, or of walking the rest of the way to where he now stood. It was as if the enormity of what he was involved in had just hit him for the first time. It was pouring, and he felt the water trickling down his face and the back of his neck and running off his nose. He somehow believed that the weather was symbolic-as if God himself was shedding tears for one of his children who had gone astray, and for whom the way back might not be easy.

Sam had spoken to Colin three times by phone since their last meeting and knew there was a car somewhere close by, each with at least one of Colin's men in it. That, if nothing else, gave him some comfort; however, what they would do once he was inside the flat, Sam did not know.

Max Jordan himself welcomed Sam into the apartment. Also, there was Henri, and another character unknown to Sam. He heard sounds coming from within the flat, indicating more members were in attendance. Remembering Colin's instruction to feign ignorance, Sam looked quizzically at Jordan, and Henri effected the introductions. Sam felt a presence behind him and turned to find Rab grinning at him.

"Come in, Paul," said Jordan, laying his arm around Sam's shoulder. "I understand you want to be part of our group. Well, I think we can arrange that. You've already shown how eager you are, and I can see no reason you shouldn't play your part. We need fresh blood, don't we?" The rest of the group agreed vigorously, while Rab, it seemed, sneered at him, rather than showing similar approbation.

"There's only one more small thing we want you to do, and after that, you'll be a fully involved member, ok?"

"Aye, sure," agreed Sam. "Anythin' ye want us to do, ye just have tae ask."

"Well," continued Jordan, as he motioned for Sam to take a seat, "we want you to deliver this parcel for us." He nodded to the wrapped package on the floor in the middle of the room and noticed with silent alarm that the group, although appearing friendly, stayed well away from it.

"Aye, sure, whit is it, like? A prezzie, or somethin'?"

"Yes, that's it. That's precisely what it is," confirmed the gang's leader. "And we want you to deliver it for us. It's for a... friend of ours. You don't mind doing that, do you?"

"Naw, not at all," replied Sam with as much enthusiasm as he could muster. At all costs, they must not see fear. He must not show them he knew what was in the box, that he was to be the carrier of destruction and death.

"Where do ye want me to take it?" he asked, trying to hide his latent fear. It was Henri who responded. "Our friend works locally. It is his birthday today, and we want to give him a surprise. You see that we have marked on the box who it is for. All you have to do is to hand it over to the receptionist. None of us can do it because he knows us, so it would spoil the surprise if he came out and recognized us." Sam regarded the box again, and saw the inscription on the wrapping, although he could not make out the recipient's name. "When do ye want me tae deliver it, man?"

"Well, now's as good a time as any," replied Jordan. Both he and Henri well knew of the volatility of the device and wanted it out of the flat as soon as possible. If things went to plan, the bomb would go off later that day, by which time the French couple would be well on their way to Paris, and the rest of the crew would have melted into the shadows. Sam, or Paul, as they knew him, would be the only one to take the fall. The authorities would spend a long time hunting them down, but this little arsewipe would be doing a long, long spell in Barlinnie.

Sam watched while Jordan and Henri gingerly lifted the device and put it into a large canvas hold-all.

"Ye's are takin' awfy good care o' yer friend's present. It must be valuable."

"Aye, well, he's having a party after work the night, and we want it tae go with a bang," replied Rab.

Despite themselves, Jordan and the Parisian could not help laughing at their friend's wit.

"It's rather fragile, so please don't drop it," cautioned Jordan. "It was also quite expensive and we couldn't afford to replace it, so please take care, won't you?"

"Are youse no' coming wae me?" asked Sam.

"Rab will go with you, just to make sure you get there all right. It's such a rainy morning, and we don't want our friend's present to get wet."

"No, I'll bet you don't," thought Sam.

At this, the gang's driver looked up in surprise. "This wisnae part of the deal. How am Ah suddenly getting' into the act?" he asked.

"Because we can't take the risk of the b... of the present getting damaged in the rain. You're the driver. You go."

The decision was final, that much was clear, and Rab knew enough not to argue with Jordan or his French counterpart. He had seen what happened to those who did.

"Go on, go now, and you'll be back in twenty minutes. Rab, you need to go in with Paul to see that he gets it away without problems. Just stand at the door, that's all. Paul can do the rest."

So they were still playing the same game. Only he, Sam, would be close enough to be recognized. The driver, although inside the building, would presumably be far enough away, so only a scant description would be available, especially with his anorak hood over his face. In fact, if he behaved in just the right manner, they might not even have taken him for an accomplice at all, just someone who had come in for a minute to shelter from the driving rain. By accompanying him inside, it would not allow Sam to warn the member of staff what was in the parcel without tipping his hand.

"So, this pal of yours, whit's he like?" asked Sam as they headed down the stairs.

"Aye, well, Ah don't know him that well, like."

"So you could take the parcel in, then. It disnae have tae be me, does it?"

At this, Rab lost his temper. "Look, pal, if you want tae be in the group, ye have tae learn tae do as ye're told, and Max said it wis you that had tae deliver the bloody thing, ok. No' me."

They drove down Duke Street in the rain, crossing over High Street where the road they were on changed its name to George Street. Sam noticed that only one windshield wiper was working while sitting with the package perched precariously on his lap. He hoped to God that Colin's men were behind him, and, he realized, if they weren't, he might not have time to give them the location of the device. It was due to go off later that evening if the Frenchman was to be believed. Sam turned around just once but did not see any following vehicle. Where the fuck were they? He was afraid to repeat his actions in case Rab became suspicious. After all, they were only delivering a birthday present.

Suddenly, Rab swung the car to the left, swerving into Montrose Street and throwing Sam wildly around the back of the vehicle. Rab realized the monumental stupidity of his actions and turned round in time to see Sam trying to keep the hold-all in an upright position, automatically clutching the bag close to his chest.

"What the fuck was that all about?" Sam shouted.

For the one and only time in their short acquaintance, Rab apologized. However, Sam felt it was more to himself than his passenger. "Sorry, mate, had to swerve for a bloody dog, but don't worry, I'll make sure we get him on the way back." His driver's attempt at black humor did not impress Sam. What was he thinking about? Was he really prepared to risk blowing them both to smithereens in the middle of one of the busiest thoroughfares in Glasgow to avoid colliding with a stray? Rab then turned right at a more sedate pace into Cochrane Street, where he continued for a short distance before pulling in and parking.

"OK, this is it. Let's get this done before the fuckin' rain gets any heavier."

Rab opened the rear nearside door to allow Sam to exit the vehicle without also having to juggle with the explosive device. "OK. Just follow me. It's only aroon' the corner. Shouldn't take us longer than five minutes, then it's back to the flat." The driver entered through the revolving doors, ensuring Sam was behind him. When both were through, Sam ran into the building as quickly as he could to avoid a further soaking, but, more importantly, to avoid any more rain than necessary from falling onto the canvas bag. Sam did not want to risk blowing up half of Glasgow, and himself most of all. He sensed Rab was waiting behind him, observing him. Sam took less than two minutes to explain to the receptionist what was in the bag, and she happily agreed to see that it got to its intended destination.

They conducted the return journey in silence. He had seen no one follow them to the location, or back to the tenement. Everything was so uncertain, and Sam had no way of knowing whether Colin or any of his team were even in the vicinity. They reached the door to the flat, which was already lying open for them. "Well?" asked Jordan, nodding to the driver.

"Aye," Rab replied. He signed to show them it had all gone to plan. Cans of lager and bottles of scotch were already open and being consumed. "Ah had a feeling that Ah wis being followed, but it wis probably mah imagination," he whispered to Jordan. "Ah had tae do a wee body swerve, just in case."

"Here's to tonight's party." toasted the gang leader.

They all chorused, including Sam. He was desperate to go, to get to a phone box, and warn Colin, but knew it would look suspicious if he took his leave now. He had to stay until the bitter end and hoped to God that the end didn't come sooner than expected.

It was three o'clock when Sam finally thought it would be acceptable for him to leave without arousing suspicion, as, by this time, some of the gang had also dispersed.

Although he had had a bit to drink and was not as astute as he should have been, he was still alert enough to remember the danger. Using the phone box across the road from the flat, he called Colin.

"Thank Christ you phoned," the Special Branch officer shouted down the line. "I was afraid something had happened to you. Are you ok?"

"Yes, I'm fine," Sam replied, his voice still heavy with all the alcohol he had consumed.

"Listen, Sam, this is really serious. We lost you going down George Street. Do you understand? We don't know where you planted the bomb. Where is it, Sam? Where did you take the explosive?"

"You lost...? What do you mean 'lost'? I don't understand... I thought..." Sam responded in some confusion.

"Never mind all that," Colin screamed. "Come on, Sam, I need you to focus. Listen to me, where did you go from George Street? Can you remember? Please, Sam, please try to remember. We have very little time. The bomb could go off at any minute. Please, you must have some idea. How far down George Street did you go? Did you turn left or right? For fuck's sake, Sam, try to sober up. Which way did you go?"

Sam could only repeat with incredulity, "You lost...? How could you lose...?"

Colin could see he was getting nowhere with Sam in his current condition. "OK," he responded in frustration. "Just stay where you are. I'll come and get you now. Just stay there for five minutes, and I'll pick you up. Do you understand?"

"You lost, you got... lost, but... you want me to stay by the phone box?" Sam asked, trying to concentrate.

"Yes, Sam, just give me five minutes." and with that, the Special Branch officer cut the line.

Unfortunately, five minutes was three minutes too long. Unseen by Sam, Max Jordan was watching him as he left the tenement and entered the phone box. Jordan's first thought was that he was calling for a cab. That would not be unreasonable, considering the condition he was in. But what if it was not a taxi...? What if...?

Jordan hurried down the stairs and crossed the street just in time to hear Sam shout how he was lost. Or was it that he had lost? Or had gotten lost? Had Rab got lost on the way to planting the device, and if so, who was Sam telling? This little prick had a lot to answer for. The radical dragged Sam from the phone booth and began kicking and punching him, his feet connecting heavily with Sam's groin, and his fists pummeling into Sam's face, arms, and stomach. The onslaught happened so quickly Sam had no time to react or to defend himself. "Who the fuck were you talking to, you little arsehole? We told you what would happen if you betrayed us, you little cunt." So saying, Jordan dragged Sam back across the road, still beating him about the head.

Sam was now desperately trying to sober up while struggling wildly against the bigger, stronger man. His mind was racing. How much had he heard? Sam had to stall for time, and if he'd ever acted in earnest in his life, that time had to be now. By this time, they were inside the close mouth, and Sam was still being roughly shoved up the stairs, Jordan punching and kicking him remorselessly from behind. Finally, they reached the apartment door, where he pushed Sam inside.

"Max, what…?" began the Frenchman.

"This little bastard's sold us out."

"What do you mean, 'sold us out'?"

"He was on the phone. I heard him! I heard him say it! 'We got lost.' I heard him say it with my own two fucking ears. Go on, you little shite, say you didn't. Who were you talking to?" He had now got a taste of blood, Sam's blood, and it was a taste he savored.

Play the part, Sam. Behave the way you did with Andy. Be the person. Act as he would act. Think as he would think. Do as he would do, become the character. It's your only way to get out of this. His whole body was aching, and his groin felt as if he had caught it in a vise. Both of his eyes were hurting badly, and he was having trouble focusing. Sam felt as if he would pass out, but knew that if he did so, there was every possibility he would not waken again. *Stay awake, Sam, for fuck's sake, stay awake!* he screamed inside his mind. The metallic taste of blood was in his mouth and streaming from his nose. He looked wildly from Jordan to the Frenchman. "'ot the uck's uck?'

'ot's owing on? 'ot 'ave I 'un?" He could no longer speak coherently because of the savage beating he had sustained about the mouth. If he could not make himself understood, he was surely done for. They would not waste time trying to make him out. They would just finish him off, and leave his body in a ditch, or behind some other tenement building far away from this one.

"Who were you talking to, Paul?" asked Henri. Sam wondered in his distress if they were playing 'good terrorist, bad terrorist.' Using all his remaining strength and determination, Sam replied, "'y 'ate. I 'os talking to my mate. I was as'ing 'im to gum an' 'et me. That's all it 'os. My mate." The last word being forced out.

"But I heard you, you little prick. I heard you say 'we got lost.'"

"No, dat's not what I said. 'Las' night vos de night og our 'ub 'arts 'ournament. We 'ere claying de 'ion and 'istle."

"What the fuck's he saying?" asked Jordan with undisguised impatience.

"He's answering your question, my friend, and if you hadn't been as free with your fists, I'm sure it would make a lot more sense." Turning to Sam, the Parisian continued, "So who were you talking to just now, my young friend?"

Sam made a throwing motion with his least damaged arm. "'arts. Darts." Sam articulated the word desperately.

"What the fuck has darts got to do with anything?"

Now that he felt he had gained a little time, Sam answered again, more slowly, trying to regain control of his speech. "We were playing the 'Lion an' Thistle'. Darts. Rivalry 'et'een teams. We 'ate 'em an' they 'ate us. We lost to them." Forcing out the syllables was hurting him tremendously, but Sam realized he had to make them understand him, make them believe him.

The Frenchman laughed, "Darts. You were talking about darts."

Sam regarded him curiously. His mouth was now badly swollen and throbbed almost unbearably. Through his pain and discomfort, he tried to make them understand. "'ot do 'oo t'ink I 'os 'alkin' agout? 'oo ving I 'os dalkin' do de dops?" Do 'oo vink I'm vuckin' 'tupid?" His voice rose in anger and desperation. "Dey're still 'ookin' vor me avter knocking dat tolis ov 'is 'orse. Crust gee, vonin' de dops is de last ving I vant do 'ight 'ow." The blood had stopped flowing, but his clothes were now severely drenched. Jordan, too, had Sam's blood all over him.

"What if he's done a deal with them, Henri? Sold us out to avoid prosecution. Knocking a police officer off his horse is small potatoes to what we..."

"Enough, Max. Don't forget, our friend here knows nothing about that. No, I think we have to believe him."

"But you didn't hear him; his voice, it was so... passionate!" Even Jordan was now having doubts about his interpretation of the overheard conversation.

"And when your beloved Rangers beat Celtic, are you also not... passionate?" Henri smiled. "Is this not so?"

"Yes, but this was... different. You didn't hear it. It was in his voice..." but his argument was faltering, trailing away. Could he have been mistaken? Had it just been two friends discussing a darts match?

Sam breathed a sigh of relief. He'd done it. He'd pulled it off. Fuck it, but he was good. He was the fuckin' best! And then there was nothing but darkness; darkness and oblivion. Jordan was still holding Sam roughly by the collar and was about to release him when the door suddenly burst open. Colin rushed in, his gun already un-holstered and in his right hand, aimed directly at Max Jordan "Let him go, you bastard!" screamed the Special Branch officer at seeing Sam's shocking appearance.

"And who the fuck are you?" sneered Jordan with contempt.

Henri at once understood what had happened. It didn't take a genius to work it out. "You were right, my friend. Our buddy here was working for the police. Here's one of Glasgow's finest." He snorted as he backed away from the Special Branch man.

"That's right, mon ami, and you're both under arrest."

"For what, exactly?" sneered Jordan. For roughing up this bag of shite? Yeah, ok, I'll come quietly. Now, are we going to get this done?"

At that moment, six armed police officers came bounding up the stairs, coming in through the front door. Standing immediately behind Colin, their rifles raised to shoulder height, with the muzzles pointing directly at Henri, Jordan, and the remaining cell members.

"Oh, my, this little cunt must mean a lot to you. Six armed officers? Who is he, the Chief Constable's son?"

"Where is it?" Colin screamed, noticing that Jordan now had a knife held to Sam's throat and that the blade had pierced his skin, causing a dribble of blood to escape. "Where is what?" returned Henri, smirking sarcastically.

Colin sighed in exasperation. "I've no time for this malarkey," and turning to the front two officers, signaled them to come forward. "Open that casement window," he barked. The nearest officer did as he was bidden, and then Colin stepped past Jordan and grabbed the Frenchman roughly by the collar. Dragging him towards the open window, he hoisted Henri through the aperture, so that his head and upper body were protruding into space.

The Parisian screamed, aware of what Colin had in mind. He struggled to get out of Colin's tight grip, but the detective's determination overcame Henri's fear.

"No!" he screamed, "you cannot do this. You are British police officers. You do not do such things!"

"Yes, I am a British police officer, but the unit I work for has its own way of getting things done. We don't play by the same rules as the rest of the Force. Now, unless one of you tells me where the fucking bomb is going to go off, our French friend will have a nasty accident while trying to escape."

"No, no, wait. Please don't... I'll... tell..."

"Sir, you can't do this. It would be nothing short of murder, and I can't accept this order." The officer looked to his colleague for confirmation, who was also shaking his head wildly.

"Don't you understand?" screamed the Special Branch man. "These bastards are about to explode a bomb somewhere in the middle of Glasgow, and if we don't find out within the next few minutes, it'll be too late. God knows how many people will die." Despite Colin's plea, both officers remained resolute. Neither would help Colin with what he was about to do.

Jim Brennan, the officer who had opened the window, faced off with Colin, ignoring Henri's continuing screaming and thrashing. "Sir, this would be downright murder, and there will be an investigation. Now, you may not care if your career goes down the toilet for this piece of crap, but I do. You'll bring the whole service into disrepute, as well as probably serving time in the next jail cell to these maniacs. Even if you do turf him out the window, how, exactly, is that going to help us find the bomb's location?" Pointing to the remaining gang members, he continued, "They're more afraid of these two than they are of us. They won't tell us, and he can't very well tell us if he's dead."

"We're playing for high stakes here, Jim. I'm sure if this bastard takes a flying header out the window, it'll do wonders to loosen the tongue of one of his other friends," Colin responded.

"No, sir, I still can't let you do this." The Special Branch officer could see there was no way of budging Brennan and his colleague, and presumably the other officers, from their position. And, he had to admit to himself, there was a lot of logic in what the officer had said. He hauled Henri back in, throwing him across the room. "OK, let's see if we can do this another way." Colin's frustration was evident in his voice. He turned to face Jordan, who still had his knife held at Sam's throat. Walking a few steps forward, he pointed his gun at Jordan's temple. "You can see what I see, right? This bastard has a knife held to the throat of an innocent civilian. He's already drawn blood. In my book, that's attempted murder, so if I shoot him now, I'll be saving the life of his victim. Does that satisfy your moral indignation?"

The police officers looked at each other in confusion. "Sir, with the greatest respect, all we see is one terrorist about to kill another terrorist. Who is...?"

Being careful to take his finger off the trigger, Colin pointed the gun at Sam. "He isn't a terrorist; he's one of mine! I planted him in this group, and he's been working for me! We wouldn't be standing in this Godforsaken flat right now if it wasn't for him. He's a braver man than any of us. Now, do I have your permission to do my fucking job?"

It was then that Jordan spoke up, taunting them while still holding onto his captive. "You can shoot me if you like, but you're the one who'll hear the 'boom' when it goes off. Oh, I can't wait to see your face. With all your planning, and even getting this little arsewipe into our group, it won't help. So go on, Mr. Detective, fire away."

At that point, Sam came to, unaware of the drama that had unfolded around him.

"I might hear the boom, but I'll fucking make sure you don't." And with that, Colin turned the gun butt around. He began to pistol-whip Jordan about the head, making the terrorist let go of his hostage as he tried to protect himself from the onslaught of the detective's blows. As Colin could see Sam slowly awakening, he stopped hitting Jordan and knelt beside him. "Where is it, Paul?" the detective asked quietly, remembering to use Sam's alias. "Where is the bomb?" Sam whispered into Colin's ear, so faintly that the police officer could barely hear him. Two words; it was enough.

The Special Branch man raced past the remaining four armed police officers, down the three flights of stairs, rushing to his car, which was parked outside the tenement. He screamed into his car radio, "This is Oscar Charlie, I repeat, Oscar Charlie. Put me through to the bomb squad now!" There was an abrupt break before he was transferred. Before the radio operator could respond, Colin screamed into the microphone, "Bomb Squad, this is Oscar Charlie. I know where the device is..."

CHAPTER 14

As he was being escorted past Sam, the would-be terrorist hissed at him, "This isn't over. No matter where you go or what you do, I'll find you. I'll fuckin' find you, and I'll finish what I should have done just now. No matter what it takes, I'll come for you, next week, next month, next year, ten years. You won't ever have a peaceful night's sleep again, you treacherous cunt. Someday..." and turning to the Parisian, he barked, "You'd have told them to save your own neck. You bloody... traitre! You're no better than that little bastard. I'll get you too, just you -"

The rest of his tirade was cut off by one of Colin's team, yanking him by his collar through the front door and down the stairs, while two of the other officers hustled the Frenchman out the same way. Sam was wiping off specks of spittle from his face, but he could still hear Jordan ranting as he was being led, none too gently, out of the building. Once most of the terrorists and officers had gone, Colin examined Sam.

"Don't worry about him. He's all piss and wind. He's going to be well out of your way for many years, and so is Henri. Besides, he only knows you as 'Paul McGregor', not Sam Nathan. He can try to find you all he likes, but as long as he doesn't know your real name, you'll be ok."

Sam wished he could be as confident as Colin sounded, but Jordan's words would haunt him for many months to come. Yes, Jordan would go to prison for a long time, but not forever, and he looked and sounded like a man possessed. Max Jordan was prepared to blow up a famous Glasgow landmark with hundreds of people inside. He would surely not think twice about murdering one more person, especially the one who had betrayed him. This was something he needed to talk to Colin about. Surely, there was something the Special Branch man could do.

The only remaining member of the group still to be taken away was Rab McIlwee, Sam's erstwhile driver. He was just sobering up when he heard Colin talking to Sam. So 'Paul McGregor' as they knew him was called Sam Nathan. This information would earn him some Brownie points with Max Jordan. Now they knew who he really was, it would be easier to track him down and kill him—slowly and painfully.

"We'd better get you to a hospital, get you checked out, and make sure you're ok," continued Colin with concern.

"I'll be all right," Sam winced, his power of speech recovering a little. "A good night's sleep, and I'll be fine. Please, I just want to go home."

"I know," replied Colin, "but Jordan's hurt you pretty badly. You can't possibly go home in that state. I need to make sure he hasn't damaged you even more than you look. It won't take long, I promise, then I'll run you home myself; promise. Besides, we need to get you plastered up and ready for this evening. It's going to be an interesting night."

"What do you mean, 'this evening'? Haven't I done enough already?" Sam asked, looking down at his distressing condition.

"No, Sam, there's one more thing you need to do."

"Oh, fuck, look at me. What more can I do for you in this state?"

"You can come with me to the City Chambers for seven-thirty. Oh, by the way, do you own a tux?"

• • •

On the way to the hospital, Colin filled in the blanks. When he had arrived at the phone box and found the phone hanging off the cradle, Colin knew the teenager was in trouble. The Special Branch officer raced back to the car to radio for help before running over to the flat, assuming correctly that Sam somehow must have gotten into difficulties. He also explained the motive behind the group's choice of target. There was to be a big reception that evening at the City Chambers in George Square to celebrate UNICEF's twenty-fifth anniversary, the United Nations children's organization. The organization had been established at the end of 1946, and there had been a rolling silver anniversary celebration of that event. It had spanned every continent, and it was now Glasgow's turn to hold the ceremony.

Many very important people, including ambassadors from a number of countries, would be there, not to mention many politicians and diplomats from the U.K. and overseas. Representatives from children's charities and other official bodies, as well as local dignitaries, were also invited; over two hundred souls, not including the catering and council staff. It was just too good an opportunity to miss. This would really have put their name on the map. Had this atrocity gone to plan, they would have joined the elite group of world terrorists, like the I.R.A. and Baader-Meinhof. They would be respected, revered, even. They would be in the 'big time,' able to issue threats and demands; the world would notice them.

The subversives had addressed the package to the Lord Provost, Sir Donald Liddle, who would chair the assembly, with the instruction that it was to be opened at eight p.m. Everyone would assume that it was a gift from a well-wisher, a contribution to the international charity. They had timed the device to detonate at seven forty-five to ensure that it would already be situated beside the dignitary, killing not only him but those nearby. That the explosion would injure or murder so many famous people, not to mention the damage done to such a prestigious building, would be catastrophic. This was their goal. The greater the chaos and deaths, the more seriously the world would take them.

· · ·

Although Jordan had beaten Sam severely, most of his wounds were superficial, and the bruising and swelling would recede through time. He had also sustained a broken nose and a couple of bruised ribs, but these, too, although painful now, would eventually heal completely. The nursing staff would have preferred to have kept Sam in a ward overnight for observation, but Colin insisted he had to take him away. The doctors asked for no explanations, nor were any expected. This was a Special Branch officer, after all. He could shut down the whole hospital with one phone call if he wanted to. Best to give him his own way. If anything happened to the boy later because of his injuries, well, they could always point the finger at the detective inspector.

The medical staff discharged Sam with some painkillers and instructions to visit his G.P. if necessary. It was time they were no longer here. It was time to go.

• • • •

Sam's parents were not in when he got home, for which Sam was relieved. The last thing he needed was for them to see him in this condition, especially when he would be going out again later that evening, just a couple of hours after sustaining such a savage beating. Colin had dropped Sam at his home and returned to collect him just after seven o'clock, by which time Sam had gently and painfully bathed much of the blood off himself and changed his clothes. He would hide the garments he had been wearing and either launder them himself or throw them away.

He had had to admit to Colin that he had only ever seen a tuxedo in movies, and far from owning one, wouldn't even know where to get one. Colin had smiled at this confession and told him not to worry, just to be ready, and he would arrange the rest. And he did not disappoint. The security man arrived with a tuxedo, a dress shirt, appropriate neckwear, and black patent leather shoes. This event was, after all, a 'black-tie' affair.

Colin and Sam arrived at their destination shortly before seven-thirty. Once inside the building, Colin accompanied Sam up the Carrara marble-lined main staircase and directed him to a corridor, instructing Sam to change in the toilets. The teenager was too overawed by his surroundings to argue about this demand and soon transformed himself, the pain now thankfully receding a little. His only problem had been arranging the bow tie, with which Colin helped him.

Emerging from the gents' lavatory, Sam took stock of where he was. The chamber seemed enormous to him and was the largest room he had ever been in. It measured over one hundred feet long by almost fifty feet wide and was lined with murals showing the city's history. The arched ceiling, towering far above him, was over fifty feet high and was also covered in paintings. Sam imagined that this must be what the Sistine Chapel looked like.

There was a rectangular top table, which would have been thirty feet long. It was already covered in spotless white tablecloths, on top of which were placed bottles of wine, flower baskets, glasses, and wine goblets, as well as carafes of water. Dotted around the rest of the floor space, almost at random, were twenty-five round tables, each laid out with places for eight guests. Sam wondered at which table he was to be seated. He had not noticed the seating list in his bewilderment, which was just to the left at the top of the staircase. Had he done so, he might have been perturbed to learn that his name was not on the arrangement plan. His presence there was for a different reason. As television cameras would be present, Colin felt it would be safer for Sam if he should not be there as a guest in case they showed his picture in later news broadcasts.

In the taxi on his way over to the event, Colin instructed Sam not to discuss his role with anyone. If asked what his connection was with the function, he was merely to reply that he had raised much-needed funds for local children's charities. Colin told him to act modestly as if it were embarrassing for him to discuss it further.

The security authorities had decided that most of the assembled guests should be ignorant about the calamity which had almost befallen them, and of Sam's role in preventing it. That publicity was bound to find its way quickly into the news arena, and Colin was determined for Sam's safety to keep the knowledge of his involvement to a minimum. Sam accompanied the detective into the main reception area, where the assembled guests regarded him with curiosity, and sometimes, by rudeness bordering on the offensive. He distinctly heard the words 'boxing' and 'St. Andrews Hall' mentioned.

"If only they knew," thought Sam. "They fucking well wouldn't be looking down their noses if they realized a lot of them wouldn't be going home tonight to their nice fancy houses and hotels if it hadn't been for me." He noticed waiters circulating with trays of champagne and other staff carrying platters of canapés. The other invitees and serving staff avoided him, unsure whether his presence was official or if he had somehow gatecrashed in uninvited. Sam didn't wait to be offered. It was the least they owed him, he reckoned. And where was Colin? He had escorted him in, then made his excuses and left. Sam felt self-conscious, especially about his appearance. His face was still swollen and bruised, and his nose was bandaged. No wonder he was attracting so many strange looks. He needed Colin, right here, right now.

As if on cue, the officer beckoned to Sam from a doorway off the reception hall, to which the teenager hastily responded. "Sam, there are a few people here who want to say thanks for what you... did. The guests you're about to meet are the only ones apart from me who know the truth. Are you ready?"

Sam nodded in assent and followed Colin into the anteroom. A few bare oblong tables lined the walls with several folding chairs stacked neatly against them. As well as these, there were perhaps a dozen or more formal red velour upholstered, and high-back chairs also placed in order beside the tables. None of the assembly was seated, each milling around the center of the room, murmuring to each other, awaiting Sam's arrival. He recognized most of the eight or nine guests as politicians and celebrities he had seen on T.V. and occasionally read about in the newspapers. One of these was Sir David McNee, current Chief Constable of the City of Glasgow Police and Colin's ultimate boss. He, also, had spent some time in the Special Branch before attaining his present position.

When Colin discovered McNee was to be a guest, he had no choice but to explain his and Sam's role in preventing such a major catastrophe. McNee had expressed outrage that his subordinate had gone to such unbelievable lengths by recruiting a civilian and such an inexperienced and callow youth. His anger was only tempered because they had averted the disaster. McNee confided several things to Colin. Although a large device, capable of inflicting any amount of carnage, the mechanism itself was a simple one and did not present any significant problems for the bomb disposal unit. Still, it had been a close thing.

Colin gave silent thanks to a God he did not believe in for delivering them from such chaos and mayhem. For reasons best known to himself, the Chief Constable had alerted the more senior invitees to the foiled plans. When it became known that it was an eighteen-year-old who had thwarted the plot, each wanted to express their gratitude personally, hence, Sam's hastily approved invitation. One by one, they extended their hands in greeting, and each offered their appreciation in their own individual way. In particular, one guest seemed to want to know more about Sam's background and asked if he might have a minute or two alone with him.

After the rest of the dignitaries had left the antechamber, the statesman turned to Sam. Sam could see the beginning of tears forming around his rheumy, tired eyes, and he noticed that he was trembling, with flecks of spittle dribbling from the sides of his lined mouth. He had been drinking heavily, and he slurred his words so badly that Sam had to strain to hear what he was saying. At first, Sam could not understand what the man was talking about. He was obviously in a heightened emotional state, but whether this was because of the alcohol or that he had come so close to death, Sam could not be sure. After once again expressing his thanks for Sam's bravery, he began to speak of other things. None of it made sense, and Sam tried to pull away from the older man's grasp, but the statesman was stronger than he looked. Despite his inebriated state, he held Sam firmly while gripping the shoulders of his tuxedo jacket. Pulling him closer until they were almost nose-to-nose, he forced Sam to look into his worn and weary countenance. The stench of alcohol from his breath was almost overpowering, and Sam had to turn his head away. He could only shake his head in abject disbelief at what the older man was telling him as saliva ejaculated from his lips, covering Sam's face with his drool.

For several minutes, the one-sided conversation went on, the older man holding up a restraining index finger, silencing him when Sam tried to interrupt. Eventually, the man finished, and Sam stood deathly still, numbed almost senseless by what he had just been told. The statesman released his grip but kept his eyes firmly on Sam. By now, the older man was crying, his eyes rimmed red, warm tears coursing down his deeply lined face.

Sam was so dumbfounded by the revelations he had just heard that he could not speak. Words wanted to come, and so many questions were forming inside his head, but at that moment, he did not have the articulation to give them a voice.

The statesman, shoulders bowed, turned to leave, weaving unsteadily towards the door.

"Wait!" Sam shrieked. "Please... wait. I mean, why me? Why me?" The statesman turned slowly, his right hand clutching the doorknob. "Do you really have to ask? After the exemplary way you conducted yourself? It's only you and others like you that can stop it from happening. I'm too old and no longer have the courage or the strength. You must stop it. You must!"

"But how?"

The old statesman merely gave Sam a wan smile before turning the handle and leaving the room. "Providence, perhaps." And with that, he was gone, leaving the adolescent in a state of horror and disbelief.

The events of the past few weeks, the preceding few hours, and now this monstrous disclosure had all but unhinged his young mind. Everything he thought he knew, everything he had been comfortable with, had all been a sham, an illusion. Nothing made sense anymore, least of all the man's insistence that only he, Sam, and others like him, whatever that meant, could put an end to the madness.

The teenager raced out of the room and caught up with the senior statesman. When he opened his mouth, it was not him who spoke.

"How do you know?"

"I can't tell you."

"Then how can I believe any of this?"

"It is true, I assure you. Do you think I would lie about something like this?"

"Why are you telling me? What do you think I can do? You're the one with influence; it's you that's got the title, the contacts. You're the, what's it called, the establishment. If you can't do anything about this, what the hell do you think I can do? I'm a nobody, I'm a fuckin' nobody!" and Sam, too, began to cry. "How dare you lay this on me? What the fuck am I supposed to do? What can I do? This is way, way too... too... big for me to take in. What right do you have to tell me these things? Who else knows?"

"No one. Not a soul, except the person who told me, and the madmen who... It could be..." the old man faltered.

"It could be..." Sam prompted, almost sure he already knew the answer.

"Yes, damn it, it could be very dangerous knowledge to possess."

"And yet, you still told me, me! Someone you don't know, have never met, has no connection to, nothing! Why the hell did you do it? Why disclose this... this, God, I don't even know what to call it, why me?"

"You don't understand. I... I was in the same situation as you. That is, I didn't know until... until...."

"And which bastard spoiled your night?

"A friend."

"A friend? Some fuckin' friend, eh? With friends like that, I'd sooner take my chances with the Gorbals Cumbie."

"I beg your pardon...."

"They're a local gang. They hurt people, but believe me, not as much as you've just done."

At that moment, Colin reappeared. Sam knew that if he could confide in anyone with the knowledge the old man had just revealed, it was the detective. He would trust that man with his life, and hadn't the detective just saved his life earlier this very evening? Colin would know what to do. He was, well, he was Colin, but before Sam could blurt out his secret, the Special Branch man broke in.

"Sam, I'm sorry, but I must get back to Turnbull Street straight away. Something urgent has come up, and I have to leave, but I've arranged a taxi to get you home. It'll be here in a few minutes. Thanks for coming, and I'll speak to you again soon. Bye for now." and with that, the detective was gone.

"But Colin," Sam wailed, "I need to speak to you...." his voice trailed off as he realized Colin would not have heard him. His mind was now a whirlwind of emotions, made all the worse by not even being able to share his knowledge with the one person who would know how to handle such incredible information. He trembled and felt faint-like, only an immense effort of will stopping him from collapsing on the spot.

• • •

More upset was awaiting Sam on his arrival home. As he got out of the taxi, he noticed the living room light was still on. His parents were never up at this time. They always retired at around ten o'clock. Dad! His father had been complaining of feeling unwell and of pains in his chest and arm. Oh fuck, NO! As he opened the front door and rushed into the room, his mother's face seemed to confirm his worst fears. She had been crying, her eyes still red and raw from the tears, her face puffy and strained. Her next action, however, stunned him. Despite his visible injuries, she rose from her chair and slapped him as hard as she could across the face. The force sent him reeling backward into the sideboard. The pain he felt at that second was indescribable, but what he experienced next was much worse. She was clutching an envelope - his envelope. She had found his letter and had been sitting up, waiting for him, nursing her fury.

Still clinging to the message, she rushed at him again. "You bastard, you little fucking bastard! You mamzer! You've betrayed us. Again. What is it with you? Have you got a death wish or something? Are you trying to get yourself killed? You'll certainly kill us! Just tell me, Sam, what have we done to you to make you hate us so much? Five years ago, when you wanted to go to Israel, remember? You promised us, your father and me; you promised us you would never, ever, do anything like that again. And now, what do I find? That you've got yourself mixed up with a bunch of mishiggahnah goyim who are going to do some terrible thing, and that you're part of it? That you're up to your neck in it. Tell me it's not true, Sam. Just tell me it's not true." She sobbed again, the tears once more trickling down her lined and worried face.

"No, Ma, it's true. That is, it was true, but it's over now. It was over earlier today. I swear, Ma, I promise. I'll swear on a siddur if you like." he replied, about to make his way to the drawer where his parents kept their prayer books.

"And those bruises on your face. That was those goyim too, eh? You can swear on a thousand siddurim; I still wouldn't believe you. You're a liar, Sam. You're a filthy, beitzedik liar. I'll not believe anything you say ever again. I want you out of this house tonight. I can't take this anymore. You're not the son we raised. You've become something else, I don't know what, but you're not my little Sameleh. He's gone. I want you out of my house. Now!"

"Ma, you don't understand. What I... did. I had to do. I've saved...."

Millie Nathan held out a warning finger. "Don't you dare! Don't you dare tell me you had to do anything. What did you have to do? To get yourself fucking well killed? Is that what you had to do? What's next for this family, eh? A brick through the bedroom window? A rag with petrol stuck through the letterbox?" his mother screamed.

He saw there was no use in trying to explain. She was not in the mood to listen. "Does... dad... know?"

"No, he doesn't. Not yet. I only found this... thing a little while ago while I was tidying your room. I don't know whether to tell him. The shock might kill him. I mean it, Sam. He's not well. What do you think would happen if he found out what you'd been up to, eh? Chicken soup doesn't cure everything."

"If you want me to leave, Ma, I'll leave, but not tonight. Please! Where can I go at this time of night? Where can I go?" he pleaded.

"Right now, Sam, I couldn't care less. I can't bear to look at you, never mind have you under the same roof, but you're right. I can't have you walking the streets at this time of night, but tomorrow, Sam, tomorrow, I want you to leave. Your father and I need some peace and quiet in our lives, especially your father, and we can't have that while you still live here. How can we relax when we might come back one day to find our home burned to the ground? All because of you, you mamzer. Now get out of my sight. I don't want to see you again."

"But Ma, where can I go? Where will I live?"

"I'll phone Auntie Gertie in the morning. You can stay with her until you find a place of your own. I'm going to bed now, but God knows if I'll sleep. You can do whatever you want. Good night." And with that, she trudged out of the room; a woman suddenly made old before her time.

Sam stood in the living room for a couple of minutes, reluctant to stay in the house where he was no longer welcome, yet equally disinclined to wander the neighborhood so late on. Eventually, he decided it might be best if he went out, even for a little while, just to clear his head, to give himself space to think.

Millie heard the front door closing, but just turned around and cried into her pillow.

The streets were dark and deserted, and a light drizzle was falling. Sam wished the rain was more torrential to wash away the guilt and remorse he was feeling at that moment. Despite the trauma of the last few minutes, he could not help calling to mind the elderly politician's words and the terrifying information he had imparted. He tried to think logically about the totally illogical. If the older man was correct, other people, influential people, had to know, surely. It was unthinkable that Sam alone had been entrusted with this awful secret. Still, if it were true and were made public, the consequences would be incalculable. And even if he could, or had the desire to shout it from the rooftops, who was he? An eighteen-year-old nobody with a fame complex? No one would believe him; not only that, he was likely to be ridiculed without mercy. The politician would probably deny any such conversation ever took place. He had no proof, no evidence, and, if the politician were right, there would undoubtedly be no trace of any.

But what if the reverse was true? What if they took him seriously? What then? It might even trigger the very thing the old man foresaw. No, he had to be wrong. The statesman had no reason to lie to Sam. He had just saved the man's life, for God's sake. So, it had to be true. But what if... what if... the old man had got it wrong? What if the old man had misinterpreted the intelligence he had been given? Yes, that was it. That had to be it. The man was elderly, and judging by the skinful he'd consumed earlier, might even have been 'confused' at the time. The relief he felt was almost palpable.

Despite the earlier upset with his mother, Sam almost felt light-headed, such was the weight lifted from him.

Safe now, knowing that he had reasoned out his nightmare, Sam undertook an intellectual exercise. What if the politician had been correct? Just supposing, as outrageous as it now seemed, these cataclysmic events were actually to happen? Decisions would have to be taken high up, very high up; in fact, they would have to be taken at the very top.

The very top. Oh, fuck! Oh, Jesus Christ, the very top. It was as if a bright, blinding light had suddenly gone on inside his head. It blocked out everything, the brightness, the pain! So many things, so many ideas, so many answers! Suddenly, everything was clear, and inside his mind, Sam could see forever. It was as if the total sum of man's accumulated knowledge had erupted with an earth-shattering explosion inside his head. But this data was slowly fading, only one indisputable truth remaining, refusing to leave him, demanding to be heard! The statesman had been telling the truth, the absolute truth, but even he did not understand the full implications of what he had divulged. Only he, Sam, had divined this, of that he was sure.

By some freak of inspired deduction, he had pieced together the answer to, and the reason for, one of the abiding mysteries of the previous decade, the murder of the American President, John Fitzgerald Kennedy! He turned over in his mind all the information he had come into and what he already knew about the slain leader. No matter which way he considered it, the result always came back the same. Some crazed lone shooter hadn't murdered the president, and although Lee Harvey Oswald might have pulled the trigger, he didn't kill Kennedy. The decision to do that had been taken at a much higher level, and it was now clear to Sam that Oswald was not the only man to have Kennedy's death on his conscience. Who knew how many more individuals had been involved but who, unlike Oswald, would be way above the law and would never be brought to justice?

He had been wandering aimlessly, letting his legs and feet take him where they may, and, as if awaking from a dream, found himself at his local shopping mall. There was a bench nearby where Sam sat down and began to sob. It was all too much, far too much for one person to take, his liaison with Colin, and his subsequent recruitment and involvement with Jordan's group. The beating, the fancy reception, its hideous aftermath, and the revelation he had just sensed.

Now, the estrangement from his family. Had it all been worth it? Would he do it all again, had he had the power to see into the future? He thought about the two hundred and fifty people in the hall and all that he'd been through during the last two weeks and concluded that he really didn't know. Despite the lives he'd undoubtedly saved and the destruction he had prevented, he just didn't know.

But what would he, could he, do now? Tomorrow, he might not even have a roof over his head. He trekked home, or to what had been his home, through the deserted streets with only the bleak, orange haloed glow of the streetlights and the soft, gently falling rain for company. It was going to be a long night, and all the way back, the thought kept nagging at him; what else could he have done...?

CHAPTER 15

He had hoped in his heart that by the morning, his mother would have relented, but if anything, she was even more adamant. So it was that he moved in with his uncle and aunt, who, although aware that something was wrong within the Nathan household, did not feel the need or the desire to become involved. Whatever the difficulty was, it had nothing to do with them. They had always liked Sam, so it was no hardship for them to accept him, but despite their attempts to make him comfortable, he did not feel at ease. After all, this was not his home, and within six weeks, he had moved out, finding himself a bedsit some distance away.

Eventually, the Frenchman, Jordan, Rab, and most of the other subversives were brought to trial. Police found enough evidence in the flat to ensure a conviction without Sam having to give evidence, despite him being the procurer of the bomb's timing mechanism and the bearer to its intended destination. He was unaware at the time that Colin had gone to great lengths to ensure his anonymity, even appealing to Sir David McNee to put pressure on the Procurator Fiscal to drop any charges against Sam. Despite Sam's valiant actions, McNee had only reluctantly complied, and the P.F.'s office acted as he requested. As far as McNee was concerned, it did not matter that Sam had ultimately saved many lives, maybe even his own. A crime was still a crime, whether Sam had been working under the direction of a senior police officer.

McNee's reaction upset Colin, but at last the Chief Constable had finally, albeit belatedly, seen sense. Still, the main thing was that Sam would avoid any prosecution. That was all that mattered. It was the least they could do. The very least.

• • •

A week after he moved into his rented accommodation, Sam was glancing at the television news when he was shocked to see that the aged statesman was dead. He had been killed in a hit-and-run incident close to his home, just outside London. Had it only been an accident, as was thought, or had other forces struck the older man down for what he knew? The coincidence was just too convenient, and if Sam's hunch was correct, how would it bode for him? If the same people who murdered the prominent statesman had killed Kennedy a few years earlier, they would not think twice about taking the life of an anonymous Glaswegian teenager.

He deliberated and agonized for days whether to tell Colin what he knew and what he believed. He was tempted to do so, if only to share the burden of his knowledge with someone else. However, he realized that if he did so, and Colin believed him, the Special Branch man would have to take this intelligence to his superiors. Who then knew just how high up the ladder it would go? Ultimately, it might become public knowledge, and someone might even trace its authorship back to him. He had no great desire to become another road statistic, and even Special Branch wouldn't be able to protect him forever, especially from an unseen and unknown adversary. And that was if they believed him at all. His information was just so overwhelming that any sane, right-thinking person would not have taken him seriously. Especially without proof, and his only link to this information was now lying on a mortuary slab.

He eventually met Colin again, and the Special Branch officer confirmed they had convicted Jordan on all counts, except that of hurting Sam. For Colin to get a conviction for that, Sam would have had to appear in court and give evidence under his real name. This was something that neither of them wanted, and Jordan was locked away for twelve years. The

Frenchman got a similar sentence, and Rab and other gang members were also indicted, convicted, and given custodial sentences.

Sam had to tell Colin about the rift with his parents and his current circumstances. The Special Branch man replied that it was probably the best thing to have happened, as unfortunate as this was. Unaware that Rab had overheard his earlier conversation, Colin said that it was unlikely that any of the gang would ever find out Sam's true identity. Perhaps it was better if he moved out of the area anyway and changed his name away from Nathan and McGregor. Although Colin believed that they had rounded up all the gang, there was always the possibility that one or two might have escaped and would look for him.

Unknown to the teenager, Colin met with Sam's employers. While not giving them the full details of Sam's involvement, suggested that a transfer to another office in a different part of the country might be appropriate, especially if a promotion was part of the package. Special Branch consulted Sam's line manager, who agreed that he would consider Sam for such an advancement. He was glad to be rid of the boy. Despite his problems and inner turmoil, the boy was just too keen and efficient. He showed he was more than capable of not only doing his own job but also that of his immediate superior.

• • •

And so it was that four weeks before his nineteenth birthday, Sam found himself in Manchester with a new job, a new flat, and a new name. Colin had given Sam a separate birth certificate, and the exams grades he had achieved at school were also now in his new identity. These papers would be all that he needed. With these, he could eventually get a passport and drivers' license, and all the other documentary detritus that it was necessary to have.

It took a while for him to summon up the courage to contact his mother to tell her of his new life and his new name, Martin Chambers.

Millie reacted with predictable horror. "It's not enough that you've brought shame and disgrace to this house, but that you have to change your name? Sam, don't you understand? Only very ill people, people who are dying, change their names. Are you trying to bring the ayin hora on yourself?" and here she spat three times before continuing, "And not even a Yiddisher name. What sort of name is Chambers, noch? You've also changed your religion? Do you want that your father should cut Kriah and say Kaddish for you? Oi, Sam, what have we done that you should torture us like this?"

He didn't think this was an appropriate time to correct his mother. That changing your name was something hundreds, possibly thousands of Jews had done when they arrived in the United Kingdom from their shtetls in Russia and Eastern Europe. It was common practice for Jews, especially for second-generation Jews like his father had done, to anglicize their names to better integrate with the community. Also, it would cut down the 'risk' of being identified as Jewish and the possibility of anti-Semitic discrimination. It was adding something to your name, usually a word associated with life or vitality, that was an accepted custom of his religion. They did this change when someone was dangerously ill to confuse the Divine decree, which ordained that the subject would die. But Sam had decided, and there would be no turning back. To avoid changing his name by deed poll, of which there would have been a record, Colin had him adopt his new identity before leaving Scotland. There, anyone could call themselves whatever they chose without leaving a paper trail, so long as it was not for any criminal or fraudulent purpose.

By making the break with his parents, family, friends, and entire life, Sam believed, hoped, that he could put the past behind him. He would start again, fresh, just another anonymous soul in a large metropolis struggling to get by. For many years he did just that, clinging to his new life as a drowning man would clutch at a piece of floating driftwood. Future events, however, would force him to confront his past and bring final closure to those events he had tried so ardently to forget.

PART 3

CHAPTER 16

May 2007

Martin's visits to Scotland had become fewer and farther apart. The estrangement with his family had never properly healed, especially as he had called himself by such a goyisher name. To avoid causing any more grief to her husband than was necessary, Millie never fully explained to him the reason for their son's sudden departure or his infrequent return visits to the family home.

Hyman died in August 1979, never really aware of why his beloved son had moved out of their lives in such an unexplained manner. Martin did, of course, come up for the funeral, but Millie would not allow him to say Kaddish at the graveside, believing him to be, in part, responsible for her husband's premature death.

Despite his frequent attempts to heal the rift between them, his relationship with his mother gradually deteriorated. He even had a Jewish girlfriend, Connie Steinberg, and for a while, it looked as if it might get serious. Despite this and the prospect of having grandchildren, Millie grew more embittered as she got older. As years went by, she became more convinced that it was her own son who had caused Hyman to die before his time. His father knew nothing about his involvement with Jordan's crew or his association with Colin. The truth was simply that Hyman had been ill, a condition which Millie had been powerless to prevent. She had to find a reason, a scapegoat, for his untimely death. Who better than her wayward, ungrateful son who had caused her so much grief, so much tzorres?

Millie never forgave Sam right up to her death in 1983. He knew she wouldn't have wanted him to be at her funeral, but he was her son, whether she still wished to acknowledge that fact. She had forbidden him to say Kaddish at his father's graveside, but she could not stop him from reciting the memorial prayer for her. He was her son.

Once Millie died, Martin had no further reason to return to Glasgow. His mother had gone back to London to live with relatives after Hyman's death, but had asked that she be buried next to her beloved husband. Martin's life was now in Manchester, and although his affair with Connie was long over, he had had liaisons with several women since, some Jewish, some not. He had, however, never found one like Connie and was unwilling to settle for second best.

The adventures he had had in his teenage years were now barely a distant memory. Time had almost faded those events altogether from his mind, even the mind-numbing disclosures of the now long-departed diplomat and the murderous threats screamed by Max Jordan. The whole geopolitical landscape had changed since those days in the early seventies; national boundaries had been altered, new nations had sprung up, countries under the banner of one administration had now found their own voice, and alliances were forged, which in the seventies would have seemed impossible.

On the odd occasion when his mind returned to those far-off teenage years, he could but smile when his late mother's words came fondly back to him. Yes, somehow, Israel had survived, even without his farkakteh help, and here he was, now a middle-aged man, with a good deal more weight and a hell of a lot less hair than he had back then. Ah, if only it could be the other way round, he mused.

Suddenly he was back and in Colin's office in Turnbull Street. Only now, sitting across the desk from him, was no longer his mentor, but Jordan and the mad Frenchman, Henri. They were talking to him, no, gloating at him, with the outsized map of Glasgow behind them, considering where to dump his body. He suddenly realized that Rab was standing behind him, holding a knife, that knife, to his throat.

"Do we slice him here, or wait 'til we get to...." asked Rab, itching to do the job.

"No, not yet. We don't want any blood here, not where they can trace it. Don't worry; it won't be long now until we finish what we should have done years ago. I made a big mistake then, but I'll fucking well not make it this time!" To emphasize this and compound Sam's terror, Jordan dragged Sam, as he was, up from his seat, punching him repeatedly in the lower back, just below his kidneys. The pain was indescribable.

He awoke with a start, looking wildly around him, almost imagining the blade still at his neck. For the briefest of moments, even as he came around, he fancied he saw Rab, Henri, and Jordan standing before him, reveling in his distress. He saw them as they were, as he remembered them, in their late teens and early twenties. Martin smiled as he slowly realized that, like him, they, too, would have aged, and would also now be in their fifties and even their sixties, if they were still around.

A dream, just a dream, he kept repeating to himself. His neck and forehead felt clammy and sweaty, but even more worryingly, his back actually hurt; in fact, it hurt like hell. As he forced his mind back to normality, he wondered why, after all these years, he should suddenly have nightmares about an event that happened so long ago in a different life. Could it have been suppressed memories, perhaps, or even deep and buried feelings of guilt about what he had done to Andy? He had kept these events so well hidden, so well-guarded against himself, that, in his mind, they had never happened, and if they did, then they had happened to someone else, not him.

Martin rose from his couch and walked around his living room to clear his mind from the disturbing images he had just dreamt. He found, however, that it was difficult to walk upright. His back did hurt quite badly, so that it was difficult for him to stand up straight. He clutched at his flanks in a vain attempt to lessen his discomfort, but found this of little benefit. He also realized that he was sweating profusely and quickly made his way back to the seat he had just vacated.

Now, he saw swirling shapes undulating before him; the pain in his lower back became even more severe. He felt he would pass out as his vision became blurry, and he vomited onto the carpet. Somehow, he realized that if he did not get immediate help and fell into unconsciousness, he might never wake up. Martin reached into his trouser pocket and brought out his mobile phone. He prayed with all his might that the person on the other end of the line would answer and summon the aid he so badly needed. The phone connected, and he could hear it ringing at the other end, but why wasn't it answering? Two rings, three rings, four rings, five. At the fifth ring, it clicked. as the voice on the other end was about to acknowledge the call, Martin interrupted, wheezing down the connected line.

"Gretel, it's Martin. Don't talk, please. Just listen. I need help. Now! I'm about to pass out. Get me an ambulance. I'm at home. You're the only one who has a k..." and then there was blackness.

CHAPTER 17

It was December 31st. 1999. Martin was alone, having just broken up with his latest lady friend. The decision to split had been mutual, but if he were to be honest with himself, he didn't want to end the relationship, at least not at that point. Martin knew it was drawing to a natural close but would have liked it to continue for just a while longer, at least into the new millennium, so he could be with someone to celebrate the once-in-a-thousand-years occasion. It was not to be. Celeste told him she had met someone else and wanted to move on. He got the impression that she was testing the water to gauge his reaction. Perhaps if Martin had remonstrated harder, he might have persuaded her to stay, but he was getting too old to play those sorts of games. She seemed almost nonplussed when he offered only mild indifference to her decision, and Martin seemed to sense that she had regretted her impulsive behavior. He had called her bluff by not challenging her, not begging her to stay, and now the ball was back in her court. She could do one of two things. Either retract her decision and suggest giving their relationship another go, or she could stick to her guns and walk away. Martin had been with her long enough to understand her character and knew that she could not now back down. She had made her bed, and now she would have to lie in it; her choice.

And so it was that on New Year's Eve, he found himself alone. Still, he did not feel like sitting in the apartment on his own. Neither did he feel disposed to join his other friends, most of whom were married or in nonmarital relationships. Instead, he did something out of character. He decided to go out and get drunk. This he could have done in the privacy of his own home, but as the saying goes, misery loves company. Martin didn't feel miserable and didn't crave company. He just wanted to get drunk in the company of others, preferably strangers, who would not pass judgment on his uncharacteristic behavior. He tried phoning for a cab, but it took several calls before finding a company that would come. It was New Year's Eve, and taxis were at a premium.

"Where to, mate?" asked the cabbie, already weaving his way into the stream of mid-evening Manchester traffic. It had been snowing earlier in the day, but this had now turned to slush, and the falling rain would eventually wash it away if it did not freeze and turn into ice. As he exited from the mouth of his apartment block and felt the cold, biting night air whipping against his unprotected face, he almost turned back. However, he decided it would be a pity to waste the ride he had fought so hard to secure.

He had given no thought to where he wanted to go to break the habit of a lifetime. It was almost like the first time he had been behind the wheel of his car after passing his driving test many years earlier. No one was sitting in the passenger seat, instructing him which direction to take and which corner to turn. It was up to him to make those decisions. So it was now. There was no lady to direct him, or a taxi driver, where to go, and he found himself rudderless. He had always left decisions of where to eat, or drink, or which hotel to stay in, up to his girlfriends, and had been happy to do so. At least, that way, if the venue turned out to be a disaster, it was their fault, not his. Not that he would ever have cast it up, at least not often.

He vaguely remembered a place he had been in a year or two earlier, but with whom he could no longer recall. He only remembered that it was near a few other pubs and was around Deansgate. What the hell was it called? Something reminded him of Only Fools and Horses. What was the pub called in that show? Nags Head, that was it.

"Um, The Nags Head Pub in Deansgate, please," he responded, still unsure if he wanted to do this.

"That'll be The Old Nags Head in Jackson's Row?" asked the impatient driver, to make sure he got the correct spot. It hadn't been the first time that someone had asked him to go to a particular place, only to discover that his fare was clueless as to its exact name and location. Then a verbal slanging match would ensue. It was New Year's Eve, and he would be busy all night. He had no time for tossers who couldn't even remember the name of the pub they wanted to be taken to.

"Yes, that's it," Martin responded with little enthusiasm. What the hell was he doing? He was about to break every personal rule he had ever made, and for what? Self-pity? Was he that pathetic? The answer seemed to be a resounding 'yes.' Twenty minutes later, he was standing outside the door of the pub, still unsure of himself. The decision to stay or leave was made for him when a party of six pushed past him to get into the bar and out of the freezing night air. They propelled Martin along with them, and it seemed so much warmer once he was inside. He looked around, hoping to see someone he knew, someone who would talk him out of committing this act of cardinal folly. The place was filling up, and if there had been anyone he recognized, he certainly did not see them.

He struggled half-heartedly up to the bar and ordered a shot of Johnnie Walker Black Label. Martin didn't drink much whisky, but liked this particular blend. He decided that if he were going to carry out his intention, he would do it with a taste and flavor he appreciated. Martin swallowed the proffered drink in one gulp, the amber liquid stinging the back of his throat as it coursed its way down his gullet. He immediately ordered another, a double this time, and repeated the process. It still stung, but not as much, as if the first swallow acted as insulation against the second. Another double followed, but he drank this one more cautiously, as if pacing himself. He was already becoming light-headed and knew he was stumbling into the state he had ordained for himself. Martin finished the last of his third drink and ordered another double. He was now becoming dizzy, and his inner voice told him that was it. He had had enough and should stop now, but he was determined to see what he had been missing during all those years of self-enforced sobriety. Martin dismissed the sanctimonious echo inside his brain with a shake of his head.

"Fuck this," he thought. "I set out to get shit-faced, and that's zackly what I'm go'n to do." He lifted the glass in front of him, determined to at least put one more to bed before the alcohol took over.

He had raised it to his lips and was about to deliver another dose of liquid fire to his stomach when a female voice said, "Excuse me, I think that's my drink you're holding." Martin turned slowly to see where the sound was coming from, unsure if it was directed at him. Facing him with a bemused expression on her face was a woman who would be a few years younger than Martin. She was slightly taller than him and held her bearing very well. She wore a purple sleeveless knee-length cocktail dress, with a heavy woolen beige coat slung over her right arm, a sequined black clutch bag held in her left. Green stud earrings, which complemented her striking green eyes with just a hint of brown, completed her ensemble. Her auburn hair was parted in the middle, with each side cascading over her ears and resting neatly on her bare shoulders. The lips were fuller than Martin usually preferred, and her features he would describe as handsome rather than pretty. Her nose was too masculine to make her into the beauty which she might otherwise have been. She was staring at the drink in his hand, and he realized he had inadvertently lifted her glass of Chardonnay.

"Sorry," he responded, trying to smile his way out of his mistake. He handed her the glass of white wine. "Must've picked yours up by mistake. I'm sure I told my right hand to pick up the glass of scotch, but he never listens to anything I say. Got a mind of his own." Where the hell was this coming from? he wondered to himself. If this was what too much drink did to your vocal cords, he would return to being an ardent teetotaler.

"That's ok," she replied. "I would have thought that someone with an accent like yours would know the difference between a glass of wine and a measure of scotch. "Despite having lived in Manchester for over thirty years, Martin had not lost his Glasgow accent, although it was now tempered with Mancunian tones.

"No, really, I'm sorry. I set out to get drunk tonight for the first time in my adult life. I didn't intend to steal anyone's drink, never mind...."

"Never mind...?"

"N... nothing. Sorry, if I finish that sentence, you'll think it's a come-on line, which it wasn't meant to be."

"Why don't you let me judge what is and what isn't a come-on line?"

"I only meant... I mean... I... my name's Sam, no, not Sam, Martin. That's it. Martin. Who the hell's Sam?" He had almost let his guard down, something he had never done before, but he had never been this intoxicated before, either, at least not since his teenage years.

"Damned if I know," the woman replied. "My name's Sophie, no, not Sophie, Gretel. That's it, Gretel," she answered, mocking him. "But I wish it was Sophie. I hate my name. It's so old-fashioned."

"I'll change my name to Hansel if it would help."

She smiled back at him. "I think you've changed your name enough times for one evening, Martin, or Sam, or whoever you are."

"Let's stick with Martin. Um... can I buy you another one of those?" he asked, pointing at her now half-empty wine glass.

"Well..." she hesitated.

"I'm sorry. You must be waiting for someone. I don't want to...."

"No, well, yes, I am waiting for someone, but you can still buy me a drink if you like. She should have been here half an hour ago, and I don't like to be kept hanging about."

Martin was about to make a vapid remark about only being used to make her companion jealous when he arrived, but Gretel had thrown a spanner in the works when she announced her friend was also a 'she.' Suddenly, he didn't want to be drunk anymore. He wanted to be sober more than he had ever done in his life.

"Why did you decide after all these years to get blitzed tonight? Is it some kind of millennium fever, or have you just decided to enter the twenty-first century on an alcoholic high?"

"Long story..."

She glanced at her watch. "Looks like I've got time for a long story...."

Martin suggested telling her his 'long story' over a meal, but not in this pub, which was becoming more busy and rowdy as the night wore on. Gretel said she knew a little Italian restaurant nearby, which would be a quieter place to hear a 'long story.' She explained she had by now given up on her friend coming to meet her. If Ginny came later, well, Gretel had given her enough time and, besides, she could have phoned or texted if she knew she was going to be late.

It had become even colder by the time they left the pub, and Martin helped her on with her overcoat, despite the restaurant being only around the corner. He did not want his new companion to freeze to death, at least not before he could turn out his tale of woe.

Over a late supper, they talked and got to know each other. Gretel told Martin that she was a psychologist, a doctor who treated trauma patients. She specialized in those with a history of abuse or neglect and others whose mental state was affected by severe injury. They just seemed to gel, almost symbiotically, and it seemed like no time at all that she was opening up to him in a way she had not done for many years. She told him she enjoyed cooking and painting in her spare time, mainly watercolors, and explained that she had also tried her hand at pottery, sculpting, and even glassblowing. Martin noticed that all her pastimes were creative. Gretel replied that it was cathartic to create something tangible out of basic, even raw ingredients.

Once they had finished their meal and were ready to leave, Martin offered to call a cab for her, but she had only planned to have two glasses of wine as she had brought her car, which she had parked in a nearby street.

"Why don't I run you home instead? It would save you trying to get a taxi. They'll be few and far between, especially at this time of night on New Years' Eve."

"No, that's ok. I wouldn't want to take you out of your way."

"Please don't tell me your mother told you not to accept lifts in cars from strange women," she grinned.

"No, nothing like that. I just don't want to inconvenience you, that's all. And as for being 'strange,' you're probably the most intelligent woman I've ever met."

She accepted his accolade with what she hoped was unassuming modesty and kissed him on the cheek, whispering into his ear. Martin smiled at her and asked her if the offer of a lift was still open. She took his hand, and they both left the restaurant to find her car.

He got out when they reached his apartment, having already planned to see each other again the following Saturday. They kissed once more on the cheek, and he watched her drive away, heading for home. As he walked up the stairs to his flat, Gretel's whispered words came fondly back to him, "If I weren't a lesbian, I would drag you back to my place right now, you gorgeous man." And she meant every word.

And so, they had forged a friendship that night, one which they both appreciated and cherished. Each was free to pursue their particular forms of romance; one never enquiring of any personal or intimate details from the other. Unencumbered by petty jealousies, they took delight and found comfort in each other's company, purely for company's sake. He once let slip that he thought of her as his 'intellectual superior,' which was one of only a handful of times in their relationship that she became angry with him. She tried to explain that it did not make her anyone's intellectual superior just because she had a Ph.D. These days, they almost handed out doctorates with cornflake boxes. This sentiment, in turn, upset him, as it was now as if Gretel were patronizing him.

Whether his other friends knew of her sexual orientation, Martin neither knew nor cared. He only knew that he had found someone with whom he could share his innermost thoughts, fears, and hopes, and believed that she was of a similar opinion. He was sure in his own mind that this was a friendship that would go the distance.

CHAPTER 18

He awoke slowly, his eyes blurry, and his mouth as dry as old sandpaper. He knew at once that he was not in his bed, and the ambiance felt strange, yet somehow familiar. As he came to, he understood. No, he wasn't at home; he was in hospital. This much he could discern, but why couldn't he move his left hand? It felt as if it was clamped in a vise. He turned his head slowly to see what was causing this restriction and then smiled. Of course, it had to be that. What else could it be? Gretel was sitting beside him, his left hand gripped between both of hers.

"Hello, you," she whispered. "You gave us all quite a scare."

Martin could see that her eyes were puffy and rimmed with red. She had been crying, and Martin guessed that she had not slept for some time, either.

He smiled dreamily up at her. Through eyes that were barely open, and a parched throat, he responded, "Hi. How long have I been here?"

"They brought you in two days ago, my love. The longest forty-eight hours of my life," she said, as she squeezed his hand.

"What the hell happened? I was in my flat, felt funny, and I think I remember calling you. Did I, or...?"

"Yes, darling, that's exactly what you did, and I'm so... so..." She couldn't finish her sentence, her emotions overcoming her ability to speak. She had been so determined not to cry in front of him, but now he was awake and conscious and back with her, she could no longer hold herself in check.

Now that he was more alert, and as his senses slowly returned, he was experiencing discomfort. Martin had a tube going into his nose, and another one entering his right arm, presumably a saline drip. He also felt embarrassment when another tube lower down his body could only mean one thing. They must have catheterized him.

"My God, if that's how I get after a couple of glasses of scotch, I definitely must stick to Coke from now on."

She smiled back at him, relieved that not only was he awake, but his perverse sense of humor was also returning. "What the hell happened to me, Gretel? Do you know anything?"

"No, not much. They wanted to know if you have any close family, but you've never spoken of any, so I couldn't be of much help."

"Close family? Why would they... Oh, Christ, is it that serious?"

"It's better if you hear it from them, my love. They can explain better than I can, but you mustn't worry. It's not as bad as I've made you think, and I'm so sorry I scared you. I, of all people, should know better."

"Yes, you bloody well should. Tell me, please, what's wrong with me? It's not just indigestion, is it?"

"Martin, I can't. It wouldn't be appropriate. You must hear it from them. Besides, you'll have questions which I don't have the answers to. I treat people's minds, not their bodies, remember?"

"Yes, I suppose you're right, but promise me one thing. Say you'll be with me when I hear the news. I think I'm going to need someone, and that someone is you. I trust you more than anyone else I know."

Gretel assured him that she wasn't going anywhere. She told him she had called her office, explaining she had a sudden family emergency to handle and would be off for a few days. Her caseload would need to be reassigned to other staff members, although they could contact her by phone, but only in extreme cases.

"You called me family."

"Pardon?"

"You told me that when you called into your office, you said you had a family crisis. That's me. I'm your family." His face lit up like a beacon.

"Well, you know what they say, you can pick your nose, but you can't pick your family."

"But you did pick me. Gretel, I..." She put her fingertips up to his lips. She did not want to hear the words he was about to say, the words that could never be spoken between them.

Gretel felt she had to take control of this conversation; otherwise, it would veer off into tangents she did not wish to engage in. She changed the subject to deflect his thoughts and fears.

"My God, you've some imagination on you"

"What do you mean?" he asked.

"You were rambling in your delirious state, and a lot of it made little sense. How old are you, fifty-three, fifty-four?"

"Yes, why?"

"So you couldn't be responsible for the death of President Kennedy, could you? I mean, you could only have been a kid when he was shot, right?" She immediately saw a change come over him, and he suddenly seemed to become very ill at ease. He shrank away from her and pulled the bedclothes up to cover the lower part of his face.

Part of him did not want to hear anymore, but the other part screamed at him from the inside, demanding that he ask her what more he had said in his delirium.

"Martin, what's wrong? You've gone white. Are you OK? Look, I'm going to call a nurse..."

"No!" he shouted, then lowered his voice. "I'm sorry, no, don't call a nurse. It's ok; I'll be fine, honest. You were right. How could I be responsible for killing President Kennedy? I know there has always been a rumor of a second gunman on the grassy knoll, but I don't think even the most ardent of conspiracy theorists would claim the mystery shooter to be a ten-year-old boy from Glasgow, do you?"

"Of course not, but you said other things as well..."

"Oh, what things?" he prompted her, desperate to know and not to know in equal measure.

"Names. You mentioned names. Paul, Colin, Andy, Max, Rab, and Henri? Is that right? Do you know someone called Henri?"

"No, well, I did once, a long time ago, a very long time ago."

She could not help noticing that he shuddered when she mentioned the name Max, but said nothing.

"You said another name as well. You called out Sam. Do you remember, when we first met, you introduced yourself by that name, then quickly corrected yourself."

Martin reminded her that on that occasion, he was drunk, or well on his way to getting there. Gretel countered by replying that even a drunk usually remembered his name. Besides, he hadn't yet reached that stage of inebriation. He tried to dismiss her questions, and turn the conversation to other, less contentious topics, but she was now curious and persisted. Did he have a past of which she was unaware? Did this guy who hardly drank, no longer smoked, rarely gambled, and certainly did not do drugs; this plain, uncomplicated guy, have a dark secret, or secrets? Was he not all he seemed to be? She understood this was not the most appropriate time to press him, but somehow, it bothered her that her friend, her best friend, could keep something like this, whatever this was, to himself. "You don't have to tell me, but..."

"It was a long time ago," he started. "Look, I can tell you some things, but not it all. Believe me, please, when I say to you that anything I don't divulge is for your sake, not mine. I wish you hadn't heard those names. It would have made both of our lives much easier. But, I don't want to lose your trust, especially not now, so I'm going to tell you some things about myself, I never thought I would ever have to mention again..."

Martin revealed his real name, and a highly edited version of how he came to live in Manchester. He didn't tell her the circumstances in which he was recruited by Colin in the first place (much of this Martin would reveal later) because that would mean explaining the affair with Andy, which he did not want to do, especially while he was lying prone in a hospital bed.

Gretel did not, however, miss this inconsistency. How did an eighteen-year-old adolescent come to the attention of the Special Branch? Martin only told her he had done something some years earlier, which had brought him to their notice. She mused that he could only have been a young teenager when he did whatever this was.

Martin was too ashamed to admit what he had done to his friend, although, as a psychologist, he thought she might have had a professional interest. He only stonewalled and told her that this was one thing he preferred not to discuss. He also did not divulge his meeting with the old diplomat, now long deceased, and his insight into the reason for the Kennedy assassination. The least said about that, the better, but, once again, the psychologist did not fail to spot the anomalies.

"You mentioned killing Kennedy. Where does that fit into all this?"

"I won't lie to you. That's one thing I can't, I won't tell you. To make matters worse, I can't prove a word of what I do know and what I believe. If there still is any evidence, trust me, it's well hidden. Besides, most of the people involved in Kennedy's killing will probably be dead themselves by now, or at least, well into their eighties or nineties. Even if I'm only partly right in what I suspect, I don't want to burden you with this."

"Just tell me one thing. Are you saying that you know why Kennedy was murdered?"

"Yes, no, I mean... I don't know for certain, but all the pieces fit together. I could just be adding two and two and getting six. I suppose no one will ever know the truth."

"But what pieces, Martin? You said 'pieces,' so you do know more than you're letting on."

"Please, Gretel, not now. Maybe later, once I can marshal my thoughts again, but I really don't want to talk about this anymore right now. Please."

She could see he was becoming agitated and knew this would not be good for him in his current condition, so she let the matter drop. "My God, I thought I knew all there was to know about you, and now I find that I've been friends with two different people. I wish I'd known Sam. I could've probably straightened him out."

"Yes, perhaps you could have, but then, he wouldn't have had that adventure and would probably never have left his hometown. That means he or I would never have met you later. I would do that thing again ten times over if I had to. I can't think of not having you in my life, and I'm not sorry for any of it. The one thing I do regret is how I treated my parents, especially my mother. She deserved better."

"You must have been terrified, getting mixed up with that bunch of terrorists. I mean, you were never really like them, were you? You were only playing a part, right?"

"Yes, of course, it was only an act on my behalf, but I couldn't show fear, could I? I had to pretend to be like them, to fit in. Hitting that mounted policeman with a rock was an accident, but it was probably that event that secured my place in the gang. That was really something, especially when the crowd surrounded him. I never found out what happened to him, but I hope he made it out ok. Nowadays, they would class him as 'collateral damage'."

She gripped his hand again. "You truly are a strange, wonderful and brave man. How the hell did I live before I was lucky enough to have you in my life?"

"I'm sure you managed just fine. You had a life before you met me, and you would still have that life even if we hadn't found each other."

"No, darling, I realize now, I existed before I met you, but I only started to live the night you took my drink. Oh, why couldn't you have been born a bloody woman?" she asked in mock frustration.

He was about to offer, in jest, to have the 'operation,' when they saw the doctors enter the ward, doing their morning rounds. Eventually, Martin's medic approached his bed. He undid a folder bearing the name Martin Chambers and took a clipboard from the bottom of his bed.

"Well, Mr. Chambers, how are we feeling today? I see you've come back to join us. May I call you Martin?"

"Yes, by all means." Behind the doctor's back, Gretel mouthed the word 'Sam.' He regarded her in horror, but his friend just smiled and drew her index finger across her closed lips, then blew him a kiss.

The doctor's nametag read Higgins. Martin thought of My Fair Lady and Rex Harrison. He needed a surgeon, he thought, not a bloody speech therapist!

Gretel had once heard that the sex drive is the last feeling to go before death, but she knew that in Martin's case, the final emotion he would experience would be humor and the total absurdity of being buried in a thin wooden coffin to protect his lifeless body from underground predators. Who the hell did they think they were kidding? Those little buggers would still get you, and being entombed in a pine box was only delaying the inevitable.

Higgins addressed Martin somberly. "Mr. Chambers, Martin," he corrected himself. "Perhaps we could have a word in private?"

"No, Doctor, I would like Gretel to stay. If it's going to be bad news, I'm going to need her with me, and besides, as well as being my best friend, she's also a psychologist. Right now, I need her more than a bloody elocutionist."

Gretel drew Martin a bemused glance and wondered if he had lapsed back into a state of delirium. He only smiled at her and asked Higgins to continue.

"Ok, Martin, it's like this. A couple of days ago, you experienced what we call an abdominal aortic aneurism." Martin reached out to find Gretel's hand, preparing for the worst. They found each other's fingers and entwined them tightly. Higgins continued, "Normally, this is no big deal, and there are many ways we can treat this condition. However, in your case, the aneurysm ruptured, leading to a severe loss of blood. Believe it or not, another two minutes and you would have been beyond our help. It was as close as that. If you hadn't made that call when you did, I assume to this lady here, and she hadn't answered and responded right away, you would have been dead before you got to the hospital. As it is, you arrived, as they say, in the nick of time, and we've done what we can to repair the damage. We would have preferred to have used endovascular surgery, but there was no time. It may have given you a better long-term chance of survival, but we had to act quickly. Our only other option was open surgery, so I'm afraid you've got quite a large scar on your abdomen. Unfortunately, I can't give you any favorable long-term prognosis. Hopefully, you will get better, and we'll send you home in a few days..."

Gretel interrupted him, "No, doctor, he's not going home. He's coming back to stay with me until he's fully recovered." She stated this so forcefully that Martin knew it would be pointless to argue, at least in front of the doctor.

"What I'm saying, Martin, Doctor O'Hara, is that we hope you will get better, but it may only be a matter of time before this happens again. We've put in a stent which will help, but I can't promise that it will work indefinitely. I'm sorry, but you may be living on borrowed time. At this stage, we just can't be sure."

Martin wanted to ask so many questions, but they were all jumbled up inside his head, and he could not articulate what he wanted to say.

Fortunately, Gretel was prepared. "Doctor, I treat minds, not bodies, but Martin has never complained of being unwell, or of having any pains. How could this just happen?"

"As a doctor yourself, you'll understand the term 'asymptomatic'. Some conditions, like this one, don't give us any prior warning. Martin could have had this problem for years and been completely unaware. The only time it would have shown up is if his doctor had found it during another medical examination. But, if he feels otherwise healthy, and doesn't visit his G.P. regularly, then there was no way he, or anyone, could have known."

"What's the cause?" she asked.

"Any of several factors. Smoking, bad diet, raised blood pressure, high cholesterol. They're the main reasons."

"Ok, so what can we, that is, Martin, do to mitigate this from happening again? Surely there must be something."

Higgins could see the desperation in her face; her entire body language was begging him to give her some hope, however small, however slim. "Are you on any medication at the moment?"

"No, nothing," he responded.

"Ok Well, I'll be writing to your G.P., but I would suggest that you get your blood pressure and cholesterol checked. We'll monitor that here, but you've just been through an extremely traumatic experience. Your blood pressure will still be low as we've had to transfuse four pints of blood into you, so, likely, any readings we take won't be accurate, anyway. Better to wait until you're home, that is, with Doctor here. See your G.P. as soon as you can. If both or either your blood or cholesterol readings are above normal, then you will need to take statins to pull down your cholesterol level and a course of blood pressure reducing medication. Your doctor will discuss this with you, and hopefully, we'll not see you back here again, but as I said earlier, we just don't know. I'm afraid that's the best I can do. Oh, the one question I should have asked, do you smoke? Please tell me you don't!"

Martin smiled. "Well, I used to smoke, but stopped about four years ago. Don't even have an ashtray in the house anymore. Good boy, see?"

"Yes, you are a 'good boy', but if you smoked for a long time, then the damage may already have been done. There is extensive research, however, which shows that the body can repair itself, once a smoker stops, so who knows, you may outlive us all yet. Well, I don't think there's much more I can tell you at this stage. Just rest up and take it easy. We'll monitor you for the next few days, and as long as there are no contra-indicative signs, we'll chuck you out on Friday." and with those parting words, the doctor moved on to his next patient.

"Where the hell did he learn his bedside manner? At the Doctor Crippen school for charm and diplomacy?" Martin wondered aloud, then continued. "I've just realized the most important thing of all. My God; you saved my life. If it weren't for you, I wouldn't be here. I hope you know what this means..."

"What's that?" she asked.

"You're stuck with me now. How can I ever...?

She shushed him. "Just get better, you silly man. You can take me out to dinner once you get your strength back, but in the meantime, just lie quietly and relax. Listen, now I know you're past the worst, I do need to go home and get showered and changed. I'll be back later, I promise. Is there anything I can get you? I can swing by your flat if you like, if there's anything you need."

"No, I don't think so."

She stood up, preparing to leave.

"Gretel...?"

"Yes...?"

"You... nothing. It's ok, just go."

CHAPTER 19

On his release from the hospital, they argued about where Martin should go. He felt strong enough to return to his own place, but Gretel insisted he should come back to stay with her, even if only for a few days. He finally agreed, realizing she would only worry all the more if he returned to live by himself. They stopped at his apartment long enough to pick up some clothes and toiletries before driving back to her house.

Martin explained that he was concerned about her reputation, having a man staying in her 'bachelorette' home.

"This is the twenty-first century, Martin. Besides, I'm sure a few of my neighbors have twigged that I play for the same team, if you get my meaning. It will surely set the tongues wagging when they see a man, yes, a man, enter my front portal, no sexual pun intended."

"Did anyone ever tell you that you've got a filthy mouth?"

"No, well, not for at least two weeks."

"I guess we need to set some ground rules..." he began to fidget with unease.

"Martin, you're my best friend. There are no 'ground rules.' If I want to invite a lady friend back, I will do just that. Likewise, should you decide to have a girlfriend over. In that case, I shall do the adult and sophisticated thing and be very discrete, ok? Unless she's quite attractive, of course. The one thing Martin, that you and I will never do is share a bed. You will use the guest bedroom and only the guest bedroom. Is that quite clear?"

"Well, er, yes, I suppose so, but I only meant that I didn't want to get in your way in the mornings. I was just going to suggest that I should stay in bed until you've had your shower and so on."

"Oh." The embarrassment was almost palpable.

"You know, for a trick cyclist, you don't half jump to some strange conclusions."

Martin told her later that he would have loved nothing more than to share a bed with her, to show his love for her intimately and physically. He had to use all his powers of self-control not to rise to her unintended bait.

Over the next few days, he felt himself getting stronger and did not want to impose on his friend any more than was necessary. He was also finding it more difficult, especially as his health improved, not to express his true feelings for her. It was becoming almost unbearable, living under the same roof as the one person in the world he cared so deeply for and being unable to tell her how he felt.

A week after he had arrived at her home, Martin thought it was time to go back to his apartment. He would tell her that night and began to pack his things. Gretel saw his valise in the front room as she walked in through the outside door. "So, you're leaving me," she said. "Typical man. Get what they want, then it's 'wham, bam, thank you, lesbi-an.'"

"If only you knew," he thought sadly.

"Ok, let's have a quick bite to eat, then I'll drive you back. No hurry, is there?"

Martin offered to take them both out, reminding her of the deal she made with him in the hospital.

"I haven't forgotten, and you still owe me that meal, you bastard, but not tonight, ok?"

Martin could sense a tenseness in her voice but could think of no reason to account for it. He knew she enjoyed having his company, but must also have realized that he would need to go home sooner rather than later, so his packed case shouldn't have come as a shock. He studied her face, trying to discover why she appeared so strung out. Had there been any crisis at work? He wondered. Any of her patients who had been giving her a particularly hard time.

"What's wrong?"

"Nothing. Nothing's wrong. It's just that I... I've got used to having you here, that's all. I'm just sad that you're going."

Martin told her he wished he could believe it was just that and would have been flattered if that had been the case, but he knew it had to be more. After all, they would still see each other regularly.

"I've been thinking about that adventure you had, what you told me about in the hospital."

"And...?"

"I've no right to pry. It's your business and yours alone, but it's been bugging me, this thing about the Kennedy assassination. I know there's a lot you haven't told me, but I still don't know why. Martin, I do respect your right to privacy, but it's just been gnawing at me. Good friends, best friends, shouldn't keep secrets from each other, especially over something that happened so long ago. How can events that occurred so far back in the past bear on our relationship?"

"You don't understand. I was just a kid then. A young teenager, but I did something really dreadful, really awful."

"But no one died, right?"

"No. No one died," he conceded, "but it came damned close."

"You? You almost died? When you were an adolescent?"

"No, not me, someone else."

"Who, Martin? Who almost died?"

"Why? Why do you need to know these things after all this time? What difference does it make now?"

"Because when you were delirious, you mentioned more than names, you spoke about things, events, places, but you weren't making any sense. I only know that deep down, it must still trouble you, still hurt you. I only want to help you, Martin. Let me try to exorcise those demons still within you."

"Always the shrink, eh?" he responded, turning his head away. "Look, whatever happened occurred a long time ago in a different life. I'm not a fourteen-year-old boy anymore. I'm a grown man, and I've put those days behind me. Now leave it alone."

"Ok, I will, but please just answer one question, then I'll ask no more, I promise."

"What's your question?"

"Did you kill someone when you were fourteen?"

She saw him grimace, and for a moment, he was back in Andy's house on that unforgettable afternoon.

"No, not deliberately."

"You killed someone...?"

"No...no, I didn't."

"But you almost did?"

"Yes." he would offer nothing more. The memories were flooding back, and they were still painful.

"Martin, I have to ask. Was it deliberate? Did you try to kill someone?"

"No."

"So, it was an accident?"

"You said one question."

"So it was an accident," Gretel persisted.

"Yes, it was a bloody accident, and, no, no one died, so please now, leave it alone."

The psychologist studied Martin silently for a few moments, trying to make sense out of it all. Rather than clear up the situation, this only made it more confusing. Martin almost killed someone but didn't, and whatever these actions were, they brought him to the attention of Special Branch five years later. What did he do, a fourteen-year-old boy, that could make him a person of interest to the secretive police department such a long time after? By his own admission, it was an accident, not attempted murder, and even if this were the case, surely the regular police would have been called in. Why involve the Special Branch?

As if he were reading her mind, Martin blurted out, "Ok, I'll tell you. I'll tell you everything, but once I do, I can't un-tell you. Do you understand? Our friendship will probably end after tonight once you know what I did."

"Martin, I doubt anything you tell me could make me want to end our relationship. Especially over something that happened when you were only a kid. Do you think I'm that shallow?"

"No, I don't, but perhaps you, of all people, will find it interesting as well as appalling."

"I don't understand."

"No, but you will…," and so Martin told her the complete story of what he did to Andy, right from the beginning.

"Well, as a study goes, that's some tale. You applied Pavlovian type methods, and probably achieved in a few weeks, what it would take trained psychologists months to accomplish. Phew. No wonder you didn't want to tell me. Remind me never to piss you off. But where does Special Branch come into all this?"

So Martin explained their need to get someone to infiltrate the terrorist group, and how they intended to scour Glasgow University seeking an ideal candidate. By a sheer fluke, Andy was the first student they approached. He declined their advances, the events of almost four years earlier coming back to him. He told them about Sam, as he was called then. But, as Sam realized later, this was not so much to help the authorities as it was in the hope and expectation that the terrorists would discover him and deal with him accordingly. She could only gape at him, shaking her head in amazement. Martin realized now he had told her that much, he may as well divulge the rest. So he told her about the beating, and how he had almost made it out of the flat on Armadale Street. He would have disappeared into thin air, but for Colin's untimely arrival, and how Jordan threatened to get him, no matter how long it took.

"OK, you can take me home now. If you don't want to, I'll understand. Just call me a cab now."

"All right, you're a cab. Don't be so bloody stupid and stop feeling so fucking sorry for yourself. How dare you think I would end our friendship over something you did when you were barely out of short trousers? And despite what you did to your friend, you more than made up for it by preventing a massive disaster. As a human being, it concerns me you almost cost your friend his life, but as a psychologist, I say 'wow.' I might write a paper on this."

"No, please, don't. I don't want this ever to leave these four walls."

"Relax, Chambers; I was only joking. I don't know what to call you now. Is it Martin or Sam?"

"Martin; always Martin. Sam Nathan no longer exists, except on my birth certificate. My original birth certificate," he added.

"How many birth certificates do you have?" she asked.

"Only two, one in my name, my original name, and the other in this identity."

"OK, Martin. Think I prefer Sam," she shrugged, "But Martin will have to do, then. You still haven't told me how all this ties in with Kennedy. It does all tie in, doesn't it?" Martin confirmed that, yes, he was told certain things about American military strategy in the Cold War, by one of the V.I.P.'s whose life he had saved. Why the old statesman had told him, Martin never knew. He only realized that the president would have known about these war plans and would never have approved of them. That was why Kennedy had to be eliminated. He had to make way for a Commander-in-Chief who would go along with the strategy formulated by the Joint Chiefs-of-Staff and others inside and outside the Pentagon. They had, Martin believed, secretly sounded out Johnson, who had no such qualms or reservations. Once they knew Johnson would not be an impediment, the train was set in motion. They would assassinate Kennedy, and his Vice President would take over. Did Johnson put two and two together? If he, Martin, had done so, then surely the new president did as well. But he probably realized that if he went public with his suspicions, he would meet a similar fate to his slain predecessor. Better to let someone else, like the Mafia, or the Soviets or the Cubans, take the flack and the blame. But what were those plans that the President was killed for trying to countermand? That was what the old statesman had told Martin, and it was the only piece of the puzzle left.

Slowly and hesitantly, he let it all come out, bit by bit, until it was told. Gretel carefully considered what Martin had just revealed. Now she understood his reluctance to let her in on his secret. It was for her own good; she could see that now. Perhaps it would have been better if she hadn't known after all. This was heavy-duty stuff, and she was only a psychologist. No one had trained her how to handle highly classified intelligence. Yet neither was Martin, and he had borne this information in secret for over thirty-five years. Had he not been born Jewish, she thought, he might have been a priest.

Martin could see her watching him, regarding him, pensive, her eyes widening slightly as an idea came to her. "Have you ever heard of an author called Robert Ludlum?" she asked Sam.

"Yes, he wrote The Bourne Identity. I might have read it once. Pretty far-fetched."

"I love him. He's one of my favorite authors."

"I'm surprised you've got time to read, what with your job, and your painting and glassblowing and all. What about him?"

"Yes, I still manage to read occasionally, anyway, Ludlum wrote a book called 'The Chancellor Manuscript.'"

"So...?"

"It's about a young historian called Peter Chancellor, who researches high-level conspiracies. Anyway, he finds out certain things that happened between big business, government and the military, corruption, graft and so on, only he doesn't have enough hard evidence to turn his findings into a treatise, a serious exposé, so what does he do?"

"He scrunches it all up, chucks it in the fire, and becomes a manager at Tesco's?"

"No, you dummy. Chancellor turns it into a novel, a work of fiction. He takes the information he has gleaned, uses his creative instincts and a bit of imagination. Before you know it, he's got a bestseller on his hands, several bestsellers, if my memory serves me correctly."

"So let me get this right. You want me, someone who's never written a shopping list, to turn out a bestseller based on the events I've just told you about?"

"Something like that, yes."

"You're mad, a mad psychologist. You are a fruitcake short of a few raisins if you think I'm going to even consider doing that."

"Why?"

"Why? First, I can't write. I don't mean that I'm illiterate; I just can't write a story. Second, I don't have the time. I've got a business to run, ok, not a very successful one, but a business none the less. Third, I don't think I want to tell the entire world all about my dirty washing. You're my best friend, and you were right. We shouldn't keep secrets from each other, but that doesn't mean that I have to prostrate myself before every Tom, Dick, and Harry. Some things are just meant to be kept private, and this is definitely one of those. Ok?"

Gretel was prepared for this and came out, all guns blazing. "You're not seeing the big picture here. If the Americans were up to no good, surely everyone has the right to be told. Even if it was over forty years ago, don't you think we should all know what might have happened."

"But that's my point. It was a long time ago. The world has changed since then. Whatever strategies and tactics the Pentagon had planned then would have all changed by now. No one would treat it with the same seriousness that they would have back then. The world has moved on. The Cold War is long over."

"So there's no danger of any fallout if you'll pardon my pun. But this is more than unbelievable; it's mind-blowing." Her next statement almost floored him. "Look, Martin, I'll be perfectly blunt. We don't know how much time you've got left. Do you want to die without leaving some sort of legacy?"

He regarded her in shock, scarcely believing what she had just said. She was his best friend, his soulmate. How could she say such things? He could only shake his head, saddened by the way he felt she was treating him.

Gretel realized almost immediately that she had overstepped the mark. It was her Irish roots, she explained, impulsive and forthright. Call a spade a spade. Martin knew she wouldn't have hurt him for the world, and she instantly regretted her words.

Despite Gretel's less than diplomatic way of explaining her reasoning, it sank home, and in some perverse way, through some distorted logic, Martin realized perhaps she had a point. Maybe people did have a right to know. Possibly he was just tired of carrying such a heavy load by himself. Perhaps it was time to share. He sighed heavily.

"I don't know when I'm going to get the time to start this thing, but ok, I'll give it a go."

But Gretel had other ideas. "Listen, I know you have little time. Neither do you have any writing experience, but I do. I write reports all day long, for God's sake. Why don't you and I collaborate, you know, write it together? It would give us an excuse to see more of each other, that is, if you still want to see me after what I just said."

He told Gretel later that he almost admitted to her then and there that he wanted to spend every minute of the rest of his life with her and never let her out of his sight. His only reply was, "OK, but not tonight. I do need to get home. Let's meet up on the weekend. I could spend it here, and we'll make a start."

And so it was decided. They had a quick meal, then Gretel drove Martin home. Despite his initial reluctance, he admitted he was looking forward to spending the weekend with her. It would be fun, Martin thought, even though he would be confined to the spare room.

CHAPTER 20

They discussed the idea of where to set the story and initially thought of perhaps making it all happen in London. Neither of them knew the metropolis well, and they realized it would slow down their momentum. The story would just get bogged down in trying to find bits of the city where the events might have taken place. They were both reluctant to set the work in Martin's hometown, as this would just literally be too close to home. Where else should it be located but in the place they both lived: Manchester? It made sense, and at least both of them knew the city. Naturally, he would have to alter the main characters' names, and of course, the locations would now be Manchester suburbs, but he was comfortable with this. When they got down to starting on the manuscript, one thought kept bothering Gretel. Why had this never come out? Someone must have known; someone should have been brave enough to put their head above the parapet. Martin reminded her that if he were right, Kennedy did, or was about to, and look what happened to him, poor bugger. If those who wanted this issue kept secret had no problems with killing a president, what chance did anyone else have? And if other people were not afraid for their own lives, then more dire threats could be made. Cross us, and we'll not only make you disappear, but we'll also do the same thing to your nearest and dearest, your wife, your husband, your families, your children. They were compelling and persuasive arguments for keeping silent.

Although they were writing the story from actual events, Gretel realized they would still have to do some research to make the story more authentic. At one time, this would have meant trawling through library documents and newspaper archives. However, thanks to the wonders of modern technology, they could now do this from the comfort of Gretel's office at home.

• • • •

A couple of weeks after they started the project, she was poring over some conspiracy websites when she came across an article that almost floored her. Martin looked up as he saw the look of disbelief on her face. With her eyeglasses perched halfway down the bridge of her nose, Gretel beckoned him over. "Martin, come and see this. It's quite astounding, and I can't believe what I'm reading."

Martin joined his friend at her computer desk as she pointed towards the screen. Leaning over her shoulder and reading partly to himself and partly out loud, he learned that in the late 1920s and early 30s, the American military planned to attack and annex Canada. "… they planned to build secret bases from which they would fly paratroopers to invade Canada. Meanwhile, blockading their ports with American battle cruisers, preventing military support from British troops." Martin continued reading, occasionally looking at Gretel. "Can any of this be true? I mean, it's all so… fantastical. Britain was, is, America's staunchest ally. Why would the United States turn on its closest friend? It beggars belief."

"Yes, it does, but it was the only way the U.S. believed it was going to supersede Britain as the dominant world power. They seem to have been quite far along with their plans before they abandoned the project. It even had a code name. They called it 'War Plan Red.'"

Martin drew up a chair and stayed beside her as they read more accounts of formerly highly classified American military and political subterfuge. According to an anonymous retired C.I.A. agent, The United States almost caused a war between the Soviet Union and China back in the late 1950s. The writer explained that the planners and strategists inside the

Pentagon were extremely concerned. They worried that both Communist superpowers would enter into a pact similar to the Axis agreement between Germany and Italy during the early part of WWII. However, this would be much more serious, as the world now had nuclear weapons. The J.C.S. fretted that a military alliance between the two nations would see the Chinese sweeping east and southwards, conquering southeast Asia, and eventually invading Australasia. The Korean War was an early forerunner of what was to come. While the Chinese were busy in this theater of war, the Soviets would surge westwards. They would mop up those countries not already under Russian occupation, eventually mounting a sea and air assault on the United Kingdom. This strategy would isolate The United States as Central and South American countries also fell to communist insurgency and ultimate control. "My God, Martin, this almost ties in word for word with what you told me. I knew you weren't lying to me, but reading this just validates what you said." They continued to read. The Americans were already hard at work, clandestinely trying to create a breach between the two communist nations. The C.I.A. attempted to destabilize their association by secret economic, political, and even military intrigues and wanted to push their friendship to breaking point. To this effect, a platoon of American soldiers, some of whom spoke Mandarin, and others who spoke Russian, dressed as Soviet troops, and were secretly conveyed to a remote border point between the two countries. The Mandarin-speaking soldiers shouted insults at the Chinese forces, who traded abuse for abuse, believing they were addressing their Soviet counterparts. To stir things up some more, the Americans went one step further and dropped their trousers to 'moon' at their Chinese adversaries. This action was one step too far for the Chinese troops, who were more than just angry by these gross actions. They were incensed, and a few soldiers fired their weapons toward the offending soldiers. But this was where the story got even stranger. One version said that the Americans were about to return fire when an officer realized they were all carrying U.S. carbines, not Soviet rifles. If the Chinese recovered any ammunition, it would lead to some very awkward questions, so the order was given not to respond. Another version of the tale stated they had accomplished their objective simply by outraging the Chinese to the point of making them discharge their weapons. The third version was the most frightening. The Americans, dressed as Russians, retaliated to ramp up the pressure to cause maximum mayhem and only stopped when they realized the situation was getting out of control. Chinese officers did not understand what was happening. They believed that this was a plot, a first 'salvo' by their communist 'allies' and perhaps even a diversion to invade their country. Maybe they were at war. Word soon reached their political masters, and the Chinese demanded an explanation and an apology. The Soviets would, understandably, have denied any such action took place, which the Chinese would have refused to accept.

The C.I.A. officer later learned through intelligence channels that this incident went all the way up to Mao and Khrushchev, and it strained relations between the two leaders throughout this period. Although other factors, such as ideological differences, affected their eventual separation in the early 1960s, the anonymous writer was assured that this incident played no small part in that rupture.

"So, if this report is accurate, then the Americans almost caused a war to further their military and political aims. If so, then it's not outwith the realm of possibility that they would have done what you've asserted," she said.

"Looks like it, wouldn't you say?"

Martin continued to retell his adventure for Gretel to annotate. As he did so, more of those long-ago events came back to him, and despite the passage of so many years, he almost felt as if they had only just happened.

Within two months, Gretel had prepared a typed finished draft, and she agreed to edit it herself before submitting it for publication. She had done some homework on how to get a novel published, especially a first effort, and her investigations had proved worthwhile. First, it would need to be typed, preferably on a computer, so they could email it. This also meant that she would have established a timed and dated electronic trail in the improbable event of anyone plagiarizing their work. This was a given. Who would even dream of offering a handwritten or even a hard-copy story these days? Second, the grammar, syntax, and spelling had to be as accurate as possible. Prospective authors inundated publishers and agents with their works every day. They would not waste time on those efforts where the writers did not even check if their manuscripts made grammatical sense. Next, the work should be around four hundred pages; a publisher would consider anything less as a novella. At around an average length of two hundred words per page, the story should be around eighty thousand words long. An established author could, of course, write much more than this. It was more expensive to publish a long story rather than a short one. The novice writer would be a literary unknown, so less was sometimes more. Last but no less important was that the story had to be interesting and innovative. Gone With The Wind had already been written. There was no need to write it again.

The next matter they needed to work out was the title of the manuscript. This issue taxed them almost as much as writing the story. It was the only time during the entire enterprise that they raised their voices. As the entire story was about Martin's past, he felt that his title suggestions should get priority. Gretel countered his argument by saying that it was her suggestion that Martin should put his knowledge into print. After almost an entire afternoon of bickering on this point, they came to a decision. They agreed to each think of five titles which they would write separately on small pieces of paper and fold over, so the details were hidden. They would then pass each other their title ideas, and in the unlikely event that both came up with the same suggestion, this would be the one they would submit. Failing this, each would score the other's titles out of ten. They had enough trust and faith in each other's honesty, affection, and integrity to believe that neither would deliberately mark down a heading out of misplaced pride or jealousy. The title which scored the highest rating would be the one that they would use.

As he read Gretel's ideas, he realized she was so much more literate than him. He had been a fool even to think that he could do better than her; after all, wasn't she the one who transcribed his words onto written pages. He was about to tell her all this when she looked up at him, smiling, regarding him over the rims of her reading glasses. "Well, Chambers, you never cease to surprise, if not amaze me. Believe it or not, I think we've found a winner."

Just for a second, Martin didn't understand her. He looked at Gretel in some astonishment. "What do you mean?"

"This title. It's good; no, it's great. In fact, I'd say it's the best."

"Which one? I mean, I... I just took it for granted that it would be you who came up with the best title; I mean, you're the one with the 'ology,' the smart one, the...."

"Oh, come on, Chambers, don't be so modest. Learn to take praise when it's offered."

"No, well, yes, it's just that, Christ, this is a first. You're not just saying this, are you? Please, Gretel, please be honest with me."

"I am being honest with you. This is a superb punchy title. It sums up the entire book without giving anything away."

"Well, I just thought that so many people who were around Kennedy turned out to be false friends and allies, especially those who wanted to, you know...."

"Obviously. No, it's a good title. Let's go with it."

"OK, so The Judas Conspiracy it is."

The last item they discussed was under whose name they should send it. Martin understood that although the story was essentially his, Gretel had done most of the hard work. The psychologist, however, did not want to compromise her professional career. What they had written was, despite being based on actual events, a work of pulp fiction. After a bit of arguing, they decided on a joint name, but neither liked 'Martin O'Hara' or 'Gretel Chambers.' Gretel, especially, was not inclined to adopt another surname. Too much like being an old married woman, she believed. Suddenly, she let out such a shriek of laughter that Martin thought she had taken ill. She told him the soubriquet they should offer the work under, and Martin could only shake his head in wonder at her bizarre and distorted sense of humor.

"Well, why not?" she asked, pouting in mock petulance. After all, the name sums up the essence of who we both are."

"Yes, but... Les Straight...?" He could hardly articulate the name without laughing.

"Well, you're straight, and I'm...."

"For that matter, why not call ourselves 'Dick Van Dyke'? After all, I've got the 'dick,' and you...."

"You are joking; please say you are joking," Gretel responded. Martin quickly confirmed that he was only having a bit of fun at her expense.

And so they had agreed. They would offer this, their first, and probably only collaborative work, as this androgynous character, 'Les Straight.' And God help them both!

Gretel said that she intended to send the work to an agent to test the water. She knew it was as professional as any first attempt could be. If it were rejected, it would not be because of the author's lack of command of the English language. Gretel knew how to formulate sentences and paragraphs. Martin, however, didn't want any 'middle-man' getting in the way. He knew they had written a bloody good book, or at least Gretel had, he emphasized, and didn't see why they couldn't send the work directly to a publisher.

As much as she loved this man, she tried to explain patiently, as if talking to a child, that publishers were notoriously poor judges of what was and what wasn't a good read. Her researches had told her that most publishers usually only accepted works from existing, established authors. How many times had publishers rejected J. K. Rowling before someone had the good sense to see the earning potential of the boy wizard? They bickered a bit before Gretel finally got her way, as Martin knew she eventually would.

To prepare for this event, Gretel had already created an email account under the pseudonym of Les Straight. She had also found the contact details of several literary agents and sent each of them a synopsis and the first two chapters. She hoped this would whet their appetite but would not send them the rest of the story until she had a request, in writing, to do so.

Of the six companies she sent the inaugural work to, five responded with kind remarks but rejected their offering. One or two explained Kennedy was now considered ancient history and had no relevance to modern life. Also, the conspiracy theories surrounding his demise had been flogged to death, and the public was not in the mood for any more half-baked hypotheses. The rest simply said that the piece they had received was well written, but they did not handle this type of story.

The sixth company thanked them for their submission but advised Gretel that they would be closing down soon and were accepting no more manuscripts. They suggested a couple of other concerns that might be interested. One had already responded, but she filed away the other's name. Who knew? It might come in handy one day.

CHAPTER 21

Naturally, they were both sad about getting five straight rejections, but Gretel, ever the optimist, reminded Martin that the last company only could not help them because of its imminent demise.

"Maybe we made a mistake," Martin said. "Maybe no one wants to read about stuff from almost forty years ago, even as a story. Sorry, but if you thought that getting this book published would get you on the fast track to early retirement, you sure as hell got that wrong."

His friend was hurt by these remarks, which she felt were so unworthy of him. "I never thought that at all," she responded, surprised at her friend's unkind words. "First, I like my job, and I have no plans to retire, now or in the near future. Second, although I hate to blow my own trumpet, I am quite good at what I do. It gives me tremendous satisfaction to see people who have come to me with emotional or psychological problems, and leave my office, eventually, as whole and healed. You cannot understand what that's like because if you did, you would never have made those crass remarks."

Martin realized he had hurt her, something he would never have done deliberately. "No, I didn't mean it like that, and you should know me better. God, you lesbos are so touchy..." The suddenness of this last exchange startled her, but she knew at once he only made it to lighten the atmosphere between them. He would never cast up her sexuality in such a derogatory way. Gretel's response was to throw a well-aimed scatter cushion at his head. "Next time you say a stupid thing like that, Chambers, it won't be a fluffy pillow, it'll be a lead pipe." They discussed whether they should pursue their objective and send the manuscript to more agents, even perhaps, despite her misgivings, to publishers themselves. Or maybe they should abandon the whole idea altogether and call it a day. It had been a splendid exercise, and Gretel knew they enjoyed working together, despite some creative differences. Maybe they had overestimated her writing abilities, and perhaps she wouldn't be the next Agatha Christie after all. And yet, deep down, they both knew she had turned out a well-crafted and articulate piece of work.

"I bloody well hope you're not the next Agatha Christie. She disappeared for a while, didn't she? I don't want you lighting out on me. Who would I phone if I collapsed again?"

"I don't take kindly to remarks like that, even if you did make it in jest." Gretel retorted. It brought Martin's condition too close to home, 'the elephant in the room,' which neither wanted to discuss.

In the end, they kept going, and Gretel found a few more literary agencies. She also researched which publishers might be best suited to considering their story. She knew, however, if it came to the bit that it was a publisher who offered them an advance, Martin would never let her forget it. He would become insufferable. Gretel thought with some humor and asperity; that lead pipe might come in handy after all!

She decided perhaps part of the problem with getting their story accepted was that it took quite a while to get to the main point. Maybe the first two or three chapters weren't enough to generate interest. Gretel discussed with Martin the possibility of sending the entire manuscript. At least this way, there could be no excuse for the agent or publisher to say they hadn't seen enough of the story. Martin saw the logic in her argument and agreed that the next batch of companies should get the complete document. Unfortunately, all the agencies they found insisted they should send only the first fifty pages, together with a plot synopsis. No one wanted an entire manuscript. "To hell with that," said Martin. "Let's send the entire book to one or two, just to get a reaction. You never know."

So once again, the psychologist went through the exercise of emailing the story to those agencies she had researched. She also remembered the company that the agency that was going out of business had referred her to. Within a few minutes, she found their website and contact details.

After several more weeks, most of the second group of agents had responded, again rejecting their effort. One of the last companies to reply was a firm called 'Swansong Literary Agents', the one suggested previously by the now-defunct company.

• • •

A few days earlier, after reading the emailed submission, the proprietor of Swansong Literary Agents, Leighton Swan, picked up the phone and dialed a number. He realized it would be very early in the morning where he was calling. He also knew that the recipient would not mind the inconvenience of the hour.

Because of this call, the deputy director of one of the United States' Intelligence agencies spoke on a secure line to a senior politician, a former Army general, now a Capitol Hill senator.

"Brian, it's Roger. I won't waste time with small talk and chit-chat. Something's come up, and you will not believe what...."

Former U.S. Army General Brian French had known Deputy Director Roger Oppenheimer for several years and never failed to be impressed by his dedication and professionalism. If he said that this was not the time for idle gossip, it had to be something pretty big.

"Go on. I'm listening."

"Are you alone?"

"Yes. I'm in my home office. Alice is still asleep."

"I've just had a comm from London, from one of our low-level guys there, Leighton Swan."

"Swan... Swan... wasn't he the guy...?"

"Yes, it's the same Swan. After what he did with Brooklyn Bridge and all, we gave him a sinecure posting. We felt it was the least we could do. The guy was seriously burnt out. Anyway, we set him up as a publishers' agent, and you will not believe what he has just told me. Prepare yourself."

"OK, what?"

"He's just been sent a book detailing Operation Atlantic Tornado!"

"What?"

"You heard me. Someone has sent him a book, a novel, and it's all about Atlantic Tornado."

"That's impossible. No one knows about that, outside a few old diehards like you and me, and we were sworn to absolute secrecy. God, after all this time, there can't be more than five or six of us left. After the fiasco with Kennedy, we don't even tell the White House incumbent anymore. How can this be possible? Are all players accounted for? Any off the field?"

"Yes - and no - as far as I can tell. I made a few discrete calls before phoning you. This manuscript has come completely out of the blue."

"Give me the details."

"Well, as far as I can make out, Swan received an unsolicited email with an attachment. Contained within the attachment was an entire story, a novel, based around Atlantic Tornado. It doesn't mention the operation by name, but the details are identical. Swan was going to forward it to me, but I don't think we've set his internet up for secure comm, so I've told him to hold off in the meantime."

"If it's a novel, could it just be an enormous coincidence? Could someone just have thought this up in their head, with no prior knowledge?"

"You should know better than that, Brian. There's no such thing as coincidence in our game, only a connected sequence of events that we haven't yet found a link to. And besides, he also mentions Kennedy...."

"What? Unbelievable! No one, I mean, no one knows about that. This is impossible, insane."

"Well, insane or not, it's out there. Someone knows."

"No, this is all wrong. If whoever did this really knows the truth, they must realize that going public is a death sentence. We can't ever allow this to get out, and they must know that. That's why this surely must be just a gigantic novel of chance. Wait a minute; do you think the Russians or the Chinks could have gotten wind of it, and this is an attempt to discredit us?"

"The thought did cross my mind, but if it is either of them, why wait until now? Surely the time to have done that would have been years ago, but I guess it's still a possibility. I'll take soundings."

"Who's the author?"

"It's a guy called Les Straight."

"Do we know anything about him? Has he written anything else? Who the fuck is he, and how the hell did he get a hold of this information?"

"Whoa, slow down. I only got this information a short while ago. I reckoned it was more important to make sure no one from Atlantic Tornado hadn't leaked first. What was the first rule when confidential knowledge was made public? Always look to the most likely, so that's what I did, but trust me when I tell you; it wasn't any of our guys. You can be sure about that."

"OK, now we've eliminated the obvious, we need to have a quiet word with this Les Straight. We need to know how he came by this intelligence, and more importantly, find out if he's blabbed to anyone else."

"There's no time for those niceties. Mr. Straight needs to be silenced now before he can do any more damage."

"But surely we need to know how far this has gone. We can't plug a leak until we know how large the leak is."

"You don't understand. It's unlikely that Swan was the first agent he sent it to. He's probably touted his manuscript to God knows how many other agents or publishers. For all we know, any number of them might think this is a story worth publishing, especially in the light of its contents. Even now, he may be getting offers. We need to stop him before this goes any further."

"We could use Swan and his contacts to see if anyone else has seen the story and get their reaction."

"OK, I'll get on that immediately, but in the meantime, we need to do something about this Les Straight."

"Do we know where he lives?"

"Nah. We only have an email address. We could, of course, locate him through this, but we'd have to go through our Brit chums, and I don't think that would be wise considering the circumstances, do you?"

"Probably not."

"Well, whoever he is, we can't permit anyone to walk around with this intel inside his head, no matter how he came across it."

"I agree. We need to issue a 'TEP' notice, but we can't risk agency, and I mean any agency involvement. We don't want a repeat of...."

"Don't remind me. Don't worry; we've got a few outside contractors we can use for 'arm's length' business."

"You'd better get started then."

"I already have."

CHAPTER 22

Gretel had decided that if all prospective avenues that she had approached the second time also declined their novel, then that was it. They would waste no more effort on it, at least for the time being. Although her practice had not suffered, Gretel felt she was not allowing her patients all the attention she should have given them. Her mind occasionally strayed to the now unlikely possibility of seeing their work on bookshelves. They also discussed vanity printing. Yes, they could achieve a certain degree of literary success by self-publishing. However, Gretel felt that as a professional, she needed to be taken seriously, though anonymously, and needed the approbation of an objective third party. In other words, she needed someone else, apart from Martin, to tell her that, yes, she was accomplished and didn't need to spend her own money, or Martin's, in bringing a book to market.

• • •

Six days after Swan made his phone call, Gretel received an email from Swansong Publishing. It read, "Dear Mr. Straight, we have just reviewed your novel entitled 'The Judas Conspiracy,' and would be interested in discussing this work in more detail. I wonder if you would be kind enough to contact me to arrange a mutually suitable time for us to meet. I look forward to hearing from you shortly. Regards, Leighton Swan."

Apart from assuming that she was a man, which was, she supposed, quite understandable, it thrilled the psychologist to get this message and she wasted no time in forwarding it to Martin.

An hour later, her mobile phone rang. It was Martin. "Well, I suppose I'll have to get myself a tux," he started.

"Why?"

"I can't go to the Pulitzer Prize Awards in a pair of denims and a 'Hug me, or I'll fart' T-shirt, can I?"

"Whoa, Tiger, calm down. They only said they wanted to meet. Could be for any number of reasons."

"OK, smart-ass, apart from the obvious, name one."

Gretel thought for a few seconds, then answered, "Nope, I guess you're right. Infamy and misfortune, here we come!"

"Um, shouldn't that be..."

"Yes, just my idea of a joke. Wow, we did it. You and I. We did it."

In reply to Martin's question of whether Gretel had already contacted the company, she responded that no, she hadn't, as she wanted to speak to him first. Despite all their previous attempts to get the work into print, they hadn't worked out which one of them should go to any initial meeting. Citing her other professional duties, she suggested Martin should be the one to attend. Gretel knew she could trust him not to pass the work off as entirely his own. His honesty and integrity were beyond question, not to mention his obvious affection and respect for his good friend.

They would spend the weekend going over the manuscript one last time. Gretel, as 'Les,' responded to Swan's email, sending a blind copy to Martin, suggesting a meeting for ten a.m. the following Monday.

Gretel had already exhausted all the local agencies and publishers, and Swansong was in central London, having a WC1 postcode. Martin considered driving down, but being well aware of the traffic situation, even with Congestion Parking in place, decided to take the train to Euston. The journey would only take a couple of hours, and it would also give him the time and opportunity to re-read the manuscript one more time, just to iron out any final bugs that they might have missed, unlikely as this was. He could catch a train around seven in the morning, which would arrive between nine and nine-fifteen a.m. It surely wouldn't take him an hour to get from Euston to Swansong, even in early morning rush hour traffic.

They decided he should stay over on Sunday night, and she would drive him to Piccadilly Station first thing the following day.

Their plans, however, hit a significant obstacle on the Monday morning. Whether it was stress or excitement caused by the thought of the impending meeting or deterioration in his condition, Martin could not be sure. He only knew that he was in pain once again and could not make the trip that morning. Naturally, Gretel insisted on postponing the whole exercise, her priority being Martin's unsettling condition. It was more important to get him to the hospital. He could phone Swan and explain. Surely he would understand and re-schedule their appointment for another day. But Martin had a better idea. Why couldn't Gretel go after all? Swansong had never spoken to or seen 'Les Straight.'

'Les' could be a diminutive for Lesley, the female version of the name. Martin had done his homework on this and named several lady authors who used abbreviated first names. There was the crime novelist P. D. James, and the science fiction writer, D. C. Fontana, to name but two.

Gretel tried in vain to argue that she had a busy schedule and would be pushed for time just taking him to the hospital, never mind taking the day off to go on a 'jolly' to London. Martin retorted that after all their hard work in producing the finished article, and especially the effort she had put in to get an agent, did she want to see it all go to waste? He would be fine, he said, once he was in front of a doctor. Only please God, not Higgins. Despite her anxiety for him, this remark made her smile, and she finally relented.

"OK, you bastard, I'll drop you at the hospital, then make my way to the station. I can phone the office from there with some cock and bull story. You owe me big time for this, and I will make sure you effing well pay." It was only those friends who you truly cared for and who reciprocated this affection with whom you could use such language. She smiled, before continuing, "Seriously, Martin, I am worried about you. You will be ok, won't you? You won't do anything... foolish, will you?"

He looked at her, puzzled. "What do you mean, 'foolish'?"

"Do I have to spell it out, you dozy bugger? Die. I don't want you to…"

"As Oscar Wilde said, 'Die, that's the last thing I shall do.'"

"Oh, Martin, you are completely incorrigible."

"Well, don't 'incorridge' me, then. Now, can we please get to the hospital? This pain is getting worse."

"Martin…"

"No, I'll be ok. It's just a twinge, honest."

He would not let her go into the hospital with him, instead urging her to catch the train that would take them both to their 'fortune.' Gretel promised to phone the hospital after she left Swansong and would be back as soon as possible. She blew him a kiss, and he answered with a slight wave of his hand and a smile as he made his way through the hospital's front entrance.

She had already discovered that the nearest train station was at Moston, a twenty-five-minute drive from the hospital. However, she did not know if it had a Park and Ride facility. It was not an area of the city that she knew well. She thought if memory served her correctly, that if worst came to worst, she could find a space to park on Hollinwood Avenue or one of the side streets nearby.

Gretel arrived at Euston later than she had expected, having had to take the detour to North Manchester General, and had to catch the following train. She had considered phoning ahead, as a courtesy, to advise the agent that she might be delayed but decided against doing so. She wanted to spring her gender on them as a surprise. Despite her earlier quiet misgivings, she was able to hail a taxi almost immediately, most of the morning rush hour traffic having dissipated.

The cab dropped her outside Swansong just after half-past ten. She had dressed the part and wore her best business suit, a two-piece dark gray worsted jacket and knee-length skirt, white blouse, and gray fashionable patent shoes with small two-inch heels. A single string of pearls adorned her neck, matched by a pair of smaller earrings giving her, she thought, a professional air and business-like appearance. She studied herself in the window of the agency's front door before giving herself a last look of approval. "You'll do," she thought happily.

Gretel clutched her attaché case with the all-important manuscript inside and opened the outer door. The building was constructed originally as a private dwelling and had been converted to offices much later in its history. From the board to her left, she saw Swansong was one of four companies renting space on the first floor. A small aperture to her right was a receptionist's window, and she went forward to make herself known. Remembering to call herself by her 'pen-name,' Gretel introduced herself as Les Straight to see Leighton Swan. The receptionist made the required call and instructed her to take the stairs in front. When she reached the top, she saw a small blue enamel plaque attached to a door proclaiming this was the Swansong office suite.

She had promised herself that she would remain calm and not get over-enthused. Maybe Martin had been right; perhaps they just wanted to tell her to her face that they had never read such a lousy, ill-written manuscript. It would be better for all concerned if 'Les Straight' sought a less literary means of earning a living. But she knew this was not so. Gretel had read many books, both fiction and fact based, as well as several reference books about her own profession. She was sure that theirs, probably with a bit of professional editing, was at least as good as those, and perhaps better than some. She was proud of what they had accomplished together and was positive that she and Martin had written a winner. Gretel could feel her heart pounding in her chest, and it was not from the exertion of climbing the stairs. Yes, dammit, she was hyped up, and could only wish that Martin was with her to share this moment. Gretel took one final deep breath, knocked softly on the Swansong door, and an Italian accented female voice from within told her to enter.

She immediately noticed the look of mild surprise from both of the people in the room, whom she presumed to be Leighton Swan and his secretary. Swan immediately got up from behind his large oak desk and crossed the room to welcome her, smiling, taking her free hand in his, stroking it gently with his lips. Would he have done that if it had been Martin, she mused?

"I must apologize, Ms. Straight. I believe I referred to you as 'Mister' in my email," he cooed.

Gretel assured him it was an easy mistake to make, and she had taken no offense. She, too, apologized for being late, which he swept away with an easy dismissal. He invited her to take a seat in front of him as he slipped round to resume his former place, asking his secretary to organize some coffee. They exchanged a few pleasantries before getting down to the main reason for his invitation.

Before broaching the subject of the manuscript, he asked her if this was her first novel.

"Yes, it is. I've never considered myself as an author, but once I got started, the manuscript seemed to write itself."

"Indeed, but this is, if I may say so, quite a heavy subject for a first attempt." He had read her story and was intrigued by its subject. He asked her how she came to think up such a plot. It was undoubtedly a theory he had never come across and was fascinated by how she could imagine such a thing happening.

She was about to explain about Martin's involvement when Swan's secretary re-entered the office from the door behind her employer, carrying a tray with coffee and pastries. As she came through, Gretel was startled to see that there was someone else in the back room. Standing just by the door frame, someone, a man, was watching them, no, watching her intently, his eyes not wavering from her.

It all happened so quickly before the door closed again, that for the briefest of seconds, she could not be sure that her eyes were not playing tricks, but she knew what she saw. She did not imagine it. Someone was there, and he regarded her avidly, with intense hatred and malevolence. Suddenly, the whole paradigm had shifted. Who was this man, and why was he secretly scrutinizing her with such loathing?

Instantly, Gretel was on her guard. Something was not right here. Something was off, badly off, and Gretel had a distinct feeling of unease. Despite knowing that she should acknowledge Martin as the story's true father, somehow, the whole situation had now changed. She did not want to involve her best and dearest friend if this was going to endanger either of them. It was enough that Gretel should have possibly put herself in jeopardy, but she was certainly not going to involve Martin, especially in his currently fragile condition.

Gretel quickly recovered from her feelings of malaise and trusted that neither Swan nor this stranger behind the door had seen her discomfort. She replied she was a psychologist by profession and was used to hearing deep emotional problems. This story was lightweight compared to some of her clients' intimate issues. She was not prepared for intrusive questions and had to think fast, especially in the light of what had just happened. The storyline, she stammered hesitantly, had just occurred to her one night after watching a biography of the dead president on television. It detailed Kennedy's handling of the Bay of Pigs fiasco, and his response to the threat posed by the proposed siting of nuclear rockets in Cuba. One thought just seemed to follow another, and before you knew it, a book idea had been born. He seemed satisfied with her answer, before asking innocuously if she had had any help in writing the book. Perhaps it was Swan's tone or how he phrased the question, but Gretel now believed that she was being questioned, charmingly, perhaps, but interrogated none the less. The one thing she realized she must not do was to mention Martin, at least not at this stage. Not now.

"Mr. Swan, please let me be clear. I'm not a seventeen-year-old girl just out of school. I do know how to research facts and garner information and I would remind you I have a doctorate in psychology for which I spent the best part of ten years at university. I have written several theses and research papers. I do not need anyone's help in writing a book or anything else. Final."

He regretted causing her offense but, he went on, they had to be careful. A few people had offered them stories which they tried to pass off as their own work, when in fact, it was no such thing. He was sure, he smiled, that she would understand his caution, especially as it was her first attempt, and because of the very subject itself.

Gretel could feel her heart pounding again and found that she was trembling slightly. She hoped that if Swan noticed this, he would put it down to anger and not apprehension. Feeling that she was losing control of the meeting, she went on the offensive. "Mr. Swan, I came here at your request because I thought you wanted to help me get my story published, not for you to subject me to a Spanish Inquisition. Now, if you wish to help me, let's discuss it; if not, please delete my story, and I'll find another agent or publisher who isn't so invasive."

Swan held up his palms in supplication. "Please do not be so abrupt, my dear. I'm sure we can find a publisher who will be interested in your story. I'm sorry if I upset you. It was quite unintentional, I assure you. Why don't you give me a couple of weeks, no, say a month, to put this manuscript out to a few of my contacts, and I will get back to you? How does that sound?"

Gretel didn't know how to respond. Until she had noticed this unnerving person behind the door, she would have had no hesitation in accepting his gracious offer. Now she was not so sure. Was he going to get the manuscript published, or did he have some other nefarious reason for offering her this proposal? To decline would appear suspicious. After all, there must be thousands of would-be authors who would jump at such a suggestion, and she had come down from Manchester to see him. To accept would mean having to maintain a relationship with him, with Swansong, and with that man behind the door. "God help me, what am I to do?" she thought. After a few seconds, she decided. "All right, Mr. Swan, no offense taken. I look forward to hearing from you when you find me a publisher. Um, I don't want to appear mercenary, but about, ah…" She wanted to make it look as though no great harm had been done, and, why else had she come, but to get her book published and see what her story was worth.

Swan smiled at her. "Ms. Straight, we do not expect you to have done all this work for nothing. Naturally, you shall be recompensed. We normally negotiate with the publisher on your behalf to secure the best possible outcome. What you may receive depends, at least partly, on how many copies of the book the publisher believes they will sell. Our fee for doing this will come once they have accepted your story for publication. You might also expect some small advance to secure the rights to your work, so you do not offer it elsewhere. I would, therefore, ask you not to approach anyone else until you have heard from me. To do so might be considered, ah, unethical. I trust you understand."

She thanked him, then looked at her watch, explaining that she had a case conference back in Manchester later that afternoon. Not wishing to be discourteous, but she had to leave as soon as possible. Gretel asked if she might prevail on him to call a taxi for her, which he was happy to do.

The cab arrived within a few minutes, and once she had gone, the mysterious man emerged from behind the door.

"Well, what do you think?" Swan inquired.

"The woman knows more. I'm sure she does. Didn't you see how evasive she became when you started probing her? She couldn't possibly have dreamed that concoction up all by herself. That would take coincidence to the extreme."

"So, she was working with someone else?"

"Oh, yes, and I know who."

"And is it who you thought it was?"

"I don't see how it could be anybody else. I just wonder why he didn't come with her, and where she fits into all this."

"Do you think he suspects…?"

"No, don't be stupid. If he did, why would he have submitted the manuscript to us in the first place, or let her come here alone?"

"We know where she's going. Do you think we should follow her? It might lead us to him."

"I think that's an excellent idea," he answered with chagrin, as if the thought had not already occurred to him. Turning to Swan's secretary, he asked, "Francesca, my dear, I wonder if you would be kind enough to take me to Euston Station."

As he got into her car, the thoughts tumbled around in his head, imagining what he would say, what he would do, when he finally confronted his nemesis. The one person in the entire world that he had thought about every day for the past thirty-five years. The one human being he hated beyond all reason. He had read the manuscript. Despite the changes to locations and characters, only one person could have written this book. The similarities were just too great. It could not be a coincidence. By a certain Divine symmetry, he had been drawn to the one person he would have given all he owned, all he possessed, to find. The one person who had betrayed them and stopped them from carrying out their plans of destruction and carnage. The one man who had prevented them from being taken seriously as world-class terrorists. The one individual who had sent him to prison: the traitor, Paul McGregor, otherwise known as Sam Nathan.

CHAPTER 23

Fall 1980. Max Jordan had just been released from prison after serving two-thirds of his sentence. Incarceration seemed to have changed him. He had become a model prisoner and had done his time peacefully, despite being beaten, sometimes severely, by the other cons.

His actions had outraged even those hard cases who cared little for authority. This bastard came close to destroying a beloved Glasgow landmark, not to mention killing so many innocent people. One or two of them knew staff who had worked in the building. They cared nothing for the politicians and other V.I.P.s who could have been injured or lost their lives, but this piece of garbage would have hurt or murdered some of their own. No, this fucker was going to pay, and pay dearly. They would give him a very salutary lesson. You can plant your bombs anywhere else, but do it in Glasgow, and you'll be sorry, very sorry indeed. Even the warders did not seem too inclined to prevent the violence meted out to him, and Jordan spent much of his time in solitary confinement. It did not seem to matter.

Every blow, every punch, every shove down the worn wrought iron stairs only concentrated his mind on the one person responsible for putting him here. "Let this lowlife scum have their fun," he thought. "All the more payback for that little prick, that arsewipe, when I get out of here."

Despite such intense provocation, Jordan held himself in check. Getting out was all that mattered. He had a score to settle, and no matter how long it took or what it cost, he would settle it.

Convincing the prison authorities that he had turned over a new leaf had not been difficult. In fact, he had made himself out to be the victim by not reacting to the beatings. He had never even attempted to retaliate to the viciousness of the assaults, only trying to protect himself as best he could until the belated arrival of the guards. He had resumed studying for his law degree and had even requested to be isolated so he could concentrate without hindrance. It had all been so easy...

Most of his family had disowned him for what he had done, and tried to do, and had cut him off completely. Only one uncle, his father's brother, believed everyone, even someone as wicked as his wayward nephew, should get a second chance. It was unlikely, however, that he would get this fair shake in his native country. Even after eight years, memories were still fresh. There were others, outside, as well as inside prison, who would have liked nothing more than to see him suffer a nasty, painful fate. His uncle decided, therefore, that Jordan would go to the United States, where he had some influence. The American authorities would know about his past, but his uncle's associations there, not to mention a few well-placed 'inducements,' would see his brother's son enter the land of opportunity, and a 'Green Card' would be a mere formality.

Jordan understood he had no real choice in the matter, and his uncle was his only lifeline to any kind of future. He begged for some time to be by himself after leaving Barlinnie. He just wanted to see a bit of his country before leaving for good, he said. Although suspicious, his uncle agreed but would give him only three months. If he wasn't ready to go by then, he would be on his own. Jordan had no intention, of course, of saying goodbye to Scotland. He didn't care about the country of his birth one bit. After all, it was no more than an English colony. Even devolution, if it ever came, which seemed unlikely after the recent 'rigged' election, would give the Scots little more power than they had now.

No, his only reason for delaying leaving was to find the bastard who had put him in prison. He searched Nathan in the Glasgow phone directories. There weren't too many, and after his sixth try, he found Sam; that is, he found the address Sam lived at before he went to live in England. The person who answered explained that she had not long moved into the apartment Sam and his family used to occupy, and so were not yet listed under their own name. As far as she knew, Mrs. Nathan had gone back to live in London after her husband died. Presumably, her son had gone with her, but she couldn't be sure.

Well, if it were London, he would be sunk. There wasn't enough time for him to start searching the metropolis. So now he wasn't even sure where the little prick lived. Was he still in Glasgow, or had he moved to London with his mother? Or was he somewhere else entirely? Eight years had passed. The cunt could be anywhere. He could even be dead, but Jordan fervently prayed he was not. Not for what he had in mind.

He even tried a few pubs in the city center, giving his description as best he could recall it, remembering to add a few more years. No one knew or had heard of him. No, it was a lost cause. His frustration was almost tangible, and he came close to venting it on a barman, who only asked why he was looking for him. His fists clenched, and the veins on the side of his neck pulsated wildly, while his teeth ground together almost audibly. "None of your fucking business," he hissed. Some bruises he had sustained in prison were still noticeable. The barman who, himself, had done a spell in the Bar-L, recognized a fellow con and decided not to take it further. This guy was bad news, seriously bad news. He could smell the prison aroma on Jordan, and no amount of showering would cleanse it away. It permeated every inch of him and saturated his clothes.

•   •   •

Of course, Jordan's Scottish law degree was no use to him in America, but it proved one thing. Despite his background and previous conduct, Jordan had a brain. If he could get a law degree from Scotland, he could also get one from the United States. It would entail more years of study, but it pleased his uncle that his nephew seemed to want to put the past behind him. In fact, he was proud of him when Jordan announced his intention to study for the Bar. He agreed to let Max stay with him and his family until he could afford a place of his own. Under strict conditions, of course. There would be no more of his previous behavior.

His uncle also got him a couple of jobs that, although menial and way below his abilities, paid well and allowed him time to study. Jordan had no actual intention or motivation to attain his degree, despite effortlessly passing the LSAT before applying himself to his LL.M, and was only going through the motions to please his uncle. However, as he got more into it, the more he realized a lawyer could make a great deal of money. Especially if he was prepared to bend the rules and turn a blind eye or become 'deaf' at certain moments and know when to keep his mouth shut. He seemed to gravitate naturally towards the dark undercurrent of New York's criminal community. Once he had attained his degree, he sought those who would make him rich. Rich and powerful enough to return to Scotland. His fantasy was that he would do what he failed to accomplish before. Jordan would use whatever money and resources he had accumulated to find and destroy the one person he had focused his whole life on. Not only him. Maybe he was married by now. Perhaps he even had kids. He became sexually aroused as he thought of making Nathan watch while he did all sorts of unspeakable things to his family. Making him look in abject terror and exquisite anguish while he tortured his loved ones in front of his captive. He would force Nathan to watch as they died slowly, in excruciating pain, the questioning looks in their terrified eyes. 'Why?' And once he had done with them, he would look out his former friend, Henri. Maybe he, too, had a family by this time...

He had long since moved out of his uncle's house and found a brownstone apartment in the Upper West Side of Manhattan, near a few quiet bars and expensive restaurants, and close to Central Park. Life was good, and his practice was flourishing, even if most of his clients would not have been welcome at a Rotarians meeting. His office was downtown, near the city's financial hub, close to the junction of Chambers and Tribeca. Jordan was finally at the stage in his career when he saw clients at his convenience, not theirs. He could afford to turn away new business, even lucrative prospects, unless they provided him with more than mere money. He almost had enough of that now. Now it was about power. Power and influence, and soon he would have that as well.

It was late on a Friday afternoon. Normally he would have gone home by this time, being so close to the weekend, but a client's case was due to be heard in court the following week, and he had been too busy earlier to give it the attention it needed. He could have siphoned it off to one of the other partners, but this was a client he had had from almost the beginning of his career. A onetime small crook, who, like him, had risen steadily up through the ranks and was now a major player. The Feds had caught him laundering money for a high-ranking politician who had fingers in pies he really ought not to have had fingers in. No, this case had to be handled by him for two reasons. First, his client would expect no less and would not take kindly to being fobbed off on a less senior colleague. Second, and far more important, there was the politician. If he handled this case well, it was likely that the politician would remember him. Jordan would make damn sure he remembered him. This politician was popular, and if he could ride out this 'misunderstanding', perhaps one day might rise to high office. GOP or Dem, it made no difference to him. He was only interested in power, not from where it came. When you boiled it all down, one was just as bad as the other. No worse than Labour or the Tories back home.

He was in his inner office when he heard noises coming from outside, his secretary's voice becoming louder and more strained. Before he could react, they had come into his office. Two men, both tall, over six feet, and wearing identical dark suits, white shirts, and black ties and shoes. Miranda, his secretary, was behind them, struggling to get past. "I'm sorry, Mr. Jordan. They just pushed right in. I..."

"That's ok Miranda. Tell you what. It's almost four o'clock. Why don't you go home? I'll manage these two... gentlemen."

His secretary hesitated, waiting a second more for confirmation. It wasn't like him to let her finish early. Usually, he had her work more than her contracted hours, with no extra pay, bastard that he was.

He nodded, smiling. "It's fine, honest."

After she had gone, Jordan, his hands clasped on his desk, enquired, "And what can I do for you fine fellows on a Friday afternoon?" They reminded him of the Men in Black people he had heard about from science fiction and alien encounter enthusiasts. Neither man moved nor uttered a sound, just stood where Miranda had left them. "I'm sorry, do neither of you speak English?" which was, he realized, a stupid question because if neither man did, then it would have been pointless to have asked them in that language.

Again, neither man stirred. Now Jordan was becoming unnerved. Who were these goons, and why had they barged into his office? Was it a dissatisfied client? No, he had very few of those, none he couldn't handle, anyway. "Look, guys, I'm rather busy, so if you don't mind..."

"Eight million, three hundred and twenty-seven thousand, four hundred and fifteen dollars. And twenty-five cents."

"What?"

"That's what you've got in the bank, as of ten a.m. this morning. I'm John, by the way. He's... not," the first man said, as he indicated his companion. "He doesn't say very much, so I'll be doing the talking for both of us."

"You guys from the I.R.S.? Look, I pay all my taxes; you can check. I'll give you the name of my accountant, he'll..."

"We know who your accountant is, Mr. Jordan. We know a great deal about you, including the amount of income you don't declare." These guys looked serious, and Jordan knew they weren't bluffing. If they knew to the cent how much he had in the bank, then they might just have worked out how much he didn't tell Uncle Sam about.

"Based on the billable hours you declare, against billable hours actually worked, there's quite a discrepancy in your figures. What do you charge, five hundred an hour? Now, a busy guy like you, always in demand, we reckon you must work at least seventy, eighty hours a week, conservatively speaking. Forty thousand dollars a week, times fifty. See, we even give you two weeks off. Isn't that generous of us? That makes an even two million if my math is correct, which it is. But yet, you only declare billed hours at just over half that. Now, don't think we've just waltzed in here off the street. My colleagues and I, we've been watching this place for a while, seeing who comes, who goes, and a lovely assortment of rogues and ne'er-do-wells they are. I assume that you'd like to keep the money you've got in the bank, the eight million, et cetera, even if half of it belongs to the I.R.S."

"You don't sound like I.R.S. What is this, some kind of shakedown? If you've seen some of my clientele, then you'll know you've just made a big mistake."

"Max, Max, come on. Do we look like shakedown shysters? No, my dear friend, we're not from the tax department. But we could be. No, we're from a different branch of the U.S. government."

"Immigration? Look, I..."

"No, Max, not immigration. Oh, don't worry, my friend. We know how you got into this wonderful country and exactly what strings were pulled to get your worthless carcass through the door. But that's of no concern to us... at the moment."

"I'm not saying or doing a fucking thing until I see some I.D. You could be anybody; how do I know?"

"You know, you're absolutely right, Max. We could be anybody. But we're not. Let's just say that you've made a good life for yourself here, a bit illicit, perhaps, but not too bad, just the same. Certainly, far removed from the terrorist that spent eight years in a Scottish jail, who was beaten senseless, even by cons, for what you did. Christ, that had to be bad, eh? Terrorist turned lawyer. I can see that playing well in the ten o'clock news. You've been convicted of terrorist crimes. How much work do you think we'd have to do to convince the good old, unwashed American public that you've got links to Islamic terrorists? Even your crim buddies would think twice before giving money to someone who might just funnel it back to those guys. You'd be lucky if they didn't do to you what your Scottish buds did back in Glasgow. Maybe worse. These guys are scumbags, but they're patriotic scumbags. Who knows, they might find you in some dark alley with the Stars and Stripes skewered through your chest. Anyway, we'd make sure that your face appeared on every talk show and news program from here to Alaska. Oh, and we'd also take the money that you failed to tell Uncle Sam about, with interest, for starters. Oh, and I almost forgot, there's five years jail time for tax evasion. You're the lawyer. You should know this."

"Part twenty-six USC Article seven-two-oh-one, Attempt to Evade or Defeat Tax," Jordan answered, almost automatically. God knows, he had defended enough clients on these charges. He also knew that there was an additional penalty, as well as coughing up the unpaid tax, of $100,000. In fact, if these jokers wanted to get heavy, they could apply to have him tried as a corporation where the penalty was five times greater. Jordan knew he had no choice. Whatever these fuckers demanded from him, he would have no option but to play along.

"OK, what do you want from me?" he asked in resignation.

"Nothing."

"Nothing?"

"Nothing, well, not yet. But there may be the odd occasion when we want you to do little... jobs for us."

"What little jobs?"

"Nothing you can't handle."

"Look, I'm a lawyer. I can't do anything..."

"Illegal?"

"Yes, illegal."

"Like withholding taxes and cozying up to some of the filthiest scum this fine city has ever turned out."

"First, the tax thing was an...oversight. I'll make good. Honest. Second, I don't know they're guilty unless they tell me they're guilty, which they rarely do unless they have to. You know, Fifth Amendment rights, blah, blah..."

"Yeah, right, anyway, here's the deal. You get to keep the cash, the office," at this point, John threw his hands out expansively, "and you don't get to see your mug plastered all over the evening news. Also, you don't have to get intimate with those creeps you failed to keep out of jail."

"You still haven't told me what you want from me," he moaned.

"You're right, I haven't." was all John replied as he and his silent partner left his office.

There had been 'word on the street,' about a counselor with a funny accent, Scottish, or Irish, who would not flinch from using his own brand of justice to get payment from any client, reckless enough to renege out of his financial obligation, or who otherwise offended him, perhaps by refusing to testify, or by saying the wrong thing in court. Jordan made sure that everyone knew his willingness and ability to use extreme methods when it suited him. However, he was careful enough not to go too far, and the mere threats of violence were usually sufficient. Rumors were one thing, but people were in no doubt. If word ever got back to the authorities, and they could establish actual proof he could and did use intimidation, then those who provided this information, and their families, were dead. The old Jordan never lurked far away from his modern counterpart.

Despite his best efforts, threats, and acts of physical discouragement, however, inevitably, eventually, word of his non-legal activities would leak out. Jordan never discovered who had been responsible, but they got to the notice of certain people. These people realized they could use someone like this for their own purposes. Investigations revealed specific curious facts about this criminal lawyer and his unusual background; facts they could exploit to their own questionable ends.

• • •

Black Operations Domestic took a keen interest in Jordan's propensity and latent disposition for violence, despite his outward veneer as a successful, if a somewhat shady, lawyer. What could be a better cover, a lawyer who was also a thug, or conversely, a thug who was also a lawyer? He could be useful in any situation that required 'arms' length' tactics. Send in a counselor, someone with legal training, to reason with the person who needed to be reasoned with. Explain the legalities, or illegalities, of their actions or intentions, and make them aware that more extreme 'reasoning' might need to be applied if this didn't work. And so, for several years now, Jordan had been summoned whenever such methods required to be used. On the whole, it had worked out well.

CHAPTER 24

All thoughts of phoning Martin from the station or even on the train went out of her head. She only knew that she had to get back to N.M.G. and prayed that he would be well and strong enough to allow her to tell him in person what had happened. She certainly did not wish to do this on a mobile phone, especially on a crowded train. Only, even she didn't know the entire story of who this man was and why he was scanning her so intensely.

As the train left the platform, she tried to analyze what had happened earlier. They had been expecting a man, not a woman. That much was clear and was logical for them to do so, given the pseudonym she had adopted. That was the first thing, but where did that lead her? Why was it necessary for this stranger, whoever he was, to conceal himself when, if she was correct, whoever they thought was coming did not show up? Did Martin and this mystery man possibly know each other, and was he concerned that Martin would recognize him? Was he somehow connected to the statesman who told Martin about the American strategy? Did his concealment have any connection to this or not? And why hide at all?

It had to be something to do with the story. It had to be, but what? The Kennedy assassination was almost forty-five years ago. Even if Martin's intelligence had been correct, and the Americans had drawn up plans to do what was in his manuscript, surely these would have changed by now. There was no more Cold War. The chances of the events happening, for which the Americans had made contingencies, were so slim that it wasn't even worth considering. Besides, Russia had enough problems within its own borders, what with Chechnya, and so on. So, if an invasion by Russian troops was now out of the question, then what? The Americans would no longer need to deploy the strategy envisaged for such an eventuality. It was old hat.

Besides, neither Martin nor she had proof or evidence that this would ever happen, so where was the danger? As far as most people were concerned, it would be just a story—an invention based on historical fact perhaps, but a work of fiction, nonetheless. But wait. How did this man get there in the first place? Swan must have called him once he had read their novel. So, they wrote something that must have spooked someone, but where did Swan fit into this? What was his relation to the mystery man? Who was he? Did either he or Swan have links to American Intelligence? Was there still a secret embargo on any fresh evidence that might shed light on the real reason for Kennedy's untimely demise? Had Martin actually stumbled onto the truth, and was he, were they, now to be silenced because of it? It hardly seemed credible, especially after so many years, but there could be no other explanation. Someone somewhere wanted this kept under wraps. If this was the case, then Swan certainly had no intention of sending their manuscript to any publisher.

Could Gretel inadvertently have put their lives in danger by insisting that Martin reveal what he knew? But what if this was all in her imagination?

Let's just calm down and look at this rationally, she told herself. You're a trained psychologist. How would you react if one of your patients came to you with a similar tale? You saw someone or thought you saw someone, for a fleeting second, behind a crack in a door. And from this, you extrapolate this person is now out to harm you or possibly kill you. And all this for divulging secrets that were now many years old and probably worthless, even if they were real. Did this make sense? No, it didn't. It was more than likely one of the other readers, having a coffee break, standing by the door when the receptionist walked through. Get a grip, girl.

Perhaps Gretel should phone the agent back and apologize for her erratic behavior. Yes, and she would confirm that she had worked with a friend to produce the story, the person whose idea this originally was. She could always put it down to the excitement of the possibility of being a published author. He would understand. She reached into her handbag for her phone. Had she not done so at that very second, Gretel might have seen the man she had briefly glimpsed in Swansong, boarding her train. She called the agency to be advised by the receptionist that Swan had gone out and would not be back for the rest of the day. Gretel decided not to leave a message, preferring to do things the old-fashioned way and apologize in person. She would try again tomorrow.

Gretel's train pulled into Piccadilly just on two o'clock. Alighting from the carriage, she made her way out of the station to head for Victoria and her connection to Moston. Fortunately for her unknown adversary, she could not find a taxi. Even the trams seemed non-existent, so she decided the only way was to go on foot.

Her tracker followed at a discrete distance, only boarding the Moston train once he was sure she would have found a seat but ensuring to keep his profile away from her. When her train reached Moston Station, Gretel seemed to be the only person to get off. Jordan waited until she was a good seventy to eighty yards in front of him before following the psychologist. His anonymity was paramount, and he dare not risk being seen and identified, no matter how slight the risk. He waited for as long as he could, then walked behind her at a distance. Gretel was still unaware that anyone was following her, and she was inadvertently leading him to his quarry. However, it did not seem to occur to him that she would be driving, and it caught him out when she got into her car. He found his anger rising. How could she? How could she? So near, and yet... he wondered if she had somehow discovered that he was trailing her and led him on, knowing he could not follow her any further? No, the thought was absurd, but his close pursuit was not without promise. He had the make, model, and color of her vehicle, although the license plate was just too small to read from that distance. That this woman was a psychologist, he already knew, presumably employed by a local health department. However, the possibility did not escape him that she may have also been in private practice. With a bit of patience and ingenuity, it shouldn't be too hard to trace her.

When she arrived at the hospital, Gretel found Martin waiting for her. She did not want to alarm him with her vague suspicions about a mysterious man. She had reasoned it out and had concluded that there was no such person. It had all been her imagination, probably caused by the excitement of the occasion; leave it at that. Besides, Martin would have enough to worry about. He told her that, yes, they had examined him, but the doctors could find no cause of his earlier pain and discomfort. It did not seem to be anything to do with his condition, and the best they could come up with was that it might be a troublesome gallstone. They asked him if he had seen his G.P. since his release from hospital, and, yes, he confirmed, as Higgins had predicted, his doctor had prescribed a forty milligram statin and a five milligram blood pressure pill.

On the journey back to his apartment, Martin kept plying her with questions about how the meeting went with Swansong. Gretel only gave Martin a highly edited version of those events. She said the agent felt that he could get their novel published, and he would forward their work to a few of his contacts in the business. They should know within a month whether they had a book deal. Naturally, he asked how much they stood to make and wondered, humorously, if he would have to become a tax exile. Gretel smiled wanly at this remark and reminded him they had not yet signed a contract, never mind made any money.

The word 'contract' made Gretel suddenly realize that Swan did not ask her to do likewise. Although she had no experience in this business, surely, she thought, he would have wanted to make certain that she did not offer the manuscript elsewhere. An oblique reference to not contacting any other potentially interested parties did not seem very professional. Why did he not get her signature? If he thought their story was good enough to be published, why did he not secure her commitment with a legally binding contract? Suddenly, her worst fears came back to her. Surely, it was not just an oversight on his part. If it was, then he was a lousy businessman. Gretel remembered the saying made famous by the movie producer Samuel Goldwyn, 'A verbal contract isn't worth the paper it's written on.'

Something was wrong here, definitely wrong, but should she tell Martin? No, she decided, not yet. She would spend the rest of the evening researching Swansong and its proprietor. He had an American accent, and she wondered if this was important. Well, there was the all-important Kennedy connection. Somehow, she thought it was. Maybe she would get some sort of clue what they were all about and perhaps even their very legitimacy as literary agents.

•   •   •

Meanwhile, Jordan, too, had been busy. He had taken a train back to Piccadilly and found an internet café nearby. The lawyer looked up Greater Manchester Health Authority to discover the locations that offered psychological and counseling services. By trawling through them, he had found seven possibilities. These would do for a start. He scanned all of them on the off chance that one would mention Doctor Les Straight, but was not too disappointed when he did not find any such reference. Some pages also showed photographs of staff members, but the psychologist's picture was not on any of these. It was now getting late, and he did not yet have a car or a place to stay. He would need both, as he did not intend to return to New York until he did what he came to do. He found the false documents John had given him, passport, driver's license, and credit card with a $5000 limit, all printed with the name Harry Baines. Any transactions he needed to make while he was in the U.K. had to be made with those documents. Jordan didn't mind this arrangement. Why not let Uncle Sam pay for his trip? After all, he was going there on official business. John had insisted that under no circumstances should the lawyer take his own documents, just in case of any unforeseen difficulties. As 'Harry Baines,' he could and would disappear once his mission was over, and he was back in the States. If they caught him with his real identity, this could pose unnecessary difficulties and make him mortally expendable. Jordan said he understood, which he did, of course, but he was no fool. He realized that once he had done his job, he would be of no further use to them, and they might revoke the documents they had just supplied. Then he would be stranded in what was now to him a foreign country without the means to get back home.

Did they take him for a complete idiot? Of course, he would carry an alternative passport, a fake he had one of his clients obtain for him. This one would identify him as 'George Humphreys', resident of Boise, Idaho. This document was his insurance policy, should the Department decide that he had outlived his usefulness. Of course, they might have also requested a 'watch' notice on his Max Jordan documents, hence the need for an alternate identity. They might not kill him, but they could make life difficult for him.

And that was another thing, thinking about insurance policies. When this whole mess with John had begun, Jordan felt he would need to cover himself, just in case. In case of what, he wasn't sure, but he would not let John and his silent crony have the last laugh. No siree. The counselor called his fellow lawyer and friend Morty Schumacher and told him he would post him an envelope from time to time. Under no circumstances should he open these envelopes unless he didn't hear from Jordan at least once a fortnight. Morty knew his friend well enough to understand what this was. It was Max's way of staying alive. Schumacher assumed the information the letters contained was details about his criminal clients. If he disappeared or had a nasty accident, he would leave instructions on what he should do, anonymously of course, with the contents. More than that, Morty didn't need or want to know. As a precaution, Morty was to burn the previous envelope, only keeping the most current.

• • •

There was a Premier Inn next to the station. It was rather basic for his tastes, but it would suffice. Jordan did not intend to be in the city any more than a day or two. He didn't expect any trouble hiring a car, despite having only an American driver's license. He would get a local map from the car rental company and make sure that the vehicle he hired came with a GPS device. If necessary, he would purchase one. He would use the evening to get familiar with the area and have a decent meal. He considered finding a woman for the night, but decided that he needed to rest. There was also a phone call to make. Tomorrow was going to be a big day.

• • •

Swansong Literary Agency - besides giving the contact details she was already familiar with, the website supplied very little information. A small boutique literary agency specializing in 'off-the-wall' and non-mainstream literature. Is that what their novel was? Off-the-wall? Non-mainstream? It listed the owner and associates who presumably read and edited the manuscripts. There were only three souls, much less than the other agencies she perused before going onto Swansong. The website did list a few random books that it had been responsible for getting published and a couple of obscure authors, of whom she, at least, had never heard. It certainly didn't brag about how they had found an unknown and turned them into a literary tour de force. Indeed, the website was very bare, almost as if they were reluctant to announce their very existence.

Gretel wondered why they had even bothered to go to the expense of having created an internet site in the first place when it was so poorly managed. It gave little background on the proprietor, Leighton Swan. It mentioned only that he was Canadian (ah, Canadian, not American) having lived and worked in Toronto before coming to London in 2004. Unlike other biographies, it did not list his previous companies or Swan's prior experience as a literary agent. Was this something he had done in Toronto? Had he been successful? Why had he come to the U.K. in the first place? Who knows?

Her previous research told her about The Writers and Artists Yearbook, the bible for all budding and established novelists and writers. She would make time in the morning to go to her local library. Maybe they would have a copy. If not, she would buy one. She wanted to see if they listed Swansong as a source. Perhaps it would shed more light on the company than she had discovered online. Either way, the results could be very interesting.

The Writers and Artists Yearbook would not tell her that Swan was not Canadian but American. Gretel had been correct the first time. Leighton Swan had been on the periphery of American Intelligence for many years. He had been a crypto-analyst, a code breaker for the C.I.A., deciphering secret messages intercepted through covertly monitored emails, phone texts, and postal mail. Word and letter patterns, algorithms, cryptic ciphers, and all the rest were his meat and drink. He had successfully broken the codes of terrorist cells, planning to cause mayhem in various parts of the country. One particularly nasty attack was to have been on the Brooklyn Bridge at Friday rush hour. Extremists would plant explosives at different locations along the bridge's superstructure and detonate them when peak hour traffic was at its heaviest. Although the blast may not have been great enough to cause the bridge to collapse, the deaths, carnage, and destruction would still have been incalculable. It would almost have rivaled and maybe even surpassed 9/11 in its sheer wanton ferocity. To make matters worse, other attacks were to be launched in New York itself to coincide with the bridge's destruction. This havoc would stretch the emergency services to breaking point, and, unable to cope, the city would have to shut down. The chaos would be astronomical, and the National Guard and maybe even troops would need to be called to restore and keep order. All this would take time. The looting, disorder, destruction, initial lack of control, and the profound shock of it all would live in the American psyche for years, possibly generations.

But a couple of clever and dedicated men had foiled the terrorists' plans, one of whom was Leighton Swan. Because of his work's sensitive and highly classified nature, he knew his country could not honor him publicly for what he had done. Besides, being identified would make him a marked man. However, the pressure took its toll, and Swan felt he was getting 'burnt out.' As a token of appreciation and being awarded the Distinguished Intelligence Cross, they offered Swan a new posting, one that would take him away from that level of undercover work.

Getting the D.I.C. was no mean feat. This honor was usually only awarded to those agents who had shown exemplary valor in the field, facing immediate life and death situations. The government decided in this case, however, to make an exception. Because of their outstanding work in saving so many lives and property, both analysts were awarded the medal in a secret ceremony.

An agency connected to the C.I.A. was setting up a small network of covert agents in Britain to garner low-level intelligence. It would be the kind of information that might be blurted out carelessly or indiscreetly over a bottle or two of wine and which might, ultimately, lead to more considerable advantages. A politician's wife might be dissatisfied with her husband's 'performance' and seek more satisfying pleasure elsewhere. This information, in itself, was not significant, but suppose this politician was a senior minister or high-grade civil servant. In that case, his wife might be 'persuaded' to 'borrow' or photocopy some of her husband's official papers. Not cooperating might lead to any number of nasty and unwanted complications.

Of course, they already had intelligence sources posted within various echelons of the U.K. Government who provided them with high-grade confidential information. This would be a similar thing, just on a lower level. The Soviets had been doing it for years, and it was often said, and not always light-heartedly, that the Kremlin knew British defense secrets before the top brass in the M.O.D.

So, someone in Echelon decided that Swan would set up shop as a literary agent, keeping his ear to the ground. As an agent, he would get invites to many literary soirees. All he had to do was keep his eyes and ears open for any small tidbits that might come in useful.

At one time, only those politicians and civil servants whose careers were over or who had retired wrote their memoirs. Any information in those reminiscences was well out of date by the time it was published. Nowadays, those same politicians and senior government officials couldn't seem to wait to get their names into print and rushed to find publishers even while still in office; shameful, perhaps, but a sign of the times, no less.

Until a few weeks previously, however, this seemed to be an exercise in futility. Yes, he had heard the odd piece of scandal, but not of enough interest to take to his handler in Chelsea. She would only have made some derisory comments and sent him away, feeling like a schoolboy chastened for not keeping up with the rest of the class.

But now, dropped onto his lap, so to speak, had come this manuscript. Although Ms. Straight had submitted it as a work of fiction, Swan knew it had to be more than this. There were just too many details that he knew for a fact were accurate and that even a seasoned author could not know of without some inside help. Something wasn't right here, and he needed to act. No use in going to Symphony, his Chelsea contact. She would only claim the find as her own and would keep him out of the loop. No, this one he would have to follow up by himself. He would need to contact Washington. So he did.

CHAPTER 25

One morning, a few days earlier, John came into his office, unannounced as usual, and asked him if he would like to take a vacation. Jordan was immediately wary of this invitation. John would never offer him a holiday without some ulterior motive. "Yeah, you got me," John admitted, "but cheer up, it's an all-expenses-paid trip back to the Motherland. You're going back to, what do you guys call it, back to Blighty."

"The English call it 'Blighty,' not the Scots," Jordan answered with some bitterness.

"Well, whatever you call it, you're going back tomorrow."

"Tomorrow?" Jordan screamed, "That's impossible. I... can't. I've got...."

"We know what you've got. We've seen your diary and have been in touch with the relevant courts. Don't worry; we've worked it out. You'll only be away for a few days; then it's back to business as usual."

Jordan knew it was useless to argue. They still had too many holds over him, and he could not find any reason to forestall them.

"OK, what's the deal this time?"

"So glad you see things our way. It's a book, a book we don't want to be published. But it's more than that. You see, even if you can persuade the writer to give up on the idea of getting the book into print, the problem is that what he wrote about is still inside his head. He'd be walking about with stuff...." John pointed to his temple, "that we would rather keep from being talked about. Ever. No, this time, using your usual brusque methods may not be enough. This time, you'll need to do... more."

"What do you mean, more?"

"You know what I mean."

"Now, wait a minute. Roughing someone up, threatening, intimidating, sure, I've done those things, but now you want me to - to murder someone. No, no way. That's not going to happen. You can do what you like to me, but I won't kill anyone for you!"

"Oh, please cut the sanctimonious bullshit. That's exactly what you threaten to do to those people who cross you. You tried to 'off' two hundred people once, if I remember correctly. Surely one little teensy-weensy murder won't affect your sensibilities."

"That was a long time ago. You know that. Besides, I'm in my early sixties now. I'm too old for that crap. Find someone younger with more moxie."

They were prepared for his forceful resistance, but John had an ace up his sleeve. He had a whole armful of them.

"OK, here's the deal. Do this one job, and it's over. We walk away, and you never see me again. Your debt's been paid in full."

"Christ, this must be one hell of a book. What's it about?"

"You don't need to know anything about the book or its' contents. All you need to do is what we want. In this case, the less you know, the better."

"So, you probably don't know, either." Jordan snorted contemptuously.

"May I remind you, Mr. Jordan, that I have your balls in these," and the agent held out his cupped right hand towards the lawyer. "It would not pay you to ridicule me or hack me off." And so saying, he made to squeeze his hand into a tight fist.

For a few seconds, Jordan couldn't speak, but then he found his voice. "So, the unpaid taxes, the terrorist shit, jail time...?"

John made a show of blowing his fingers apart. "All gone for good. Pwoof. Our only other condition is that you stop all the intimidation malarkey. You're right. You are getting too old for that shit. No more threats, no more violence. Once you come back, that all stops, and the slate's wiped clean."

"What time's my flight?"

CHAPTER 26

Jordan had had a restless night. He was so close to confronting his hated adversary, so near, he could almost taste it. He didn't yet know who this woman was, purporting to be Les Straight. Could she be his wife? It wasn't important who she was; she was associated with him. That was all that mattered. Swan was aware of Jordan's mission and had furnished him with a weapon, an Argentinian Bersa Thunder.380 semi-automatic pistol. It was similar to and as accurate as a Walther PPK, but less conspicuous. Besides, giving him the Walther would make him think he was James Bond, and this lowlife was no Bond. The Bersa had a seven-round magazine already inserted. Knowing Jordan's history of violence, Black Ops Domestic gave him only one spare clip. If he couldn't accomplish his mission with fourteen bullets, the Department really would need to sharpen up its act!

Once he had arrived in England and discovered who his quarry was, the ex-terrorist protested he didn't need a gun. He wanted the satisfaction of taking this one with his own bare hands. A firearm was too impersonal, and this was a very personal matter. Despite his protestations, however, he quite liked the idea of carrying a gun. It gave him a sense of power. If nothing else, it would show that treacherous bastard Nathan or McGregor, or whatever he called himself these days, that he meant business. He would brandish it if he had to, maybe just to cow the little fucker, to terrorize him, before committing the deed himself.

Despite his penchant for violence, Jordan had never used a firearm, preferring to get much more up close and personal with his victims, but this would be different. Nathan and this woman would need to be killed as much for his pleasure as for more pragmatic reasons. He might even incapacitate them with a couple of shots, then finish the job in person. Slowly and painfully. When he admitted to Swan that he had never fired a gun, Swan's only reply was that it was easy. Just make sure the safety's off, point it at your target, and pull the trigger. Like most guns, it had a small front 'blade' sight attached to the end of the barrel, as well as a rear notched one for greater accuracy if he had to shoot his target from a distance. Swan, however, was aware that Jordan would want his victim to know who his killer was. The only way to accomplish this was to get up close. The closer the better, in fact.

Although it was a small gun, its 'stopping power' was more than sufficient to do the job, and if he did it correctly, the manuscript's secret would die with its author. To make sure that Jordan did not shoot himself accidentally, Swan took the precaution of also giving him the twenty-three-page owner's manual. He could do no more. The rest was up to him.

Like most new gun owners unfamiliar with carrying a weapon, Jordan kept fingering it inside his jacket pocket. He could scarcely believe that he was holding a gun, a gun that could kill people, any number of people if you had enough bullets. But he only wanted to kill one, or maybe two, and he would have plenty of cartridges for that. Fourteen would be more than adequate. But before all that, he needed to find his way to Manchester International Airport. There was someone he had to meet.

• • •

Gretel found she had a break in her diary the following day and had no appointments from ten a.m. until after lunch. This gap would give her enough time to visit the local library and look up Swansong. The reference book was two years old, being the 2005 edition, and didn't list Swansong. That either meant that they chose not to be or that perhaps the company didn't exist in 2005. She then remembered that Swan had not come to the

U.K. until 2004. Hence, it made sense that his agency wouldn't yet possibly have had enough time to be included in that edition. There was a bookshop nearby. Now was as good a time as any. She realized she wouldn't get the opportunity later, as she had arranged to see Martin that evening. No, they didn't yet have the 2007 issue, the latest one available was 2006. That would have to do.

She quickly scanned the pages, and, surprise, surprise, there was a listing, but it offered very little else that Gretel did not already know. Well, that was a waste of time. No, wait a minute, there was something. The yearbook listed another agency at the same address, the same offices as Swansong. Gretel hadn't noticed it yesterday in her excitement and rush to get to the agency. This arrangement wasn't entirely unusual, but maybe there was a connection between the two companies. A quick phone call should sort this out. She dialed the number listed for the enterprise calling itself Kent Professional Book Promotion and Editing Services.A few minutes later, more things were falling into place, and the psychologist realized she would need to see Martin before their intended rendezvous. In fact, she would have to see him right away.

• • • •

Jordan scanned the Incoming Flights board and saw that the plane he was looking for had just landed. It wouldn't be long now. He would enjoy the brief wait, dreaming of how the two of them would torment and torture before, well, before - and then she was through. It had been thirty-five years, but she had hardly changed, at least in his eyes. She was how he remembered her that last time in the flat, on that final, fateful day. "Marie-Claire, you look terrific. How have you been?"

"Très bien, my old friend, my old comrade, and how are you? You look well and prosperous. Life must be good in New York. The legal profession, it pays well, eh?"

"I get by."

"Oh, I'm sure you do more than 'get by.' You must have some very influential clients, n'est-ce pas?"

Jordan did not feel inclined at that moment to let his companion know the kind of people he was providing legal services to. He would explain all that later once they had accomplished their task. She must be tired after the flight, he said, and invited her for coffee at one of the airport restaurants. Her reply shocked and amused him.

"Please forgive me, Max, but my experience of English coffee is not favorable, especially in airports and train stations. Perhaps we could wait until we get back to the city. I'm sure Manchester has some fine coffee houses, but not as exquisite as Paree," she added, smiling. She thought of Maxim's at the bottom end of the Champs-Élysées and the other fine establishments on the wide boulevard itself. However, even some of these were now past their best.

On the way back to the city, the pair played 'catch up.' They still corresponded regularly and had done so since Max got out of prison and had stayed in touch ever since. When he asked her about Henri, her eyes misted over. Yes, the Frenchman had returned to Paris after his release from prison, but he had not fared as well as Max. Henri, too, had had a hard time, even more so because of his nationality, and he was never the same. He had made a half-hearted attempt to go back to his former ways, but found that the world had moved on. He had gone strange and seemed to want to carry on the class struggle, waging a one-man campaign, and it was for this reason, he attempted to bomb the Bourse, the French Stock Exchange. The French police believed he had set the timer incorrectly, or that it malfunctioned. For whatever reason, it exploded before he got there. He was blown to bits inside his car.

Ah, well, scratch one, thought Jordan. It's just a pity that I can't kill that arsewipe Nathan twice to make up for it.

It had only been a stroke of luck that the authorities had not rounded up Marie-Claire up with the rest of the gang. She was on her way back from the off-license after buying more celebratory drinks when all hell broke loose. She did not even want to go, as the last time she tried to purchase alcohol, the counter assistant refused to serve her, not believing her actual age because of her diminutive stature. He only handed over the bottles and cans when she produced her CNI, which, although printed in French, showed her date of birth and her photograph. She saw police officers entering the tenement and rushing up the stairs. How the authorities had discovered them, she did not know. She only realized that there was nothing she could do now to save her comrades. The Parisienne walked away from the building, still carrying the bottles of liquor, tears slowly falling down her cheeks.

She had made her way back to Paris, expecting to be stopped by the police at any minute, either in Scotland or at Portsmouth or on her return to France. But it was as if, by a miracle, she could walk straight through the ferry terminal at St. Malo without incident. The ones who were caught, they had not betrayed her; they had not given her up to lighten their own sentences. She would remember them, all of them.

Unlike her male companions, Marie-Claire was well into her twenties at the time of the failed bombing attempt and was now in her late sixties. Despite still being a radical, she had long since come away from extremist politics. She was especially disillusioned when Mikhail Gorbachev caved into the Western capitalists and allowed communism to crumble in the land of its birth. Marx and Engels must have been spinning in their graves, despite Marx himself being buried in Highgate Cemetery, London, in one of the very heartlands of capitalism. What an irony. She had become a tireless fighter for women's rights, especially the right to have abortions for unwanted babies. The French government even prevented rape victims legally from seeking such drastic solutions. She frequently had run-ins with various politicians and government lawyers, the French judiciary, the police, and the Catholic Church. She had made a name for herself, working tirelessly for the cause she so passionately believed in, but her days of taking direct action were over.

Despite fighting for the rights of French women to have control over their own bodies, even if this meant the taking of unborn life, she had realized that murdering those who deserved to be killed, those capitalists, bankers, newspaper owners, and politicians who made the lives of the people, the proletariat, so miserable, for their own selfish purposes, only made her, and her kind, look more like the murderous thugs they indeed were. The public had had enough of the wanton violence. It would no longer tolerate with equanimity the actions they had taken, and so she had long since given up the class struggle. But even then, there were exceptions. A score had to be settled, and a debt had to be repaid.

• • •

Gretel contacted Martin and insisted that she had to come over right away. All thoughts of her job, pressing though it was, had now gone out of her head. She had to see him immediately, and, no, she could not discuss what she had to say over the phone.

Forty minutes later, Gretel was sitting in Martin's apartment, a cup of hot coffee in her trembling hands.

"OK, so run that by me again. I need to hear it more than once if I'm going to make sense out of this."

His friend started from the beginning, explaining how she saw someone staring at her from behind Swan's door, then putting it down to an overactive imagination. She had become agitated again when she realized Swan hadn't asked her to sign a contract, at first dismissing this as an oversight, then connecting the two incidents. She then repeated the information she had just relayed, as much for her own benefit as Martin's. Even Gretel, herself, could not believe what the proprietor of Kent Professional had told her and had to hear it again, even from her own lips. It was the only way she could rationalize the intelligence he had furnished her with earlier.

"Yesterday, around quarter-to-ten, Bill Kent entered the communal building which housed their respective businesses. There was a man in his sixties at reception, asking for Leighton Swan. He had a distinctive accent, Scottish, but with strong American overtones. He seemed to be in a hurry, appeared very agitated, and kept looking at his watch. When the receptionist asked who he was, he replied as if she should already know. He was very discourteous but gave his name, anyway. It was Jordan. Max Jordan."

"How the fuck did Jordan find us, I mean, me? What's his connection to Swansong? What the fuck's going on?"

"I don't know, Martin, I just don't know. I've been turning various ideas over in my head, but whatever scenario I come up with, it makes little sense. That's the least of our problems right now. We can worry about the connection later. We need to think about our next moves."

"Surely, it's obvious. We need to phone the police. Our lives are in danger. Mine anyway, probably yours, too. We can't do this on our own. We need to contact the Manchester cops. That's our only hope."

"Wait a minute. Before we do that, let's think this out...."

"Yes, and while we're doing that, he's going to come crashing through that bloody door, intending to finish what he started thirty-five years ago."

"No, wait! There has to be more to this. There has to be! Just take a minute to think things through."

"OK, what?"

"I don't know! Just keep quiet for a minute and let me concentrate. We know Jordan's here, and we assume he's come to get you. But how could anyone have made the connection? We changed all the names and locations, and we made sure we didn't use any surnames that even remotely sounded like his. It's got nothing to do with him recognizing his description. It can't be unless he and Swan already knew each other, and Jordan had told him about his background. But the coincidence of us sending the story to someone who just happened to know one of the protagonists, well, it's staggering. I refuse to believe it."

"But didn't you say that when the receptionist asked who he was, Jordan behaved as if she should already know?"

"Maybe she was a temp. perhaps she hadn't worked there for very long. Who knows?"

There was one way to find out, but they had to be quick. Time might not be on their side. Martin would have to do it, in case the receptionist recognized Gretel's voice. The receptionist's name was Trudy. Martin argued they didn't have time to play these games, but his friend insisted. It might bring them one step closer to who knew what, but it was necessary.

"Hi Jan, it's Vincent. How are you?"

"I'm sorry, you must have the wrong number. This is Vennart Buildings."

"Yes, that's right, but I'm sure the last time I called, I spoke to Jan at reception. Is she there?"

"No, there's no one here by that name. I'm the only receptionist, and my name's Trudy."

"Oh. Ok, Trudy, sorry to have bothered you."

"That's all right. Can I help you?"

"Ah, I phoned a while ago, and as I said, I thought I spoke to Jan. I work for a contract cleaning company, and Jan, well, I thought it was Jan, asked me to phone back, so here I am. As a matter of interest, how long have you worked there?"

"Years. Started in, ah, nineteen eighty-eight."

"You know, I've just remembered. Her name wasn't Jan, after all. Sorry to have troubled you." He hung up before she could reply. Turning to Gretel, he asked, "So, where does that get us?"

"She's been there for nearly twenty years so you'd think that if he had been before, she would have remembered him, especially someone with such a distinctive accent. And she didn't."

"So, it's his first time at Swansong. He and Swan would have spoken before he came; maybe that's what Kent meant. Only that Swan was waiting for him. He didn't just walk in off the street."

"Wait a minute. We sent in the story under an assumed name, not my own, and certainly not under the only name Jordan would know me by, Paul McGregor. He was hiding behind the door, waiting to see who walked in. If it had been me...."

"My God, he might have killed you on the spot, with connivance from that bastard Swan. But it wasn't, it was me, and I'm definitely not Paul McGregor."

"Right, so they don't know if you only made up this story or if you really are connected to Paul."

"So, what do they do? They follow me! Oh, Martin, I've probably led him right to you, right to us?"

"You told them you're a psychologist, right?"

"Yes, I'm afraid so, but Martin, I...." Gretel broke down, unable to continue. He folded his arms around her waist, gently trying to comfort her. "It's ok, darling, we'll get out of this, but we need to phone the police."

"No, wait. He needs to find me because that's the only way he can get to you. What would you do? You know what I do for a living; you just don't know where I do it. He'll go round all the clinics, asking for me. Jordan doesn't know my real name, but he'll describe me and make up some story about how he needs to see me. He doesn't need to know my address, which they wouldn't give him, anyway. He only has to know which clinic I work from and either grab me when I come out and force me to take him to you or play a waiting game to see if I lead him here."

"I don't think he's the type to play a waiting game. No, he'll do whatever it takes to make you tell him where I live. He's had thirty-five years to brood over this. He'll not want to wait. God knows what his state of mind is right now. But we do have one advantage. He doesn't know we're on to him. Maybe we can use that."

"Yes, and I know how. It may buy us some time. I need to phone the office and give the girls at reception a story. It won't be too difficult. They know my... preferences. I'll tell them I had a fling with a married woman, the husband's found out, and he's coming to get me. He's a bully, and if he finds me, I'll be in big trouble. I'll just ask them to deny that I work there."

"And that's better than the real reason?"

"What do you think?"

"And they'll go along with this...?"

"I hope so. I'll ask them to phone me once he's gone."

"They'll suggest going to the police."

"I can't. I have my professional reputation to consider. The woman was a patient of mine."

"Oh fuck, this just keeps getting better and better...."

"Oh, shut up."

It was the first time Gretel had smiled since entering his apartment.

CHAPTER 27

Jordan and the French woman had decided that it would add more credibility to their story and be less suspicious if a woman was trying to find the psychologist. Marie-Claire would say that Gretel had treated her some time ago. Due to personal circumstances, she needed to see her again. She could not remember the doctor's name now but would give her description and even the make of the car she had been driving.

Although Gretel had already called Myrtle, the receptionist, to prepare her for their visit and deny any association between herself and the office, Myrtle was still very young, and Gretel had put a lot of pressure on her. According to Dr. O'Hara, it would be a man that called in, someone with a distinctive accent. She was not prepared for this small Frenchwoman, and was momentarily off her guard. Marie-Claire recognized the slight hesitation in her voice but did not pursue it, as to do so might arouse suspicion. Still, no matter the circumstances, she knew. They had found her. But why should Myrtle have wavered? The request had seemed reasonable, and Marie-Claire would have delivered it with just the right amount of charm and pathos. It might have seemed strange if she had asked her for the psychologist's home address or even her phone number, but the Parisienne had only wanted confirmation that she worked from that office. The receptionist had said she did not recognize the doctor's description, so that should have been that. What was there to be suspicious about? This could mean only one thing. Somehow, God knows how, the psychologist had found out Jordan was after her and Nathan, and she would be trying to cover her tracks. How she had deduced their intentions could wait; this was not the time for idle speculation.

Max was waiting for her in the hire car around the corner from the clinic, out of sight, and she told him what had just happened. He, too, could not understand how the doctor had known about him, but if Marie-Claire was correct in her speculation, then they had to strike as soon as possible. It was two p.m. The office closed at four-thirty. They would wait for the little receptionist to come out. She would tell them what they wanted to know. Max had ways of discovering information that would shock even his French companion. He had learned a lot since going to live in New York. He also had to phone Swan.

• • •

The psychologist phoned 999 and asked to be put through to the police. Myrtle had made good on her promise to call Gretel if anyone she didn't recognize came looking for her. The receptionist expressed surprise when it wasn't a man, but a woman who had called, a tiny, older woman with a French accent. The police operator asked what the nature of the call was. Gretel was reluctant to give too many details to this person, who, she suspected, was a junior police officer and not experienced enough to handle such a major crime. However, she realized she had to say something, enough to connect her to someone who could help them without sounding like a complete lunatic.

"My name is Gretel O'Hara, Doctor Gretel O'Hara," she repeated for emphasis. "I am a psychiatrist attached to the Greater Manchester Health Authority." She felt she had to establish her credentials if her next statement was to be taken seriously. "I have sound reason to believe that a good friend of mine and I are in immediate danger."

Despite Gretel's reservations, the switchboard operator was trained to answer any call and did not seem fazed by what she had just heard. "Can you please tell me why you believe your life is in danger?" she asked, trying to get her to focus on just the facts. People, too often in similar circumstances, wanted to give their entire life story before getting to the salient points, which could best determine how to deal with their call. Gretel gave a quickly abridged version of the last twenty-four hours. She would only say that a man her friend had put in jail some time ago was now out and had threatened reprisals before being incarcerated; severe reprisals. The psychologist did not mention that all this happened well over thirty years previously, only that he was following her to get to him. When the operator asked her how she knew she was being followed, Gretel replied she would say no more until she could speak to a more senior officer. It was a long story, and while she was explaining all this to her, this man might be on his way to harm them. She had to speak to a detective now! Gretel tried desperately not to sound like a battered wife or a drug addict afraid for her life due to accumulated debts.

"Hold on, please, caller, and I'll put you through." The line went dead, but only for a moment.

"Detective Sergeant Singh. How can I help you?" Despite her heightened state of fear, Gretel couldn't help but appreciate the beautiful mix of Mancunian and Indian accents. "Detective Sergeant Singh, my name is Doctor Gretel O'Hara. I'm a psychologist with Greater Manchester Health Authority...."

"And what can I do for you, Doctor O'Hara?"

Gretel repeated the brief story she had just given. Singh repeated the question previously asked by the operator. "Look, Detective, my friend was responsible for putting a terrorist in jail some years ago. This man intended to cause severe damage and many fatalities. My friend stopped that from happening, and they put away this bastard and his cronies. He threatened to get him when he came out, and now he's here, in this city, looking for him."

"Is your friend there with you at the moment, Doctor?"

"Yes, I'm in his apartment."

"Can I speak to him, please?"

Gretel handed over the phone without comment. Martin cleared his throat before confirming he was there.

"Hello, Detective Sergeant Singh, my name is... Martin Chambers. I'm the person who Doctor O'Hara was speaking about."

"And please tell me, Mr. Chambers, how you are sure that this man is after you. Have you seen him or spoken to him?"

"No, not exactly, but... look, it's a long story and extremely complicated. I really can't explain it over the phone, but I need to see you now. Please believe us. This is no joke. We really are frightened for our lives."

"Can you come into the office?"

"Yes, no, I don't know. He might be watching us, watching this flat. I know I sound paranoid, but if you knew the whole story, you'd understand why." Martin suddenly felt as if he had been through this before. It was as if he was experiencing déjà vu. Then it hit him. This was how Andy must have felt all those years ago, but this was no longer just a practical joke. This was real. No one, and certainly not Jordan, would be putting a siddur through his letterbox.

"OK, sit tight, Mr. Chambers; I'll be around shortly. Hopefully, we'll get this all sorted out. Now, where do you live?"

Gretel could tell by the way Martin regarded her that he wanted to tell her something. She had to know; she had a right to know, he thought. He knew his timing was lousy, but the way things were, and even now, with the involvement of the police, anything might happen. Jordan had been waiting, brooding, nurturing his hatred for over a generation. He had to tell her now. They were sitting together on the couch, and Martin gently took her hands in his. "Gretel, I've got something to tell you...," he began.

"Oh, Martin, don't. Not now. I know how you feel towards me, and you know I feel the same...."

"No, it's not that, it's something else...."

"What...?" She could see the look on his face, and then she knew. "Oh my God, Martin, no! Please tell me it's not... that!" He slowly took her hands from his and softly cupped her face. They were both crying now, crying freely at the sheer futility of it all. "I... I wasn't going to tell you, I didn't know how to say to you, but with all that's happening, I...that pain I had, it wasn't gallstones, it was the... the aneurysm. It's burst again, and there's nothing they can do. They've found high levels of something called MMP9 in my blood. The rupture is too large for them to do much about. They wanted me to stay in the hospital, but I couldn't, Gretel, I just couldn't."

"How... how... long...?"

"It won't be long, maybe a few days, a week, perhaps."

Gretel could no longer contain herself. Her feelings of grief and sorrow were more than she could bear. This was the one man she had so much love and respect, so much devotion for, now soon to be cruelly taken away from her. If not by that maniac Jordan, then by this malicious and terrible condition. It wasn't fair; it just wasn't fucking fair!

"I wasn't going to tell you, especially now. But if they find Jordan before he gets to me, I knew you'd think that it would all be ok and that we would just get on with the rest of our lives once they put him away again. I didn't want you to go through a double... shock; I don't know how else to put it. Do you understand, can you understand, my darling?"

She couldn't speak. Gretel knew the words she wanted to say but was too emotional to articulate them. She could only nod in acquiescence.

He wasn't finished. He was dying, and it was only a matter of a few days before he.... Either by Jordan's hand or because of the illness, he had run out of time. But he wanted her to know. He wanted her to know. He took her hands again in his. "Gretel, I..."

And she did know, but now she wanted to hear it, to listen to it from his own lips, the words she knew he had wanted to say so badly, for so long. Now, Gretel not only wanted to hear them; she was desperate to hear them, more than anything in the whole world. Right now, at this very minute, there were only the two of them, and no one and nothing else mattered. "Yes, my love, my sweet, gentle, and wonderful man, I know...."He smiled. She was finally ready. "My darling, I've loved you for so long, it feels like seven lifetimes, not seven years. I only truly come alive when I'm with you. If you only knew how empty I feel when we leave each other, how my only thought is when we can be together again..."

There was more he wanted to say, so much more, but he had said enough. He had finally expressed his true feelings for her, and now, even if his life ended at this precise moment, he would die happy. "I will never leave you again, do you hear me? Not for a second. When this is all over, you and I will paint this fucking town, not just red, but every color I can think of. If I have to lose you, my love, it's going to be with a bang, not with a whimper. Do you understand?"

He smiled through his tears. He was now shivering, and it was not with cold. Reaction was setting in. It had all been too emotional, and his mind and his body could not cope. "And who's paying for this blowout, may I ask?"

"I'll put it on my credit card," Martin said wryly.

• • • •

Marie-Claire could almost see the frustration on Jordan's face as he kept watching the car's digital clock change one minute at a time, each minute seeming like an hour. She tried some small talk, but he was now too focused on what they needed to do. He did not wish to be diverted with useless chatter. Getting this girl was all that mattered. She would give them the name and address of the doctor, who would lead him to the man who had called himself Paul McGregor, but who they knew was Sam Nathan.

At 4.20, Jordan drove the car into view so he could see her when she left. Their only doubt was that she might go with a colleague. This would be a complication, but they would address this problem if it happened. They were lucky. The receptionist came out of the building by herself, and there did not seem to be anybody else around. The fates were smiling on them, on their mission. His accomplice hid in the back, bent over until she felt the car slowing down.

On a signal from Jordan, she quickly opened the rear near-side door and pulled the unwary girl in beside her, punching her in the face with her free hand as she closed the passenger door. She kept hitting her, giving her no opportunity to defend herself. She knew that if the young girl could get herself together, she might easily overpower her older and smaller would-be captor with her superior weight and fitness. Jordan drove away, but not too quickly, as much as he would have liked to. The last thing he needed to do right now was to draw attention to them.

Jordan had studied the suburb on his street map and drove to the area's outskirts, to a piece of waste ground, where no one would disturb them. Quickly climbing into the back seat, he grabbed the unfortunate girl by her hair, snarling into her face. He jammed his other hand between her legs, so she was in no doubt about what was going to happen. She started to scream, but Jordan took his bunched fist from her hair, locking it over her mouth while tightening his grip on her crotch. He didn't mean it to happen, and he had only put his hand there to emphasize his question.

He had to stay focused, but despite himself, he had become aroused. She was staring wild-eyed at her attackers, expecting to be hurt and raped. Instead, Jordan pulled his hand from her nether regions, still keeping his other hand clamped over her mouth.

"OK, listen, pet, we just want some information, then we'll let you go. Give us what we want, and you'll leave in one piece. If you don't," and he made a show of unzipping his trousers. "Now, I'm going to take my hand off your mouth, and you won't scream or shout, will you? Even if you did, there's no one around to hear you. Do you understand?"

The terrified girl could only nod furiously as she looked wildly around the confines of the car. Could she escape? Not a hope, and he'd rape her if she even tried. He might still do it, anyway, but would he do it with this woman sitting beside him? Myrtle recognized her. It was the woman who had come in earlier looking for Doctor O'Hara. They must have known that she lied to them. Oh God, this would not be good. Despite her best efforts, she couldn't help it. She couldn't stop it. She was urinating on the seat. Jordan slapped her once more, partly to emphasize what he had just said, and also out of sadistic pleasure and his increased sexual arousal.

"What's the name of the doctor we were looking for this afternoon? What's her name?" he snarled before slapping her again. The girl realized she had no choice. She would have to tell. It was the only way she would save her life, and she knew Doctor O'Hara would understand. She gave them the name they wanted. "What's her address?"

"Her... address?"

"Yes, you bitch, her address, or do I have to give your memory a jog?"

"I don't know, I swear. I don't know where she lives. Her home address will be on file, but I've never been there. We... we can go back to the office if you like. I... I 'll get it for you, but please don't hurt me again."

"That won't be necessary, my dear. Now we know her name, finding her address won't be too difficult. Thank you."

"So, I can go now?" the girl asked hopefully.

"No, my dear, I'm afraid not. We can't possibly leave you to warn Doctor... O'Hara that we're looking for her now, can we?" It was at this point that Myrtle must have known she was going to die. They would not let her live. She screamed before Jordan punched her, knocking her into semi-consciousness. "I prefer them awake, but no matter," he drawled, undoing his trousers. He would have some fun before he finished her off. Marie-Claire looked away in disgust. "If it offends you, take a walk."

"This was not part of the plan. It was only to be Nathan and the woman, no one else."

"You know we can't let her walk away. What do you think she'll do? Go home and pretend nothing happened? Don't be naïve. You know we can't just let her go."

"Make sure you use a condom." With that, she put her hand on the door handle. Jordan's lustful actions would be too much for her to take.

"Don't worry. There's no way this one will ever know the joys of motherhood."

"That's not what I meant." She answered with barely disguised disgust as she stepped from the car.

CHAPTER 28

Singh had only been a detective sergeant for six weeks, and if Martin's story was real, it was probably more than he would know how to deal with. Yes, he was ambitious, but he wasn't stupid. If these peoples' lives were in danger, he would need to take this up the food chain. His immediate superior was Detective Inspector Gerald Nish, a hard-bitten police officer of twenty-five years standing. There wasn't much he hadn't seen, heard, or done in that time, and Singh knew that if anyone could sort this out, it was Nish. He told the senior officer what had just happened, expecting his superior to rush for the door. It surprised the younger detective when Nish told him to relax; the woman was probably pre-menstrual and hyper. As for him, the poor bugger probably had to go along with her if he expected to get any. "Any what?" asked Singh innocently.

Nish looked at him wryly. If he had to ask the question, he was too young to understand the answer.

Martin and Gretel had composed themselves by the time the two police officers arrived. However, it wasn't necessary to be a detective to see that there had been some high emotion not long earlier. They both still had the telltale puffy, red eyes, and there was a general feeling in the flat that a substantial emotional upheaval had taken place. For whatever reason he was there, one thing was certain. There was a highly charged atmosphere in the apartment he could almost touch, it was so palpable. The way they clung to each other could only mean one thing. They really were terrified.

Terrified of what he didn't yet know, but that was his job. To find out. They didn't look like the kind of people who went into hysterics over nothing. She was a bloody psychologist, for God's sake. Introductions were soon over, and it was clear to Martin and Gretel that Nish would conduct most of the interview. Martin wasted no time and retold his story from the beginning; it was the only way they would believe him. At various times through his narrative, he asked them if there was anything he hadn't made clear or that they wanted him to elaborate on. They were both content to let Martin tell his story without side issues. If any points needed clarification, the detectives would ask them. Both made copious notes while he was speaking, and Martin paused several times to make sure they missed nothing he had to tell them.

When he had finished, all Nish would say was, "Well, that's quite a story, Mr. Chambers."

"It's all true, every word," Gretel confirmed.

"But if what you're telling us is real, then this man, Jordan, now has an accomplice. Someone who's helping him to find you."

"Yes. If I'm right, it's a girl, a woman," he corrected himself. "One of the gang who wasn't caught at the time. She had been in the flat but had gone out earlier. I can't remember why. She and Jordan must have kept in touch through the years, and now he's persuaded her to help him find me.

"This is all going back to the nineteen seventies. That man knows how to nurse a grudge."

"You weren't there. You didn't see the look on his face as they were leading him away. Why do you think I changed my name and came to live down here?"

"And now, after thirty-five years, he intends to take revenge. Seems a long time to have waited to come after you, don't you think?"

"Don't you understand?" Martin demanded. "Until now, he didn't know where I was. He may have looked for me through the years, I don't know, but it's only since I sent that manuscript to Swansong that all this has happened. Somehow, there's a connection between them; there has to be."

"OK, I think it's fair to say that he hasn't yet found out where you live. He only knows you as Nathan or McGregor anyway, right? So, he'll need to find Doctor O'Hara before he can get to you. Sorry to be so blunt, Doctor, but there's no other way of saying it. Perhaps it would be best if you could stay here tonight, Doctor. I know it's a bit of an imposition...."

"No, Detective Inspector, it's not, at least, not for me. You must ask Martin what he thinks, though."

Martin only nodded his head, smiling. Gretel had stayed over at his apartment once or twice before, but it was an arrangement neither of them cared for. Martin only had a one-bedroom flat, so he used the couch while his friend took his bed. He found the sofa uncomfortable, and Gretel felt guilty at turfing him out of his comfortable bachelor bedroom. "I'll need to go back to my house first to get some things," she explained.

Nish looked surprised, wrongly assuming that she would have used his bedroom and shared his bed on previous occasions. "OK, Doctor O'Hara, but just to let you know, I am taking this seriously. My sergeant and I will drive you there and bring you back here. By the way, you said that this publisher, Kent, said that Jordan spoke in a Scottish accent but with an American twang, is that correct?"

"As far as I can remember, yes."

Nish let out a world-weary sigh. "So it's possible that he's been living in the States for years and has come over here with the sole intention of...." This was more to himself, as it was to anyone else in the room.

Turning to his young detective sergeant, Nish told him to take some notes. "Contact Immigration and find out if anyone by the name of Max Jordan has come into this country in the past week. If so, find out which airport he flew into. Then check with the car hire companies at the airport and see if he rented a vehicle, and if you get a hit, make sure you get the make, model, and license plate. Also, find out how long he's hired it for. Then, get a hook into this Swansong Publishing. Find out what you can, and what cars are connected with them, just in case. I'm going to contact my mates at the Met. I think they should pay Swan a visit, and I'll also get them to have a quiet word with the receptionist and this Kent character."

Then turning to Gretel, he said, "Don't worry, Doctor O'Hara, Mr. Chambers, we'll catch him. That I promise you."

Like many doctors, Gretel did not list her personal landline number in the phone book. She was reluctant to take business calls out of regular office hours. The last thing Gretel needed was to be woken in the small hours by a patient who couldn't sleep or who just wanted to talk. Her working hours were from eight-thirty a.m. to four-thirty p.m., and that was it. She did not do overtime.

Jordan had already tried Directory Enquiries without success. In the morning, he would go to the local council and look up the electoral roll. He didn't need her phone number anyway, only her address.

They had dumped Myrtle's lifeless body where he had killed her and had buried her in a shallow grave. Pity about the back seat, though, he thought. The bitch had wet herself. With a bit of luck, they would not find her until after he had killed Nathan and the doctor and was safely back in the States. Luckily, he had hired the car under the name of Baines. He would just have to dump it and lose his security deposit. Who cared? It wasn't his money.

They both realized that they did not have to wait until the morning to view the electoral register. All this information would undoubtedly be available online. All they had to do would be to find an internet café and look up her address while they had coffee, thanks to the wonders of modern technology. Jordan did not want to risk returning to the internet café he had used earlier. Using a place like that once was ok, but twice...? That might just draw unnecessary attention, and people remember. Sometimes they remember things other people preferred them not to remember. They drove back into the city and found another spot a few streets away. While she kept watch to make sure no one was paying them undue attention,

Jordan found the site and typed in her name. Almost immediately, a result came up. There was only one Gretel O'Hara listed. He had located her. The only problem would be if she had already contacted the police. They had concluded that the psychologist probably knew that she was being hunted. She would be apprehensive when her receptionist didn't show up for work the following morning. It would only take a few minutes to deduce that if no one could contact her, she would draw the obvious connection. They had to get to Gretel tonight. It all had to be done before the girl's absence would be noticed.

• • • •

They drove to Gretel's address but found all the lights off despite being just after eight o'clock. She couldn't have gone to bed yet. No, they reasoned, she was out and would probably be with him. Jordan was desperate. He had to take a gamble. Better still, ask Marie-Claire to take it. They would approach her neighbors. There was a family emergency, and they had been trying to get Gretel on the phone. They needed to contact her. It was urgent and couldn't wait until morning. Did they know where she might be, please? It was a long shot, but it was all they had. There was no reply from the neighbors to the left of Gretel's house, despite lights being on in the front rooms. Either they don't answer the door to anyone at night, or more likely, they've gone out and left them on for security, he reasoned.

The family on the other side was more forthcoming. They were sorry to hear about the family emergency, but didn't know where Gretel could be. Then their daughter came to the door. She was a curious fourteen-year-old who, Gretel knew, had taken a liking to the man she saw occasionally coming and going to her house. The killers both knew from her actions and body language that this girl more than liked their quarry; she had the 'hots' for him. Pity, she would never get a chance to consummate the relationship, Jordan thought. She didn't know his exact address, she admitted, but she did once overhear him discussing his flat and the street it was in. Maybe they could go there and ask someone. Jordan could hardly keep the excitement out of his voice.

"Do you know this man's name?"

"Yes, it's 'Chambers.' I think his name is Martin Chambers." So the little cunt had changed his name again! Christ on a crutch, he was turning out to be a slippery bastard. Jordan looked at his watch and knew they would be too late to find any internet café still open by the time they got back to the city. "I know it's asking a lot, but as I said, this is a family emergency. I wonder if you would be kind enough to find his name in the phone book. It'll only take a minute. I realize you don't know us, so we'll stay in our car. We wouldn't expect you to let in strangers at this time of night."

Their daughter, Mel, was already halfway towards the kitchen at the back of the house where the primary phone socket and the phone were and where they kept the phone book. It had never occurred to her to look for his address, and she didn't realize it could be this easy. Maybe she should 'accidentally' find herself in his area one day, or keep finding herself in his neighborhood until they met, 'quite by accident.'

She quickly scanned the pages and found his name. The teenage girl wrote his details on the notepad they kept beside the phone and went back to the front door, from where she called the two former terrorists over. "Here, that's it. I hope you find her in time. Please tell them I said 'hi.'"

They drove away, confident now that their quest would soon be over. Within the next hour, Jordan would have his revenge, and Martin Chambers, a.k.a. Paul McGregor, a.k.a. Sam Nathan, would be dead.

CHAPTER 29

As they approached Martin's apartment block, they saw an unmarked police car, with sirens blaring and headlights flashing, squealing to a stop just yards in front. As Jordan had feared, they were too late. He would not get access to Martin's flat. "Bastard. Fuck, fuck, bastard." He slammed his fist off the dashboard in anger and frustration. "We'll never get to them now. As soon as they see anyone going into the place, they'll be out of their car in a minute. We'll never have time..."

"This is not the Max I used to know. There is always a way." Marie-Claire did not utter this remark with particular fondness or nostalgia. It was cold, mechanical, unfeeling. Marie-Claire was still disgusted by his earlier actions and had declined to eat or stay with him in his hotel room when this was over. She knew his tendency and penchant for violence. Still, what he did... yes, maybe the girl had to die, the Parisienne could see that now. But to rape her in the condition she was in, and with her body soaked in her own urine, that was plus de sacrilege, un abomination! Once they had killed this man Chambers, it would cancel her debt. She would never see or speak to Jordan again. The man was an animal; worse. Beasts only kill to survive. He murdered because he enjoyed it.

Jordan looked at her with a vulpine grin. She was going to create a diversion for him. He had such a look of malevolence about him, the Frenchwoman almost felt sorry for Chambers. She had never seen such a look of pure, unadulterated evil. "Quickly, let me out now, then just wait for your chance. You'll know when...."

Obeying her instructions, Jordan stopped the rented car. Marie-Claire stole out quietly and then ran up to the two detectives just as they got out of their vehicle. "Thank God you got here," she gasped, apparently out of breath. "I've just seen a man with a gun running into that apartment block. He just looked so mean...." She was pointing to the block two entrances down from Martin's.

Both police officers looked at each other, bewildered. "Sorry, ma'am, don't you mean the one over there?"

"No, I'm certain it was the one I've just pointed to. I just saw him run in, for goodness' sake!"

Without wishing to waste valuable time by arguing further, they raced towards the block the French woman indicated. Jordan seized his chance and bolted from his car into Martin's building. He knew he would have little time before the detectives realized she had misled them. Still, Marie-Claire's ruse would give him the valuable opportunity he needed to carry out his mission. Jordan would have preferred to make his nemesis suffer more, but it would satisfy him enough to see the astonished look on his face, mingled no doubt with abject fear, as his quarry knew his last moments had come.

The killer was climbing the stairs now, two at a time, searching for the door number. It would be on the second floor, and he no longer needed the scrap of paper provided by that silly girl. He knew where he was going. Oh, this was going to be so good, so sweet. It would make what he did to the receptionist earlier on look like a benediction. Finally, he was outside the door. He was actually outside the door. He became aroused again, but this was not the time. Chambers was not his type, and he had had enough of that in Barlinnie.

He stood for a minute, undecided whether to trick his way in or simply to kick the door down. He rapped at the door. "Mr. Chambers, it's Constable Shaw, are you all right, sir?" he shouted, changing his accent to Northern Irish. His mother had come from Londonderry. It was from where he got his radical roots.

Martin answered hesitantly from behind the door, "Yes, I'm fine, Constable, thanks."

"Do you mind if I come in for a minute, please, sir? I just need to check in person. Won't be too long."

"OK, hang on," Martin replied more confidently, and Jordan heard him un-snib the door.

• • •

Twenty minutes earlier, the red Vectra stopped outside Gretel's front door. Nish asked her for her keys. He would enter first to make sure the house was clear, and Singh would stay with the psychologist. Cover all the bases. On the way over, Singh discovered no one named Max Jordan had entered the country or had rented a car at the airport during the past seven days. He must have arrived on a false passport and could be anyone.

As the Detective Inspector entered her home, the house's front door to the right also opened. It was Melissa, the young girl who had a crush on Martin, and who had seen the car drive up. She did not recognize the vehicle but hoped to get a glimpse of him. She rushed downstairs, only to be disappointed when a different man opened the front door. Melissa hoped they had not split up, as she looked forward to the times when Martin came over, and she got the chance to speak to him, even if it was just to say hello. The teenager peered into the car, hoping to see if Martin might be inside. Well, Miss O'Hara was still there, and there was someone else, but it didn't look like Mr. Chambers. Nish re-appeared to confirm that all was ok, and Gretel could come in to pick up the things she needed. As she alighted the car, Melissa came over, surreptitiously still looking for Martin.

"Hi, Doctor O'Hara, how are you?" she asked, wondering why her friend was not with her. Gretel must have seemed uneasy and distracted.

"Hi, Mel," she replied, trying to keep the catch out of her voice. Then Melissa remembered. Maybe it was to do with that lovely couple who came earlier. "Hope nothing's wrong...."

"Wrong? Why should anything be wrong?" The woman asked, trying to keep her voice level.

"I just wondered if that couple who were here earlier had found you. I hope your family is ok"

Nish came running up to the girl. "What couple? What did they want?"

Melissa suddenly felt that she had done something she shouldn't have and was unsure how to reply. She had done enough recently to incur her parents' displeasure. She didn't want to be punished for something else, but her mom was also there when they came to the door, so if she had done anything she shouldn't, well, her mom should get into trouble, too. "They, um, said they were trying to contact the doctor. They said it was a family emergency. I told them you sometimes saw Mr. Chambers, and they asked me to find his address, so I did. I didn't do anything wrong, doctor, did I?"

She did not get a reply as all three of them raced to the car, all thoughts of getting an overnight bag now gone. Her front door was unlocked and open, but at that point, Gretel couldn't have cared less. All of her possessions were material, apart from a few awards and her degree certificates. But she could even replace these if necessary. What couldn't be replaced was Martin. Oh, Martin!

Nish retook the wheel as the more experienced driver, the unmarked car's concealed lights and sirens now flashing and blaring, arousing and awakening those in the nearby suburban streets. This never happened around here. This was a friendly neighborhood, a safe neighborhood.

The senior officer screamed into the car radio while driving. "It's D.I. Nish. Suspected murder attempt at," and he shouted Martin's address so loudly, Singh thought they would have heard him at Radio Control without the mic.

Within a few seconds, the occupants of a similarly unmarked car acknowledged Nish's call. "It's D.S. Bulliss here, sir. I'm with D.C. Paterson. We're only a few streets away."

"He's there!" Nish screamed, almost choking himself off. "He's in the flat. Get over there now!" He hung up before giving the other detective time to reply.

• • • •

Martin opened the door, his eyes staring wildly as Jordan pushed him back into the living room, the Bersa in his other hand. "How... how...?" he stammered. He slowly retreated, walking hesitantly backward towards his desk as Jordan raised the gun, preparing to fire. At this range, he just couldn't miss. "If you knew how this moment feels," Jordan began. "The abuse I took in jail, the kickings, the beatings, the knife attacks, the fucking disgusting sex attacks, the scalding water, scalding water!" he screamed, "but I took it. I took it all because one day, I knew I would find you, and that was all I cared about, and now it's come. I would have liked to have made the occasion last a bit longer, but I saw you had a couple of playmates down there. Marie-Claire won't be able to hold their attention for too much longer, so I'll just do what I came to do, and I'll go. You remember Marie-Claire, don't you? French chick. Tiny, petite, as they say en France. I called her and told her I had a bead on you. She also wanted to come and pay her respects in person, but unfortunately, she's otherwise engaged. Maybe next time, eh? Oh no, wait. I just remembered. There won't be a next time, not for you. I would have liked to have stayed a little longer, do a bit more, but it'll be enough, and every time I'm screwing some fuck, I'll think of this moment, and I'll come all the harder."

"You're too late," he said slowly, playing for time, playing for his life.

"What d'you mean 'too late?' You're here, and I'm here, ain't too late for me."

"I'm dying."

"You're lying!" Jordan spat back, aiming the gun at Martin's torso. He was going to ensure he wouldn't miss. Martin could almost feel the bullet entering his body. The searing pain sharp and heavy as the small projectile ripped through his outer clothing and penetrated his skin, then his flesh, before embedding itself in his body.

"I'm going to be dead in a few days, and that's the truth!"

"Yeah, just like you told the truth thirty-five years ago when you said you were phoning your darts mate, remember? I should have finished you then, but if I had, I wouldn't have the pleasure of doing it now."

"This time, I really am telling the truth. Look!" and Martin pulled up his shirt to expose his scarred body. Even Jordan could see that the suture scars were new. Martin let his shirt fall back down.

"How long?" Jordan asked, gesturing at Martin's wounds with his gun.

"I told you, five days, six, maybe, a week at the most."

"What is it, cancer?"

"No, it's called an abdominal aortic aneurysm. It's ruptured. There's nothing they can do."

"Do you think for one minute I give a fuck? Do you? Do you? I might only be taking a week off your life, but that'll have to do. You were wrong. I'm not too late, not while you've still got a breath left in your body. If you were on a life-support machine and only had ten minutes, I'd still pull the plug. That's how much I loathe you. You betrayed us."

"I saved over two hundred lives," Martin shouted. "Lives you would've taken without a moment's hesitation. Yes, I betrayed you. You and all your filthy, rotten gang of murderers. And I'd do it again. Again and again and again! You were then and you still are now, nothing but a piece of scum."

This tirade was too much for Jordan to bear. He leveled the gun right at Martin's chest. No! Martin couldn't allow it to end this way, not like this. Gretel was still out there, and he knew Jordan would always find a way to get at her, even with police protection. Maniacs and fanatics like him, so focused and full of hate, he would surely find a way. Martin must not let that happen. At all costs, he would have to protect his friend from this monster.

"Even at the end, you're still nothing more than a pathetic loser, a bully, and a coward. You're too shit scared to take me like a man. You've got to use a gun. On an unarmed, defenseless man, no, an unarmed, defenseless dying man. Even if you pull that trigger right now, you'll always know, in here," and Martin pointed to his groin, "that you didn't have the guts, the cohunes, to do it yourself. Some small voice will keep telling you, keep whispering to you, wherever you go, whatever you do. When you're coming inside a twenty-quid drugged-up hooker, thinking of me, that you had to use a gun... you're not even pathetic, you're worse. You're a loser, a pathetic, shit scared loser."

With that, Jordan threw the gun contemptuously onto the floor, where it landed with a dull thump on Martin's carpet. "I don't need a gun to finish you. I'll kill you with my bare hands, and come in your face as I'm doing it," Jordan yelled, and with that, he ran at Martin, screaming wildly, his hands stretched out into vicious talons in front of him.

• • •

Six months earlier, Gretel had bought Martin a letter opener. She was tired, she said, of seeing ripped apart envelopes littering his carpet. He was a businessman, not a wonderful businessman, but a businessman, nonetheless. He should open his mail with more decorum, with more finesse. So she had bought him a beautifully carved and decorated instrument, which looked quite spectacular. Unfortunately, as Martin had earlier confided to one of their friends, the only problem was that it couldn't open anything. It was useless, but, of course, he did not have the heart, or the guts, to tell her, but he liked the thought of using a knife to open his post, just not that one. He found what he was looking for in his kitchen drawer. It was a Tesco paring knife, which cost him next to nothing but worked splendidly on his mail.

He had heard the noise made by the police car as it screeched to a halt outside his flat. He went to the window to see what was going on and was surprised to see someone, a small person or a child, gesticulating wildly. Whoever it was, was directing the officers to another apartment block away from his own. As he saw the plain-clothes men darting into the entrance she had pointed to, he also spied a figure running furtively into his apartment block. Martin knew instantly that it was him. It had to be him. The fates had decreed that it was destined to end this way.

Knowing he only had seconds, Martin prepared for it as best he could, but seeing the gun as he opened the door was unexpected. It wasn't Jordan's style, as he remembered it, and threw his plans into disarray. He couldn't allow Jordan just to shoot him dead and then run. There were two officers downstairs. They weren't armed either, but they would probably be ok as long as they didn't try to be heroes. No, it was Gretel that was his worry, his only concern. Either way, Martin realized he couldn't let Jordan leave his flat alive. Even the two policemen with her were only of secondary importance to this killer, and he might only have shot them if they tried to intervene. He had to be stopped.

Martin knew that his life was over anyway, whether he foiled this evil man. He had to goad Jordan, lure him over to the desk where he kept the paring knife, his letter opener.

Just a couple more steps, you bastard. That's it, keep coming, keep coming, keep...

They both heard it together, the sounds of Bulliss' and Paterson's footsteps, racing up the stairs, as the officers finally realized the woman had decoyed them into running into the wrong block of flats. Jordan increased his pace. They would not stop him now! He would not be denied. He lunged at Martin, his hands going for Martin's throat. Now! Martin pulled the knife from behind his back and thrust it with all the force he could muster into Jordan's stomach. The killer barely noticed, being so intent, so concentrated on achieving his goal. His hands were around Martin's throat now, squeezing with all the power he possessed.

Martin knew it was over, but thought he might just have enough strength for one more jab. Wrenching the knife from Jordan's stomach, he re-thrust it back in, a couple of inches away from the first wound. He couldn't breathe, and his eyes wanted to bulge from their sockets. He was losing focus, his tongue was now lolling from his mouth, and the room was going dark, spinning, and twisting. His clothes suddenly felt warm and sticky. With the last few seconds remaining to him, he knew. It was Jordan's blood gushing from the wounds he had made. Martin had done it! He had stopped this man, this maniac, from coming after his beloved Gretel, but at what cost...?

As they arrived outside Martin's apartment block, Nish saw a car parked nose-in to the curb, its blue and red lamps still flickering behind the windscreen. The senior detective gave silent thanks that the other officers had already responded. He ordered Gretel to remain in the car, but this was her closest friend, and there was no way she would stay behind. A scant three minutes later, she wished she had taken his advice. As the psychologist alighted from the car, she noticed a tiny figure, possibly a child, in a hooded coat, lurking in the shadows. This, however, was no child. Only as they rushed towards Martin's apartment did it occur to Gretel who it was, but by then, it was too late.

Bulliss and Paterson had arrived barely seconds before them. They had burst into the room as the two antagonists slumped to the floor together in a final, synchronized display of mortal combat. Paterson remained at the door while Bulliss felt for Martin's pulse, then repeated the procedure on Jordan. It was too late. Both men were dead.

All three got to Martin's front door, which was open, and, as they looked into the flat, Gretel would not forget the shocking sight that greeted them. She had never seen anything like it and prayed she never would again. The gruesome spectacle that lay there before them stunned even the two officers. Bulliss attempted to prevent Gretel from entering the apartment. After all, it was now a crime scene, but more because he did not want her to see Martin in the condition he was in. He stopped her from crossing the threshold but could not prevent her from witnessing the horrible scene which confronted her.

Both the killer and Martin were slumped on the floor of his living room in a deadly embrace. The killer had a knife stuck into his stomach, the crimson stain spreading over his blue shirt. Blood was forming a growing red pool on the carpet, with Martin's fist still clasped around the hilt. The killers' eyes, even in death, bore a look of pure malice and absolute evil. Gretel had recently seen that look before. Martin's eyes were almost bulging from their sockets. His face had turned blue, almost purple, and his swollen tongue was lolling out of his mouth as the murderer's hands were still pressed in a death grip around his throat. Despite the unbelievable agony he must have faced in those final few seconds, Gretel could see the faint traces of a beatific smile from the corner of his lips, and she understood. He was smiling because, in those last moments, he knew he had saved her life, as unworthy as she felt of his unselfish gesture. She was the one who insisted Martin should open Pandora's Box in the first place. Her insistence started the chain of events that led the killer right to his door and to his horrible death.

Martin only had a short time left to him anyway, as he was dying from natural causes. Still, he certainly did not deserve to meet his end at the hands of this awful man, and that he did so was her fault. She would have to live with this shame and guilt for the rest of her life.

• • • •

Eventually, she gave a statement and complete account of her involvement in Martin's death, repeating most of what she and Martin had already explained. Gretel kept in touch with Nish and eventually discovered what had transpired in London the following day.

The psychologist took an extended leave of absence from work and went on vacation, but not to enjoy herself. That was the last thing on her mind, given the circumstances. She just knew that she had to get away and go over everything that had happened, and she could not do that at home, not even in Manchester. She considered going to Glasgow, to Martin's home city, but the pain would have been too much. Yes, she would go one day, but not now. Her emotions were still too raw.

Gretel found a beautiful cottage to rent in County Cork, close to her family's roots, deep in the Irish countryside. She knew if she were going to find peace anywhere, it would be there. This time, she would not be available for emergencies. For once, her patients would just have to manage by themselves. She was the one who now needed therapy and needed it badly.

As much as she tried to stop herself, Gretel could not help thinking about the manuscript and the damage it had caused. Three people had died because of it, one of them, the one person in the entire world she had adored above all others. Her first thought was to delete every reference to it and destroy the couple of hard copies she had printed. Maybe it was just too dangerous, and maybe, just maybe, there were some things that the world was not yet ready to know. But that would be the act of a coward and make Martin's death meaningless. If she did that, then it would all have been for nothing. If his life were to have any purpose, this book would need to be published. It would just have to be, even if it meant swallowing her principles and paying for it herself. Then Gretel remembered Kent, the agent in the same building as Swansong. She would try him. After all, he was very involved in this drama himself, or at least part of it. Maybe she could persuade him.

Although it was the last thing on her mind when she booked her vacation, Gretel would use the break to rewrite and update their book, so it would be ready when she got home. The psychologist did not see this as an arduous task; to her, it was a labor of love. She had taken her laptop with her, more out of habit than actually to plan to use it, but now she was glad she did. If she could not finish this undertaking now, Gretel knew she would never complete it when she got back to Manchester and the rigors of everyday living.

CHAPTER 30

The story took time to piece together, but eventually, most of it came out. They located Jordan's hire car not far from Martin's flat, where he parked it before his murderous assault. Fibers on the back seat and the floor matched those of Myrtle's woolen dress. A few days later, her body was found, the matching dress clearly establishing that she had been in the vehicle. Forensics proved she had been raped shortly before her death. However, bruises on her face and body made it evident that the girl had been forced to disclose Gretel's name, by which Jordan found her address.

Documents on Jordan's body also identified him as Harry Baines, a citizen of New York, and George Humphreys of Boise, Idaho. Officers from Scotland Yard were sent to interview Leighton Swan and Trudy, the receptionist, and Bill Kent. The one disturbing aspect of the Met. detectives' visit to the Swansong offices was that Trudy had disappeared, not showing up for work the following morning. Other detectives went to her address, but there was no reply; neither could they contact her by phone. No one had seen or heard her coming in that evening. She had just simply vanished. Bill Kent was very evasive and initially refused to help the police officers, claiming he knew nothing. They warned him that failure to co-operate could see him charged with obstructing a murder inquiry and even possibly being involved in Martin's death. Eventually, he crumbled and admitted that two men with American accents had visited him. They advised him it would be in his and his family's best interests if he had a sudden attack of amnesia. It would be for the best if he could remember seeing no one matching Jordan's physical description or remembering his distinctive accent, ever calling at the Swansong building.

The officers assumed Jordan realized he needed to cover his tracks and recalled the two people he had come into contact with when he visited Swan's office. They would need to be dealt with. Swan made the necessary call, and it was done. The Met. officer assured Kent that he need have no more fears for his family now he had come clean. They would take steps to ensure that he, his family, and his company were 'quarantined' and 'off-limits.' The officer had spent enough years on the Force to know when an intelligence operation was in progress. Had it been agents from one of the U.K. authorities, his options would have been more restricted, but Kent's assertion that his visitors had American accents almost caused the officer to burst a blood vessel. The very notion that intelligence operatives from another country, a foreign country, any foreign country, should try to intimidate a British citizen was more than he could stomach. Didn't these fuckers realize we were all supposed to be on the same side? It seemed that co-operation and goodwill were only necessary when it suited the Americans. Well, not this time. The officer had contacts in the diplomatic service, and the word was put out. Kent was untouchable. If he even caught a cold, the officer would create such a stink, it would be smelled all the way back to Washington.

Naturally, Swan initially denied knowing anyone calling themselves Max Jordan, George Humphreys, or Harry Baines. Asked how Jordan had got the Bersa recovered from Martin's flat, Swan said he knew nothing of the weapon. The serial number and any other identifying marks had been removed, and there was no way they could trace the gun back to him. The officer knew Jordan would not have chanced to bring the gun himself; the risks were just too high. No, he would have to have acquired the weapon here, after he had arrived. Unlike the States, procuring a gun in Britain was much more difficult, so the question arose—where did he get it? There was also the matter of Trudy and Kent.

Was it just a coincidence that she had disappeared the day after Jordan's arrival? Nah, it was improbable, and as for Kent, that man had been terrified. According to the timeline that the officer had established, Jordan couldn't have had anything to do with those issues. Especially as the description Kent gave for the two men who had threatened him did not match those of Swan or Jordan. This meant that Swan had to have called in the 'heavies.' He could get a court order requesting a copy of calls to and from Swan's office and his mobile phone records during the past forty-eight hours. Still, if Swan had been smart, he would have used a public payphone. Would he have been that clever? There was only one way to find out.

It seemed so far that all the evidence they had was circumstantial until they could garner Swan's phone records and have the numbers checked and eliminated. However, they did now have Kent's testimony that someone matching Jordan's description had undoubtedly been in the building.

The officer employed a tactic he had used occasionally in the past. It was highly unorthodox, but so were these circumstances. In a quiet voice filled with menace, the police officer told Swan that he would make life so difficult for him, living in North Korea would seem like a vacation. They would discretely drop word in the right places that Swansong was to be avoided. They would become a pariah company, and vague insinuations would be circulated. Plagiarism, a literary agent's worst nightmare, would be hinted at, and quiet allegations of financial irregularities would be discretely put about. The officer would ensure that the Inland Revenue went through his books with a fine-tooth comb, and they would pounce on any suspicious entries.

Swan threatened to call the officer's superiors, but the officer only smiled and said, "Prove it. It's just you and me, my word against yours, and my superiors will back me. Do you think I would come here and say these things if I hadn't already covered my arse? Three people, and maybe your receptionist, are dead because of you. A fourth person, the woman who came to this office as 'Les Straight,' would also have been murdered by that jackal, Jordan."

The officer had not sought or been given approval by his superiors, or anyone else, to make these threats. It had all been a gigantic bluff, and he hoped Swan would not call his hand. He didn't.

"Now, I am one furious Met. cop this morning, so you better tell me what I want to hear, or, trust me, you will be in deep shit." The officer was a keen poker player, and no one who knew him would play with him. He was just too good. He pushed his luck further and went on, "Don't think of going to the embassy, either. Those fuckers have all run for cover, which I believe is standard operating practice when a play goes bad, and this one hasn't just gone bad; it's gone rotten. No one in Grosvenor Square will want to know you, and if you don't believe me, call them." He picked up Swan's desk phone and handed it to him. Swan hesitated slightly, and the officer thought for a second that he had overplayed his hand, but he needn't have worried. Swan declined to make the call. God, he was good. Under this pressure, Swan gave a complete account of the whole affair.

After reading the manuscript, he realized its facts contained more than a grain of truth. Ever the patriot, Swan knew that he would have to alert Washington and let them decide what to do. There was only one course of action they could take. The author needed to be silenced before this book saw the light of day. They would have killed Martin because of what he knew and was trying to expose. The elements in Washington that Swan had contacted believed that these facts had been buried long ago and would never again be brought into the open. The political consequences could be catastrophic, despite having happened back in the sixties. Although there could not be any evidence supporting the allegations, many people would use the old cliché about there not being smoke without fire. Especially those who did not consider themselves as friends or allies of the United States. The embarrassment caused, even to the current administration, many of whom had not yet even been born, would be severe. The United States needed as many friends as she could get right now, and this issue would not help 'brand America' in the slightest.

Swan insisted he wanted nothing to do with anyone's murder or death. When he initially made the call, he only meant that someone should have a quiet word with 'Les Straight.' They should explain the circumstances and maybe even give him a financial inducement not to have the book published. He certainly never thought for a minute that it would go this far. However, his superiors in Washington were adamant that this went way beyond having a quiet drink and a chat. In fact, that would make matters worse. The writer would then know that he had locked onto something, and this would give him even more incentive and encouragement to get his work into print. But even if they could dissuade him from trying to have his manuscript accepted, the knowledge would still be out there, inside his head.

No, it was just too dangerous to have this man walking around. He had to be silenced permanently. Swan wanted nothing to do with this, he claimed, but they reminded him that he was still an employee of the U.S. government and would do as he was told, or else. They did not expect him to do the job himself, only to facilitate in its execution. Someone would contact him and explain all the details. A package would be delivered to his office, which he would give to whoever called to carry out the hit. That it was Jordan they had sent was a million to one coincidence. Jordan had only found out when he arrived in Swan's office the previous day and coerced Swan into letting him read the manuscript. The details regarding the terrorist network that Martin, or Sam as he was then, had infiltrated had to be the one he had been in; the similarities were just too coincidental.

Jordan immediately realized that they had dispatched him to kill the one man he had sworn to find and do just that. It would have been almost comical had it not been so serious. They were expecting Sam Nathan/Paul McGregor, as Jordan knew him, assuming that 'Les Straight' was a pseudonym. Had it been him, instead of Gretel, then, yes, he would have been killed, but not here, not in the office. They would have overpowered and anesthetized him. While he was under, they would search his pockets and get his address. Later, they would ransack his home thoroughly for any more copies of the manuscript and take his computer. The killers would wait until late evening when the streets were quiet and then drive him to a lonely spot where Jordan would murder him. They would burn his body and break his jaw extensively to ensure that he could not be identified by his dental records. They would also give special attention to his fingers, and sulfuric acid was to have been used to burn his prints, should they have been on file.

Such was his complete hatred, Jordan wanted to do all this ante mortem, not after he had killed him. Swan called him a beast, a sadistic beast. He denied any knowledge or involvement in Trudy's disappearance or the intimidation of Bill Kent. The officer knew he was lying about this. It was in his eyes. It was always in the eyes, but although he was worried and upset by the girl's disappearance, he had enough. He knew that the young girl deserved better. Her killer should be brought to justice, but without a body, and so soon after her disappearance, it would be difficult to make any charge stick. After all, she might still be alive and only held incommunicado until this was all over. The Met. man was also smart enough to realize that the murderers (if Trudy had been murdered) had probably skulked back into the labyrinth of shadows and dark alleyways of American Intelligence and would never be caught.

Who could do this? he thought. Who could just snuff out the life of an innocent young woman giving no more than a passing thought? It beggared belief, and the officer was almost physically sick, just thinking about it. She was someone's daughter, and he, too, had daughters.

Swan was desperate to tell the officer about his illustrious past and how he had helped foil one of the most destructive outrages the world would ever have seen. Right now, he did not think the officer would be that impressed, and he would have been right.

The senior detective knew he was holding all the cards but also knew that none of this would ever come out. He only wanted to get at the truth, which he was very good at doing. What he did with it was up to him. He doubted it would ever get to trial. Pressure would be brought to bear by the Americans. The D.P.P. would be told quietly, but firmly, to drop the case; orders from above maybe even as a quid pro quo for leaving Kent alone.

A thought occurred to him. He knew there would never be a trial, but did Swan? Unlikely. No, maybe there was a better way, which would earn him a few Brownie points with the Branch. He told Swan that he realized that in his line of work, the agent might sometimes hear 'things,' which could be of use to an interested party. The officer would quietly make all this go away if Swan fed him little tidbits of gossip from time to time. He was unaware, of course, that Swan was already doing this for his own country. It seemed a small price to pay to make all this unpleasantness disappear. He would just feed this detective the same information he was already supplying to his own side, not that there would be much of it. They could fight over it if they liked. Good luck to them.

This arrangement didn't last long, however. With his cover blown, Swan was no longer of use and the Agency retired him back to the States. Swansong Literary Agency was closed without fanfare, and a new, non-literary company soon moved in. Although U.S. Intelligence knew that Swan was aware of the manuscript's contents, they believed he was sound and patriotic enough not to say or do anything foolish. Not if he didn't want to suffer a nasty, fatal accident.

• • •

A few weeks after these events, The New York Times received a letter. It had all the paper's lawyers running every which way, and no one got much sleep for a while. It was an account, if it were to be believed, of threats, intimidations, blackmail, and violence. All perpetrated by one man, a lawyer, carried out on behalf of the U.S. government; names, dates, places, events. This was dynamite! The writer gave his name as Max Jordan, and immediately, the newspaper made efforts to trace this individual. They sent a seasoned journalist to his office, but his secretary only stated that he had gone. Where to, she couldn't say. The journalist believed she was telling the truth. She had little time for her boss. That much was clear, and a picture slowly emerged of the true character of this man. His casework had been redistributed to the other partners. One of them had filed a missing persons' report, more out of frustration at having been lumbered with Jordan's cases than out of serious concern for their missing colleague. No one particularly liked or missed him. The journalist called at the precinct where the report was made. They had made desultory and routine efforts to find him, but as no one seemed to be making much fuss about his disappearance, the file was eventually marked 'unsolved, awaiting further information.' The police office had more urgent priorities.

The journalist then tried to contact the people named in Jordan's letter. No one would speak to him. Jordan had terrified them, and even being told that he was missing, no one would talk. Missing meant just that. There was always the possibility that he might come back, and reprisals for anyone revealing what had gone on between them would be swift and merciless.

So there it was. The newspaper was sitting with a crock of gold on its lap, but what could they do with it? The alleged writer had disappeared, which was suspicious in itself, and those people named were too frightened to talk. Hence, it all seemed genuine, but without some kind of corroborating evidence, they were stuck. They certainly could not publish the names of those people mentioned in the letter. If Jordan did come back, as unlikely as that now seemed, those people would be in danger, and if they were killed, it would be the paper's fault. As well as the moral dimension, the victims' families would undoubtedly raise a class action lawsuit against them, which could bankrupt the paper. Jordan had done his job well; in fact, he had done it too well.

Other journalists, with links to the New York crime element and the security services, were dispatched to see if they could find out anything, but all came up blank. There was no 'word on the street' on this one. Jordan had just disappeared. No, unfortunately, this story, as bizarre and incredible as it appeared to be, would have to remain buried. The link between Jordan and Black Ops Domestic was a secret, known only to a very select few, and all knew that it would have to stay that way. Jordan's letter would never be published. He had failed.

•   •   •

The United Kingdom authorities had decided that, as Jordan had entered the country as 'Harry Baines', that was how he should be buried. It was a simple, dignified ceremony, more than he deserved, but formalities had to be observed, so it was done. Max Jordan had left his brownstone one day and had simply vanished.

• • •

Marie-Claire loitered in the shadows as she awaited Jordan's return. When she saw the two police officers emerging from the entrance she had led them to, and racing into Martin's apartment block, she realized things had not gone to plan. Within a few minutes, as more police cars and ambulances converged at the scene, The Frenchwoman knew for sure that Jordan would not be coming out by himself. As she watched the scene unfold, that cold rainy afternoon in January 1971 came back to her. By some twist of fate, something had again spared her from falling into the hands of the authorities. This time, there were no tears in her eyes as she slowly walked away.

EPILOGUE

(Extract from the diary of Dr. Gretel O'Hara, Clinical Psychologist, North Manchester Department of Psychiatric and Psychological Services)

August 10th, 2007

Today, I saw no patients. Instead, I attended the funeral of my dearest and best friend, Martin Chambers. It was a small, sad affair, as these events usually are. Martin was an only child and had no family to speak of, his parents having died many years ago. Even his Jewish friends were so few that the rabbi had to call in a few synagogue members to make up the minyan, the required quorum of ten Jewish men necessary to conduct a burial service under the rites of that faith.

Martin should have been interred some weeks earlier, as the customs of his religion dictate, which requires that Jewish people should be buried as soon as possible after their passing. However, because the nature of his death and the subsequent inquiry and autopsy, it has taken until now to have his body released for burial.

I still cannot help my feelings of sadness and guilt towards this lovely man when I recall it was at my instigation he revealed the information he had kept buried for so long. That he had only a short time to live anyway is not in doubt. Even had he not been so cruelly murdered by that maniac Max Jordan, he would have been gone within a few days, but Martin, of all people, did not deserve to die in the way he did. For this, I and I alone am responsible. It is a feeling which will never leave me and which I shall most likely take to my grave.

And what was that information, as unwelcome as it was for which my friend paid so dearly? Before I can commit it to paper, I must first try to get clear in my mind the background and rationale for what happened after. So, dear diary, please forgive me if I go on at length about this subject. Perhaps by doing so, I may also find it cathartic, which may help cleanse my soul. If I were a religious person and retained any vestige of the faith in which I was raised, I would visit my parish priest and ask for God's forgiveness. But when all is said and done, a priest, however kind, understanding, and well-meaning, is but human, made from flesh, blood, and bone. My innermost sentiments are so profoundly dark and full of shame that I fear that nothing less than Divine absolution can cleanse me of the sin I have perpetrated.

In committing myself to the task which has been necessary for me to bring this work to a satisfactory conclusion, I have researched as much as I have been able to. This investigation has led me to uncover the events that I will describe below, coupled with the information revealed to Martin by the long-dead statesman.

How Martin could piece together and foresee the apocalyptic nightmare that might have happened had he made his information public at the time is beyond my understanding. I only know that somehow, he had been given a glimpse into a possible horrific future that might have sounded the death knell for us all had events turned out differently. Martin had read somewhere of John Kennedy's abiding Anglophilia. My research also uncovered the perhaps little-known fact that Kennedy was a friend of the then British ambassador to the United States, Sir David Ormsby-Gore (later Lord Harlech), a frequent visitor to The White House during the late President's tenure. He was unlike his father, Joseph, who was ambassador to Britain at the outbreak of World War Two. Joseph Kennedy had no genuine regard for the British people, perhaps due to his Irish ancestry. In the 1940s, he even tried to lobby Roosevelt to stay out of the War in Europe. John Kennedy did, however, have a great affection for this country, possibly because of his trips here, while his father was ambassador to the Court of St. James. It was even rumored that Harold Macmillan procured women for him on his later brief visits as President. Even if these allegations are untrue, it is still highly doubtful that he would have sanctioned such strategies proposed by those faceless military bureaucrats in the Pentagon and their C.I.A. counterparts in Langley, or wherever such decisions are taken.

Would America have destroyed its own bases in the United Kingdom in the event of a sudden, massive, and overwhelming Soviet invasion? To be fair, one must look at this issue in the context of the era in which it might have happened. The Cold War was at its height, and the world was, at one point, barely a heartbeat away from nuclear catastrophe. I recall Martin telling me about an incident that he remembered from his childhood. The event was something that happened in his school class. It was on the day that American warships were on their way to intercept a Soviet fleet bound for Cuba with nuclear missiles on a seemingly unstoppable collision course. His teacher told her children that they might not be going back to their homes and families that night! Many of the pupils immediately burst into tears, bewildered why their teacher should say such a thing.

It was well known in military and intelligence circles during the Cold War period that American and NATO forces could not hold off a sustained Soviet invasion force with ground troops alone for any longer than seventy-two hours at best without massive reinforcements. Perhaps, one could make a strong case for the Americans carrying out such a scenario to prevent the enemy from gaining access to documents, logistics, or materiel, which could be of distinct benefit. This may be a legitimate and necessary military tactic, if somewhat regrettable. What is absolutely unforgivable is that this destruction would have been carried out, not by conventional weapons but by nuclear devices. If Martin's assertions are accurate, the Americans, Britain's closest, staunchest, and most trusted ally, would have detonated atomic bombs on British soil. It was not just to destroy, but completely obliterate, even any trace of resources that might have been of use to the advancing Soviet army. Any equipment that the U.S. troops would not have been able to carry, fly out, or otherwise leave with was to have been eradicated. It was to have been the most destructive 'scorched earth' policy in history. Lakenheath, Fairford, Mildenhall, Croughton, and, of course, Greenham Common were still very much in use at this time. Many other smaller bases would also have been targeted for nuclear destruction, not just by the Soviets but by the Americans themselves. Even Faslane, an independent British defense establishment and not American, despite its deployment of U.S.- built Polaris weapons, was targeted for destruction. As monstrous as these actions might have been, an even worse cataclysm was to have been perpetrated by our erstwhile allies. Had Britain fallen to the Soviets and the United Kingdom become a satellite Russian province, the U.S. military had contingency plans to target British cities with chemical and biological weapons. Atomic weapons launched either from their land-based missile center in Colorado, their B-class long-range aircraft, or their nuclear submarines would have rained down upon British cities. They would have inflicted an apocalyptic nightmare on London, Manchester, Birmingham, and many other large conurbations. Industrial heartlands would have been completely wiped out in a nuclear holocaust caused, not by Russian ballistics but by American missiles. Large tracts of Britain, possibly thousands of square miles, would have been uninhabitable for generations, perhaps forever, as well as the countless citizens who would have perished immediately in the nuclear salvo. Not to mention those who would have died later, enduring a long, lingering death caused by either the nuclear, chemical or biological weapons or by the radiation in the atmosphere, with little help available to ease their suffering.

How many innocent British lives, men, women, and children, would have been sacrificed to the altar of American military strategic expediency, regardless of human cost? Thousands? Tens of thousands? Hundreds of thousands? Millions?

This is the incredible and horrific secret (if it was true) that Martin had kept to himself. But knowing of Kennedy's great affection for the British people, Martin believed he would never have permitted such a grotesque and horrifying scenario to have been implemented while he was Commander-in-Chief. One can only imagine the astonishment, indignation, and outrage Kennedy would have shown to those planners in the Pentagon, and their C.I.A. accomplices, when they advised him of these proposals, and of their blinkered and myopic certainty and insistence that President or no, their strategy must be maintained. After all, this was the same President Kennedy, who refused to sanction a C.I.A. instigated invasion of Cuba by anti-Castro forces. And it was the same President Kennedy who would not permit any more U.S. troops to get involved in the Vietnam conflict. Would this same president, who repudiated conflict even towards his enemies, have allowed his military forces to unleash weapons of unimaginable horror on his closest ally? The very question itself seems redundant. Could those in the Pentagon and elsewhere have quietly approached Lyndon Johnson as Vice-President to ensure their military vision was kept in place? Would they have sounded him out to see if he was of a similar mind? The war in Vietnam certainly escalated dramatically under his presidency. If he fought to contain the expansion of Communism in South East Asia, would he have been as averse as Kennedy to see parts of Britain destroyed to stymie a Soviet invasion? It is doubtful that he would have had the same regard for the United Kingdom as Kennedy. Despite his role as Vice President, Kennedy never considered him his 'inner circle.' Had LBJ signaled his accord with the generals, and if so, did this sound the death knell for Kennedy? Did he know the fate that awaited his president on that dreadful day in Dallas? Johnson was in the same motorcade, two cars behind Kennedy. However, as a Texas politician and Vice-President, one would have expected that he would be with the President on what would be his last fateful public appearance. But was he on hand merely as a Texan politician and Vice President, or was there a more sinister reason for his proximity to the President on what would be John F. Kennedy's final day alive? Did the British government of the day know of their 'ally's' plans? Would the Americans have briefed Downing Street of their intentions? That, as a last-ditch effort to stop, or even slow down the Soviet advance into the U.K., that it would use chemical and nuclear weapons on British soil? It seems unlikely that they would have taken the British government into their confidence over such a highly sensitive and potentially politically explosive strategy (no pun intended). One can only imagine the abject terror, outrage, and utter sense of betrayal that the then-current administration would have demonstrated had they known of their ally's military strategies.

Could they even have considered this 'righteous' payback in some misguided way for Britain's refusal to commit troops to the Vietnam War? Would some in American political or military circles have seen this reluctance as ingratitude after America came to Britain's aid during World War Two and therefore justified retribution?

If this intelligence had found its way into the public arena, who would ever again trust America? If it was prepared not only to turn its back on its former major ally but to bombard it with atomic weapons, what country could truly feel safe? How much more of its nuclear arsenal might assail NATO members and other military partners, were they, also, to succumb to a Soviet (or Chinese) invasion?

America would become a pariah nation, isolated, ostracized, distrusted by everyone, and what a propaganda coup for its enemies! The flagship bearer of democracy and freedom, shown to be nothing more than a treacherous entity with thought only for its own survival. American influence and prestige could and most likely would have been irreversibly damaged.

This was now the twenty-first century, and the Cold War was long over. Although it was still not impossible, it was highly unlikely that Russia, or especially China, would instigate a situation that would lead to another intercontinental war. The world was becoming a much smaller place. All the major nuclear players had long ago come to the logical conclusion that an atomic war would be one where there could be no winners, only different levels of losers. It was almost inconceivable that the world would be plunged into the horrifying nightmare of nuclear Armageddon that so many feared in the middle years of the last century. But back in the 1960s and 1970s, if this knowledge was to have been revealed, one can only imagine with horror the potential consequences these revelations might have precipitated.

As retaliation for this unforgivable strategy, might the rest of the world have boycotted U.S. goods and even American culture and perhaps also pulled investment from the country? Would American businesses abroad be subjected to punishing taxes as retribution and imports to unsustainable tariffs? Could this have led to a slowdown and even possibly a recession in the American economy? Hundreds of thousands of jobs lost, businesses closing daily, credit harder to find, the dollar plummeting. How would the ordinary American citizen have reacted? Would America's allies have even left it out of the intelligence pooling process? Might the hawks in the administration and their kindred spirits in the military decide that the world needed to be taught a lesson? Is it possible that these events could have triggered the very act that might have precipitated another global conflict?

Were it not for the damning details contained within the 'War Plan Red' documents, one might consider that Martin's theories are just fanciful (and I sincerely hope they are.) But we must not forget that when the plan to invade Canada was formulated, it was in the era just before the nuclear age. What if atomic weapons had been available in the early 1930s? Would the United States really have deployed such weapons of ultimate destruction on its northern neighbor? Thankfully, we will never know the answer to this question.

Martin had not practiced his faith for many years and was not a member of any synagogue. He never spoke to me about family, except for his parents, so apart from myself and a few other friends, there are few to mourn him. As a non-Jew, I cannot say Kaddish for him, but I have asked another Jewish acquaintance to recite the memorial prayer and light a Yahrzeit candle on the anniversary of his death. I will also occasionally place a small stone on his grave marker, as is the custom in the Jewish religion. I hope this helps to repay, in some small measure, the love, remorse, and the debt of profound gratitude I owe to the one person I am so proud to have been able to call my friend.

I pray that you have finally made peace with your mother.

Shalom, my friend.

THE END

ABOUT THE AUTHOR

David Broadway Photography

David Philips was born in Glasgow, Scotland in 1953 and emigrated to Perth, West Australia with his wife Adele in 2009. He has two adult children who still live in Glasgow. David has had several careers including being the anonymous half of a comedy double act with an irreverent, mischievous keyboard playing robot called Mr. Hairy and it was always a matter of some chagrin that the robot stole all his best lines and got more laughs than he did. In his spare time, David plays folk harmonica, swears at the T.V. and reads, anything by Scottish authors Ian Rankin and Craig Robertson. He is also a big fan of the novels of the late Robert Ludlum. David also writes short horror fiction and is a regular contributor to Schlock, an on-line e-magazine. His anthology of 13 horror stories, *The Finest Thread*, is available as an e-book from Smashwords.com. He has also written a comedy novella called *'The McBrides'* set in his home city of Glasgow in 1972. *The Judas Conspiracy* is his first novel.

NOTE FROM THE AUTHOR

Word-of-mouth is crucial for any author to succeed. If you enjoyed *The Judas Conspiracy*, please leave a review online—anywhere you are able. Even if it's just a sentence or two. It would make all the difference and would be very much appreciated.

Thanks!
David Philips

We hope you enjoyed reading this title from:

BLACK ROSE
writing™

www.blackrosewriting.com

Subscribe to our mailing list – *The Rosevine* – and receive **FREE** books, daily deals, and stay current with news about upcoming releases and our hottest authors.
Scan the QR code below to sign up.

Already a subscriber? Please accept a sincere thank you for being a fan of Black Rose Writing authors.

View other Black Rose Writing titles at www.blackrosewriting.com/books and use promo code **PRINT** to receive a **20% discount** when purchasing.

www.ingramcontent.com/pod-product-compliance
Lightning Source LLC
Chambersburg PA
CBHW010732100726
47899CB00009B/3008